LINDA STEELE

A novel

Random Acts

Outskirts Press, Inc.
Denver, Colorado

Random Acts
All Rights Reserved.
Copyright © 2009 Linda Steele
v3.0

Cover Photo © 2009 JupiterImages Corporation. All rights reserved - used with permission.

Outskirts Press, Inc.
http://www.outskirtspress.com

ISBN: 978-1-4327-4103-7

Outskirts Press and the "OP" logo are trademarks belonging to Outskirts Press, Inc.

PRINTED IN THE UNITED STATES OF AMERICA

Prologue
1907

My parents were both killed in a freak automobile accident when I was five years old. You see, the kingbolt on one of our front wheels broke. When that happened my father lost control of the vehicle and we rolled down a steep ravine and were scattered out onto a farmer's pasture. My mother and father layed limp like rag dolls in the grass. Mama's neck was broken and I guess she was dead as soon as she hit the ground, but Papa was still alive at first. I know because when I regained my senses and ran to him, he looked at me and he was breathing like it was hard to catch his breath. I was hysterical the minute I saw him and at first ran back and forth from my mother to my father, not knowing what to do. I never noticed my own leg bleeding or felt the deep gash that ran from the top of my thigh to my knee. I screamed and I cried, but there was nobody there to hear.

Though I didn't speak a word of English, my parents were recent immigrants to the United States, I soon started running toward a distant farm to get some help for them. By the time I got there I had lost so much blood that I guess I was close to being in shock. I pounded on the door and screamed until the whole Beeghley family was at the door to see what the matter was. My first attempt to explain was in French. When they didn't understand that, I tried German. That brought a response. The family made way for a very old man with a humped back and a big white beard. Any other time his weathered face of deep wrinkles might have scared me, but that day I was beyond fear of ordinary things.

He asked me in a soft, kind voice what was the matter. Looking down at my leg he asked, "Are you crying liebchen because you have hurt your leg?"

"Nein!" I assured him and then went on to tell him about the accident. "I think my mama and my papa are dead!!"

He translated to the family then asked me, "Do you think you can be a very strong girl and show me where this happened? "

I knew the way, but when one of the women looked down at the blood on my skirt and made an exclamation, I lifted it up, saw the muscle and blood protruding through my skin and fainted. After that I only have dim recollections of what happened until I reached Dr. Barnes office. The first thing I remember is my father's best friend, Rolf VonHelldorf, and his sons, Joseph and Tom, holding me down so the doctor could examine me. I must have still been in shock because all I remember is blood and Uncle Rolf and the boys talking to me in soothing voices saying nothing. I must have passed out again because I don't remember anything else until I woke up in my own bed at home with one of Dr. Barnes' nurses, Sister Gabrielle, sitting beside me.

When I started to cry, she took me in her arms and talked to me in French. I always thought she was the most beautiful woman in the world except for my mama. She used to stop by our house and talk to my mother when she would be going past on her rounds to see sick people. Mama said she used to be a nun, but decided to wait and think about it for a while. It felt so good to have her hold me. All I wanted to do was stay there close to her forever, but finally after a long time Joseph came in to see me.

Joseph was fourteen years old. We had been betrothed since the day I was born and I already loved him. He knelt down beside us and looked at me without saying anything at first. Finally, in French he asked how I was feeling and if I needed anything. After that he was quiet and I wondered what was going to happen. The longer I was awake the more I wondered if it had all been a bad dream, until I reached under my nightgown and felt the bandage.

I panicked. "Meine Mutter!" I cried. "Meine Papa!"

They both told me not to cry because they were going to take care of me, but I didn't want them to take care of me. I wanted my mother and father and nobody else would do.

Suddenly Uncle Rolf picked me up and without saying a word took me outdoors and carried me to the edge of the woods. It was quiet there as orange and yellow leaves slowly fluttered from the tree branches to the ground. A gentle wind blew through my hair and the sun shined on Uncle's face. With a sad look in his eyes, my father's best friend told me about my parents. "Liebchen, your mother and father have both died. Their funeral will be tomorrow here at the house."

He had tears in his crystal blue eyes when I asked, "Can I see them?" without really understanding what he was saying.

"Yes, you can see them, but they won't be able to talk to you because God has already taken their spirits to heaven and only their bodies are left for us to see."

I was scared. "When will they come back?"

Uncle Rolf's eyes filled with tears and he choked. "They won't ever be coming back. We won't see them again until we go to heaven ourselves."

"Then I want to go to heaven now!"

"You can't go till God says it's time, little one."

I didn't understand the significance of the funeral, but I'll never forget the smell of hyacinths, spring flowers that somehow appeared at the funeral even though it was October, and I will forever associate them with the smell of death. My father's business associates were there and lots of people were there from the church. My parents didn't seem to have any family, though I never thought about that at the time. I was just too young to wonder about such things.

Eventually my Uncle Rolf and Sister Gabrielle were married and on the day of the wedding, they adopted me. For the next seven years we were one big, happy family with Uncle Rolf's parents moving next door into my mother and father's house and Gabrielle having three more little boys. My grandfather who I called Opa came to visit from Luxembourgh every year and even though I felt tension between him and my new father who I called Papi, it felt good to have one blood relative left. I truly enjoyed his visits. I looked forward to my twelfth summer when I would start spending my summers with Opa in Luxembourgh.

Chapter 1

Susanna

The day I was to leave Bayland and my family for my first visit to Luxumborg, my heart was heavy. Papi and Mother, my adoptive parents, and I went for an early morning walk in the woods. None of us talked. The late spring foliage was heavy on the trees and the ground smelled sweet.

Papi finally broke the silence. "I would never allow you to leave if I had a choice, liebchen. I just want you to know I love you and I can hardly stand the thought of putting you on that train this afternoon. If there was any other way I wouldn't do it."

Mother said, "I put enough paper and envelopes with stamps in your suitcase that you should be able to write twice a week. Be sure to use an indelible pencil so the writing won't fade if it gets wet. I put several in your suitcase along with a pencil sharpener. You won't forget to write?" she asked with a worried look on her face.

"I won't forget, Mother. I'll miss you and Papi terribly."

She looked away and said, "I put some pads that I made out of diaper flannel in your suitcase along with two binders in case you start your monthly this summer. It could happen any time. You have matured enough this past year for that to happen. If it does, be sure to wash the pads out as soon as possible after you change so they won't become stained. "

I glanced at Papi, mildly embarrassed. He stared straight ahead looking like he might cry if he looked anywhere else. When we reached the clearing that I always thought of as my Mama and Papa's clearing, I said good-by to my biological parents mentally and asked them to be with me on my long journey, and then we reluctantly turned back to the house to get ready to go to the train station.

The whole family went to the station with my brother Tom, my rat terrier Minnie, and me, even Joseph who I had not spoken to in weeks. As I stood by the train, ready to leave, Papi said in a very quiet and choked voice, "Be a good girl and don't take any chances with your life. You tend to take too many risks. Be safe and come home to me in August whole." Tears were streaming down his cheeks.

Mother was next. "My wonderful little girl, I shall miss you more than I can say. I'll pray for you every day. Have a good time and give each of my family a kiss for me when you arrive in France in August."

Grandfather, Papi's father, reminded me to, "Be a good girl, I know you will, but don't mind your opa unless it makes sense. He doesn't always use the best judgment so you must use your own head sometimes. Godspeed," he said as he hugged me tightly.

Grandmother handed me a box with cookies and bread and snacks to eat along the way. Included was a large bag of hard candy to last through the summer. "Have a good time with your other grandparents. We all have to share you, but it is hard when we love you so much," she said wistfully.

Last was Joseph. His golden hair was blowing, turning up gentle curls that reminded me of him as a boy. He was taller than Papi now. His blue eyes looked worried. God forgive me because I told him, "I'm sorry Joseph, I have nothing to say to you...not now or ever again," but my voice cracked as I said it and gave my feelings away. To try to cover it I turned quickly and ran up the stairs to the car we would be traveling in and never looked back. On the train Tom draped his arm around me in the seat and handed his handkerchief to me. He said nothing, but didn't look the least bit bothered about leaving. He had been graduated from law school the weekend before and was happy to be leaving for an extended vacation.

The farther we got from Bayland, the more the heavy weight of sorrow lifted from my chest. Tom joked with me and we ate cream puffs and drank hot tea in the dining car and started having fun. New York City was impressive, much bigger than Cleveland. The hotel Papi had booked for us was luxury from the front sidewalk to everything in our two bedroom suite, including the huge baskets of fresh flowers that adorned every table in every room. It wasn't often that we were allowed to feel wealthy but this time Papi had spared nothing. We ate at an Italian restaurant and stuffed ourselves, and then we went to a play. The next morning we had breakfast in our suite as we watched the porters carry our luggage out to be taken to the ship. We were shipping out right after noon.

The first two days on the ship Tom was seasick and he couldn't eat or drink anything. I had read about seasickness but never dreamed that it could be so violent. Though I had absolute confidence in my own doctoring skills, I called the ship's doctor to take a look at him because I had nothing to give him. I suggested to the doctor several treatments for settling his stomach. He ignored me but gave him Paregoric, just as I had suggested, and then pretended it was his own idea.

Our days crossing the Atlantic were idyllic. We walked the decks, played shuffleboard, dressed for dinner and ate too much. Tom chased some of the women and I played the piano whenever I could find one not being used. The captain asked me to play with the orchestra that was entertaining one evening and I had my first experience leading an audience. I never had so much fun. The crowd was enthusiastic and it fueled me like nothing ever had before! Papi would have been upset if he could have seen me pounding the keys and encouraging the people to sing along. He would have seen my behavior as unladylike, but I saw the smiles on everybody's faces and thought it was a true gift to make so many people happy. After that evening Tom steered me away from another performance, so I guess he was uncomfortable with it. I didn't argue, though any time I practiced wherever I went on the ship I drew a crowd. Having grown up at the conservatory where every student was a protégé, I never dreamed that so many people were hungry to hear good music. I wasn't shy about having an audience because I had been taught to have one, but I wasn't used to so many compliments. In my crowd we were all so talented that we didn't throw away many compliments on each other.

Our deadline for arriving at Opa's estate was June 1 so, regretfully; there was no time to stop for a visit in Rouen at the home of my adoptive mother's parents, Grand-Pere and Grand-Mere. Papi warned us that the adoption papers clearly stated that I spend June 1 through August 15, my birthday, with my biological grandfather who I called Opa. Grand-Mere sent a letter that arrived just before we left Bayland that said she would plan a birthday party for me on the 15th and that Opa was invited too. Papi told me that he would also be there for the celebration. It made me feel secure to know exactly how my life was going to proceed for the next few months, but I loved Opa, my biological grandfather, and was looking forward to seeing him too. It's not exactly like I was suffering at the thought of spending a few weeks with him. I loved him.

When we got to Luxemborg, Opa was waiting for us, his Airedale at his side. He hugged us both and took over having our baggage shipped to the house. A shiny black Rolles Royce was waiting for us complete with driver. His home impressed me then just as it had the summer I had visited with Papi and Joseph a few years before. It looked like a castle in a fairy tale book, made of gray colored stone with turrets at every corner and gables across the roof. The servants waited for us on the steps when we arrived. Some of them had smiles on their faces when I hugged them.

Opa was the perfect host to Tom and me, but at dinner that evening he made it clear that he expected Tom to be gone soon because this was his time to have me to himself. I didn't like the tone of it because even though I had been adopted by Tom's father, he was my brother. To me, that made any family of mine family of his. After all, Tom had shared all of his family with me and now I should share my one blood family member with him. I tried to voice that, but Tom interrupted me to say, "I understand, Herr Strashoffer, and I plan to be on my way in a day or two as soon as my sister is settled in comfortably. Actually," he added, "Grand Pere has plans for me in Rouen while I'm here and I'm anxious to get started.

Two days later when Tom left, I felt empty inside. Opa seemed to sense it and quickly diverted my attention to riding lessons and sight seeing. He introduced me to several children and I did appreciate the effort, but I didn't enjoy the company of most children. We had nothing in common.

After a week of feeling lost, he bought me a grand piano and put it in the sitting room so I could play anytime I wanted to. It was all I needed to bring me home. I played all day and all evening after that. I never needed anything much if I could have my music.

When I wasn't playing the piano, I was out on the grounds helping the gardeners or taking long walks with my Minnie and Opa's Airedale.

Life was genteel and peaceful. I missed my family, but knew I would be seeing them again at the end of the summer. Tom visited every two weeks, spent the night, and then headed back to Rouen. All was well until July when even in my out of the way castle I started hearing about war. There was a feeling of unease in the air wherever I went.

I asked Opa, "Do you think we will have a war?"

"No, child, not as long as you are here. The sun will shine with no shadows while you are with me."

The reassurance was good, but I still remembered Grandfather reminding me to use my own head because Opa didn't always use the best judgment. We went along in our idyllic state like that until finally on the night of August 2 I was awakened out of a deep sleep by a commotion.

Opa came quickly into my room and said, "We must get out of the city now. The Germans are invading us and it isn't safe to stay here. Quickly! Get dressed and pack only the essentials. We need to leave tonight!"

The last time I had been awakened like that my father, Rolf, was dying of a gall bladder attack and I was five years old. A chill ran down my spine. I was shaking as I unbuttoned my nightgown and quickly dressed. Minnie wagged her little stub tail and looked at me craving security, but at the moment I had none to give. In minutes I filled a suitcase with clothes and other essentials, was dressed and rushing out into the hallway. The butler picked up my bag and carried it to the waiting car. At the train station Opa dismissed his driver and took charge of our baggage. We were on a train headed for Italy in minutes.

My stomach was doing flip flops when Opa finally said, "You mustn't be afraid now. We're on our way to Italy. I have a cabin in the mountains where it will be safe for us to stay. Rolf's man who helps me at the mill, Herr Switzer, will notify us when it will be safe to come back. I shouldn't think this war would last long."

I worried about my family. "Should we send a telegram to Tom to let him know where we're going? He'll be worried if he hears about the invasion."

"Don't worry. We won't be gone long. I'll have you in Rouen

very soon and everything will be just fine."

Grandfather's parting words rang in my ears, "Use your own head." I wondered if I should have stayed in Luxemburg and gone to France.

When we arrived at our final destination, it didn't look like much. The village was small, but bustling. The first thing we did was look for a place to eat. The menu was mutton stew and bread and fresh fruit. I can't say the stew tasted spoiled; actually, it had the smell of new shoes. I had never thought of eating leather before, but it was edible and the bread and fruit were pretty good.

After we had eaten, we went to a small store. Opa bought us cold weather gear, boots, gloves, the works. I was already wondering why we needed cold weather gear in August if we were going to be back in France by my birthday in mid-August. By the time he was finished we had four horses, two saddles, blankets, clothes, and food to last for months.

We stayed at a small inn that night and left early the next morning, just as the sun was coming up. Opa had a leather pouch made so I could carry Minnie with me. It had a strap that crossed over my shoulder and allowed her to ride comfortably during the trip. I tried to remember every bend and turn we made on our journey, but after three days it became impossible. I was lost and I knew it.

The fourth day we finally came to a cozy little cabin, Opa's place. I had been worrying that maybe my grandfather was lost too, though he assured me that he knew the way. I was glad to get off of my horse and to move into the little cabin. It had been a long journey.

The first night I made biscuits like Hannah, our housekeeper had taught me and we opened a tin can that had peaches in it. Opa suggested that we have tea with our supper to stretch it farther and I agreed, since it didn't look like we had much food sitting on the table.

The mountains were beautiful and I can't say that I was miserable living in the middle of nowhere. Opa and I got along well together and I loved walking freely in the remote territory, listening to the birds, and was mesmerized by the beauty surrounding me. Minnie was my constant companion. Sometimes we looked for berries and other times we just sat on a rock and looked out upon the miles and miles of solitude. I wrote my compositions out on the paper I had brought with me while Minnie hunted for mice and whatever other small creatures happened to be around. Her occasional barking as she pounced on an unlucky bug never disturbed the melodies that constantly played inside my head. In the time I was separated from my family I wonder how many compositions I wrote. The music was endless.

It was August 15 and we were settled into the cozy lodge Opa had built back when he was a young man. "Your grandmother loved it here," he said in a raspy voice. "After she died, I used sneak down for holidays pretty often. I loved the solitude."

"Did my father ever come here with you?"

He sobered and hung his head. His voice dropped and changed to a more raspy quality than usual. "No, I'm afraid not. His holidays were always spent with the Von Helldorf's after he was eleven and before that, he either stayed at his school or spent his time with nurses." He spoke slowly and deliberately as he added, "I regret that I never behaved like a father to him, but at the time I guess I only thought of myself."

I felt sorry for him as he admitted his shortcomings. That was easier than thinking of my dead father as a lonely little rich boy nobody wanted. I reassured him. "I'm sure Papa forgives you. People in heaven understand things. Look how good you've been to me and to all of my new family."

"You're the only person in the world who seems to be able to make me feel like a decent human being," he sighed with a look of adoration in his eyes.

Changing the subject I asked, "How long do you think we need to stay here? Papi will be worried if we don't get a message to him today."

"We'll stay until the war is over. It won't be safe to go to France so we'll stay here. When things calm down, I'll take you home to the States myself if your French relatives are unable to take you. I just don't want you anywhere near the soldiers of any country. They can get mean and do things to young girls that normally they would never think about doing. It isn't safe to be anywhere near them." He patted my shoulder and added with a worried tone in his voice, "When a group of men get together anything could happen."

"Don't you think we should have sent a letter or something? Papi is supposed to come to get Tom and me today and he'll think something terrible has happened if I'm not there."

"Rolf always has worried too much. I've never seen a more nervous father in my life. I'm afraid this time he'll just have to worry because I have no plans to put you in any kind of danger just to get a letter of reassurance out to him. We're going to sit tight for a few weeks until all this blows over."

It was my birthday. I was twelve today and had never been more miserable. I hated to think of my father and mother and the boys worrying about me, but my grandfather had taken me so high into the mountains that I had no idea how to get to a town to mail a letter to them. I was quiet as Minnie and I went outside for a walk. When I was troubled, it usually helped to go walking, but today as the sun shined into my face, a sudden rift of homesickness passed over me. I wished Papi would come. I knew he would, it was just a matter of time. If he were here now, he would know what to do. As my grandfather had advised, I didn't always trust Opa when it came to making decisions. I tried to remember the trip out of the village to the cabin step by step and I wrote down what I could remember. Maybe eventually I would try to get down on my own, though it didn't take much intelligence to see that a person unfamiliar with the area could be lost and never seen again. All the walking I could do that day didn't seem to lighten the heavy feeling I held deep in my chest.

Opa had just started to worry about me when I came back to the lodge at dusk. "You were gone a long time. Be careful you don't get lost in these mountains. The nights are pretty chilly and it could be dangerous to be out without your overnight gear."

"I know, Opa. I spent most of my time sitting on a log thinking."

"Were you thinking about a song?" he smiled.

"No, I was thinking about Papi and Tom and how they must feel since I didn't show up in Rouen today."

"I'm sure they understand and as soon as it's safe, Herr Switzer will get word to us so we can go back to civilization to relieve their minds. I guess we must be missing your birthday party. I am sorry about that," he added.

I didn't think he looked or sounded very sorry and sighed as I said, "I don't mind. It's good just being here with you as long as no one is worried. Maybe everybody's already been shot," I choked, suddenly remembering the danger my family might be experiencing and then I started feeling angry that I wasn't there to help.

Opa, who seemed to sense my fury put his arms around me, "Poor little liebchen, never worry about such things. Surely they're smart enough to miss the German bullets just as we are." Changing the subject he told me, "I'm going out to shoot a deer. We need to supplement the food we have so it lasts longer. Want to come?" he smiled.

Hating the thought of killing one of God's creatures I said, "You go ahead. I love shooting things, but not animals, especially deer."

"I understand," he said as he quickly picked up his rifle and left me to sulk.

The months went by with snow drifted so high that it was often difficult to even open the doors to go outside. Thank goodness Opa had bought us each heavy mountain gear when we first came to Italy, though we seldom went out for more than a few minutes at a time because of the extremely cold temperatures. Mostly we went out to use the outside privy and to bring in more firewood. Even Minnie only went out for the necessities.

One day I asked Opa if he thought anybody could get to us before spring to tell us the war was over. I still worried constantly about my family and how they must be feeling. Most of the time I loved Opa, but I couldn't help feeling resentful that he had chosen to take us to his cabin instead of on a train to France. I felt such deep sorrow about being away from my parents, brothers, and other grandparents that sometimes I thought I almost hated him.

I thought of Joseph. On the day I was born we had been betrothed. It had always been understood that we would be married when we were grown up. We could always talk about anything till last spring when he started to seeing a lot of Carolyn Smithson. After that, he didn't seem to ever want to talk to me when we were home from school at the same time and he never came by the conservatory anymore. As a matter-of-fact, I didn't think he seemed to care about me at all. Though I had never before used my musical gifts to berate those less talented, I still didn't regret that I had done it to Carolyn. I still hated her for stealing Joseph from me, but try as I might, I couldn't seem to hate him even though he had broken my heart. I guessed I had probably made myself look small in his eyes when I tried to point out how much better I would be than Carolyn when I was grown because I was smarter and would be prettier. He was probably married by now and hadn't thought of me in months. That thought made me feel even worse than I was already feeling.

Opa came back from his evening hunting expedition looking pale instead of presenting with the usual red cheeks one had after spending more than an hour in the frigid mountain air. He sat down before taking his coat off and laid his head on the back of the chair. To me it looked as if he was hardly breathing.

"Are you all right?" I cried as I ran to him and started unbuttoning his coat. "What's the matter, Opa?"

"I'm fine. I have such a heavy feeling in my chest that it makes it hard to breathe. Nothing's wrong. Don't worry. I've decided to rest tonight and I'll go out first thing in the morning to look for some game. We don't need much. It's late February and in a couple more months we can go down and get supplies in the village. Maybe the war will be over so we can take you home. I know how miserable you've been this winter worrying about your family."

As always, I tried to make him feel better about our situation. By now I knew that he was anxious to get back to civilization, so I said, "I've liked being with you," and patted his hand. As I did it, I felt a serge of love for him sweep over me. His skin was pale and sweaty. I had read all of the medical books for the first three years of medical school and committed them mostly to memory. Joseph always bought two copies of all his books so I could read them. Mother, who was a midwife, and I had played diagnostic games with Joseph and our friend, Jacob, who were both medical students at Western Reserve Medical School and I had become a pretty fair diagnostician even though I was still a kid. Opa looked to me like he was having a heart attack. I asked, "Are you having any chest or jaw pain?"

"No, doctor," he answered, amused at what he considered my doctor game.

"Do you have nausea?"

"A little, mostly just this heaviness in my chest and I seem to be sweating even though I just came inside from the bad weather." He struggled to answer, "I'll be all right by morning. Don't worry about me."

I helped him out of his coat, boots, and leggings while he tried to act as if nothing was wrong, but he looked tired and pale and the eternal smile he had on his face when he was with me had faded. Even though he was 80 years old, he normally had a spring to his step. That was gone too. He looked as if he could hardly drag himself to bed as he told me goodnight.

With the feeling of impending death hanging over me I selfishly begged God to spare him until he could get me back to my parents, then propped him up to help him breathe more easily. I didn't want him to die, but was experienced enough with dying to believe that all the praying in the world wouldn't keep God from taking someone I loved away from me. I knew about tragedy and could feel it all around me. All I could ask for was peace for my family, including Opa, and for myself, no matter how bad things got, I thought bitterly. It would be useless to ask for more and I just hoped I could stall Him for a little while until I was reunited with my family.

In the night I opened Opa's door and crept in to see if he needed me. "Susanna," he called.

I was surprised that he was awake. "Opa, do you need anything?"

"No, but I'm having chest pain and I thought you should know. I want you to listen carefully to what I say."

He sounded more serious than I had ever heard him sound. I was scared.

"In case anything happens to me, stay here where it's safe until Rudolph gets word to you. Promise you won't get scared and leave or he'll never find you. Promise!" he ordered.

I nodded my head and said, "I promise."

"Keep my wallet so you have money. The gold coins will do you the most good so be sure you get that box of coins out of my chest at the end of the bed. You can use them anywhere until you get to Rolf and your mother. Be sure you wait here until you are rescued, don't get yourself lost in the mountains. I don't expect to see you in heaven for a long time." He shifted in his bed and went on. "Don't be afraid to kill the deer. Remember one bullet can kill a deer that will provide food for a month. The same bullet, if used to kill a rabbit will only provide one meal. When you get back with your family, remember, you are a very wealthy girl. You will own everything I have and everything that belonged to your real father. Take what is yours."

"You're going to be all right," I lied as I held his sweaty hand.

"I think so too, but we should talk, just in case. After all, I am an old man and anything could happen."

"You don't have to be old for something to happen. Look what happened to my mama and papa," I sighed then added, "but you know that. I love you," I whispered with tears in my eyes. I haven't always acted like it since we have been here in the mountains, but I do."

"I know you do. This war has upset your life and I'm sorry for it. Maybe it would have been better to take you to Rouen instead of here, but I didn't think the war would go on for so long."

"It's all right, Opa. You made the best decision you could at the time," I said, not believing it for a minute.

We stayed together in the dark room for the rest of the night with me holding his hand. By morning he seemed tired, but better. I insisted on going out to look for game, taking Minnie with me to chase up one of the rabbits that I seemed to be able to kill without much remorse. He didn't argue with me, but reminded me to wear all of my outdoor gear and not to stray far from the house.

I hated killing the animals and silently hoped I wouldn't see anything to shoot at, but Minnie was a hunter at heart, a good tracker and excellent on the trail. In minutes she had located an unfortunate rabbit and was in full chase of it. I pulled up, took quick aim out in front of it, and pulled the trigger. There was the expected blast then Minnie barking fiercely. I ran in her direction and found her standing by the lifeless rabbit barking excitedly. The poor creature was bloody and limp when I lifted it by the ears. I quickly took out the hunting knife Opa had bought me and skinned and field dressed it. I had been experimenting with a process of preserving hides thinking that we could use them to make various kinds of weatherproof apparel. This skin hadn't been badly damaged by the shot so I was careful to roll it up and save it.

A few minutes later, Minnie chased up a second rabbit. I went through the same process, always being careful to shoot a safe distance from my dog. Losing her would have been devastating. The hide on this rabbit was badly damaged. I looked at what was left of it and decided that part of it could at least be used as the palm of a mitten or the sole of a sock and salvaged what I could of it. After the second one was cleaned I took the two rabbits inside to clean more thoroughly. I had been outside for almost three hours and was beginning to get cold and tired from trying to walk in the deep snow. The only edible part of the most damaged rabbit was the legs, but still the poor little animal's life wouldn't be wasted. We would use all that we could and, since the other one was in better shape, we would have a full meal for our supper.

"It's a good thing that when I was a kid back in Bayland Grandfather and Grandmother taught me how to be a sharpshooter!" I said in an effort to be cheerful as I entered the cabin and held up the two limp rabbits. I couldn't stand to cause harm to any living creature. Thanks be to God at that time I could still take a life, though it was an effort. Even then, killing a deer seemed like a mortal sin and I couldn't even think of it.

Opa, who had been sleeping in a chair with his legs propped up raised his head to look and said, "You did real good. There's no doubt you can take care of yourself, liebchen. Your family has prepared you for life very well and I'm going to start preparing you for survival in the mountains just in case you need to know how. I know you love the outdoors, so I'm going to teach you about things I learned from my father when I was a boy. As you know, he was a mountain climber and enjoyed living off the land.

I knew he was worried about the future and whether or not I could survive alone in the mountains if he were to die, but I pretended that learning about survival would be a good game and never let on. "Good! You'll have to tell me everything. Let me get some paper and you can start teaching me now. I'll write down what you tell me."

We waited for our rabbits to roast to perfection while we talked over hot cups of mint tea we had picked at the base of the mountain early in the fall. I had become quite the cook over the past few months and seemed to be able to fix a meal from almost nothing. Often I made a kind of sourdough bread like Hannah, our cook, had taught me to make. Usually we still only ate once a day in order to conserve food. Hunger was something we lived with most of the time, but we always had enough to keep us from worrying about starvation.

As the weeks went by, I took care of Opa in his ailing health. I propped up his head and feet as I watched him have difficulty breathing when he tried to lie down and as his feet and legs began to swell, knowing that he had all the symptoms of heart failure, probably because he had damaged his heart when he had chest pain the month before. I was sure it had probably really been a heart attack. Now he was slowly dying.

One day he convinced me to shoot a deer. He knew I would never kill one for myself so he told me, "I don't think I'm getting enough to eat these days or else my body is just wearing out. Why don't you kill a deer so we have more to eat? I need to get my strength back."

I know he saw the dread on my face at the thought of killing a deer, but he must have noticed how terribly thin I had become and added, "God put the animals on the earth for His people. Liebchen, He doesn't want us to starve."

Giving him a pat on the arm, I turned to get ready to go out, taking my rifle, my knife to cut away the important parts of the deer, and a few cloth bags to put the meat into. I said nothing as I left, but it wasn't long till I saw a young buck. He saw me too. As he stood looking at me curiously, I fired my rifle and he dropped instantly with the shot penetrating his body just above his shoulder. I was definitely the crack shot that Grandfather and Grandmother always said I was and I rarely missed my target.

I mourned over his lifeless carcass until I knew I had to push myself to cut him up and get back to the lodge. Opa would be worrying about me and I didn't want him to come looking for me unnecessarily in his present condition. I hated that I had killed this gentle, majestic animal, but made an incision down his middle, then removed the animal's intestines, and kidneys. Ever so gently I removed the bladder so urine wouldn't leak into the meat.

As I worked I thought what it might be like to operate on a real human being. I had always wanted to watch a surgery. It was too bad that both Mother and Papi had absolutely forbid me to go anywhere near an operating room. Joseph and I had almost convinced Dr. Barnes to let me watch an appendectomy, but then Papi caught wind of it and told Dr. Barnes he wouldn't allow it. Papi had always disapproved of my interest in medicine. He never could understand why, with my gift of music I would be interested in anything else. It never did any good to try to convince him that I wanted to be a doctor when I grew up, because he wouldn't listen. I guessed none of that mattered anymore anyway. If perhaps Papi couldn't ever find me, I knew I would die here and never see anybody ever again.

It took me several trips to get all the meat up to the lodge in the bags I had brought with me. I took one piece of backstrap into the house and hung the rest on the back porch to freeze for another time. At least we wouldn't have to kill anything else for a while I thought to myself with relief.

That evening I sliced the meat thinly and browned it for our supper. We had more of the sourdough bread I had made the day before and ate salted nuts later in the evening. The nuts reminded me of all the times we had eaten popcorn in the evenings back home and suddenly I felt so lonesome that I went to bed early, hoping to sleep away my thoughts.

In April there were days of sunshine and melting snow and days of heavy snowing, sometimes mixed with rain. It was a messy time of year, even in the mountains. Opa was going outside every day now, but he moved slowly and accomplished little as I foraged daily for food for the horses and for us. It took me all day just to barely have enough to keep us alive. Food was short because Opa had never expected us to be here this long.

One day as we walked to our small barn to check on the horses, Opa stopped in his tracks, but said nothing. I turned to see what he was doing just in time to see him clutching his chest as his face blanched out completely.

"Opa, what's the matter?" I screamed while running to his side.

He didn't answer as he looked straight ahead with glazed eyes, and then fell down on the snow.

"Opa!" I screamed again as I leaned over him. "Please don't do this! Please!"

There was no response as I quickly unbuttoned his coat and listened for a heartbeat. The only sound I heard was a gurgle as dark brown watery material ran out of his mouth.

I looked up into the heavens and begged, "God no! Please don't take him too!"

I cried hysterically as I ran my hands through the thick, curly, white hair that had been under his cap. Never had I felt such panic since the accident that took my parents when I was five. Even back then there had always been Papi and Joseph, and Tom. Now I would be alone.

I stayed out in the snow all day that day, bent over Opa in an almost trance like way. When it started getting dark I realized I had to do something with his body. He was a big man and I was still just a girl. The ground would be too frozen to bury him so I lugged and tugged him until I finally managed to pull him up on the flat wooden sled with runners that Opa and I had made for carrying deer and firewood. With difficulty, I pulled him just inside the barn and covered him with a tarp for the night.

I sat in the dark living room of the lodge holding Minnie all night. For months when I was a little girl I had mourned the loss of my parents and I mourned the loss of Mrs. Brownson, my nurse, after that. There was the special loss of Joseph in another way, and now I had even lost Opa. I thought of the saddest music I knew. If only I had a piano to play. I sang something new that came to mind, something sad and filled with emotion.

When the sun came up, I went to the barn to check on Opa. I screamed when I saw that some animals had gotten to his body and had eaten parts of his face that had been exposed above the tarp. There were chunks missing out of his cheeks and something had attacked the orbit of one eye. It was the final devastation. There was no doubt that I could not bury him because the ground was too frozen to penetrate, but I knew I would have to do something, and then I remembered a cave that Opa and I had investigated one day. I would make a tomb for him in the cave sort of like the one Jesus had in the Bible. I would make a bed of pine needles for him and when it was ready, would hitch one of the horses up to the sled and take him there. It didn't matter how long it took, I was going to give him a proper burial. I didn't think of my aloneness or my future until much later.

It took days to get the cave ready. When it was as secure as I could make it, I took him there with the tarp now tied tightly all up and down his body so no animals could get into it. One of the horses hitched to the sled got us to the entrance of the cave, but after that I had to move the body myself. With much difficulty, I dragged his frozen body into the cave inch by inch until he was laying on the palate of pine needles I had made for him. I closed the opening with a thick closure of brush and pine.

When Opa's body was safely closed away in the tomb, I carefully went through the mass and quoted scriptures about life after death and said the rosary. After that, I went back near the lodge to look for grass for the horses. The silence was deafening. Though I didn't know it then, it had been therapeutic to have to work at taking care of Opa's body. The deep sorrow I had been feeling subsided and my work had put me in another stage of grief. Now I was mad. God had probably never had anybody angrier with Him than I was, unless it was back when I thought He was going to take my new father because of his gallbladder problem. I was furious. I looked up into the sky and screamed, "Is this what you've wanted all along? Fine! There's nobody left, unless you want Minnie too! I don't even have a piano! I'm finally alone. I'm sitting up here on this mountain with absolutely no reason to live and still I live on. Do whatever you want with me. I don't care anymore!" After that I cried while Minnie sat on guard, beside me with her ears perked up, waiting.

Joseph

*B*y April, 1915 the investigators Papa had hired seemed to have exhausted all avenues in their search for Susanna. They had followed leads all over Europe only to come to a dead end each time. Papa and Mother had lost weight and rarely laughed. It seemed that they had nothing to say to each other anymore. They were expecting another baby that month which only seemed to cause them more to worry about. I had broken my engagement to Carolyn Smithson when I realized that, just as Susanna had suggested one time when she was in a rage, nobody could come close to the woman Susanna would become and certainly Carolyn would never measure up. Susanna was not only a musical genius, but also her intelligence was superior to anything I had ever seen in any other human. If she was alive, I would regret that I hadn't been willing to wait for her whenever I looked at her. She might never have anything to do with me, but if the day came that she turned up, I wanted to be free to marry her.

Tom had begged our father to allow him to stay in France, but Papa insisted on taking him home before he lost another child to the war. Since then, my normally flamboyant younger brother had become reticent, just rattling around the offices of Von Helldorf and Strashoffer without seeming to care about anything. It was as if Susanna and her grandfather had been swallowed up into the clouds and he couldn't rest until he found her.

I was home from medical school one weekend when I asked my father for a private conference in the library. The library had so many painful memories I could hardly stand to be there. On the wall was the first Von Helldorf family picture taken the Christmas before our parents had married. Five-year-old Susanna was right in the middle of it with her big Strashoffer smile, just like her father's had been. Beside that picture was a blow up of Susanna taken that same spring, soaking wet, standing in a mud puddle in *a downpour with her curls sticking up all over her head. There was a poster size picture of Mother right before the twins were born and another big picture of us all coming at the camera on horseback with big smiles on our faces. On another wall were the new pictures of the babies who had come into the family in the last six years. On the top of the bookshelf were pictures of Uncle Henry and Aunt Frieda, Susanna's deceased parents, and a very old photograph of Papa's brother Friedrich who had died of a heart defect as a teenager. There was an assortment of pictures of our Grandfather and Grandmother Von Helldorf clustered onto one mounting and a recent portrait of them. It reminded me of times past when life was uncomplicated and free of heartache.*

I turned to look out the full length-paned window. It faced the large sugar maple trees that grew between our house and Strashoffer house where Grandfather and Grandmother lived a quarter of a mile away. The trees were beginning to look like they would burst into bloom in another few weeks as the swollen buds swayed in the April wind.

Finally Papa came in, embraced me, and then asked me to sit down. Nothing was said at first, and then it all came tumbling out as we rapidly conversed in German. "I can't live like this anymore. I'll be graduating soon and after I do, I'm going to Europe to look for Susanna. I know you have high expectations for me and Dr. Barnes is expecting me to join his practice, but I have to go and at least try to find her. Maybe I can turn something up."

"I wish you wouldn't do that," my father said in a voice heavy with emotion. "The seas are getting more dangerous for travelers every day. You might not get there safely and if you get over there, you may not be able to come back. Germany started to blockade Great Britain in February and all reports I'm seeing look like things are getting worse.

I was persistent. "I'm sorry, but I have to do this. You know how it's always been with Susanna and me since the beginning. I've always taken care of her."

I could see Papa bite his tongue to keep from reminding me that things hadn't been so good last spring when I had fallen for my old friend Carolyn. "I just can't see losing another child over there," he argued. "We're doing all that's humanly possible to find her."

I was firm in expressing my position. "I wouldn't hurt you for the world, but I have to go. Maybe your investigators don't care as much as I do. Please understand."

"I do understand," the he growled. "If I didn't have so many responsibilities here, I'd go with you. Your mother and I haven't had a peaceful moment since Susana left for Luxembourg last summer. When I start thinking of everything that could have happened to her..." He couldn't go on. The often gruff and growling giant of a man could no longer blink back the tears streaming from his eyes. I knelt in front of him and held him in my arms and shared in his sorrow.

When we finally got control of ourelves Papa asked, "Do you want me to tell your mother and Tom or do you want to do it yourself?"

"I'll take care of it when the time is right. I wanted to talk to you first. Tom will want to come too, but we're going to need to convince him to stay here. We can't be tearing the whole family apart over this and so far the little ones haven't seemed to be very affected by it."

At the table that day, Mother must have sensed that something was in the air, though she couldn't figure out what was about to happen. There was the usual confusion of dining with a six-year-old and the three-year-old twins, but there was also a quiet that enters a house sometimes even before a person leaves and all of us could feel it now. Somehow I don't think she wanted to know.

After we ate and the little boys were in bed for naps, Mother finally asked us with tears in her eyes, "Are you going to tell me what has happened? Is there bad news about Susanna?"

I answered her. "I've got to search for Susanna, Mama. As soon as I'm out of school I'm going. I don't want you to be sad, but you know how I've always loved her and there's no peace for me. I can't just sit here and wait for her to show up."

Her face looked stricken. She cried until we both worried that she might affect the baby if she didn't get control of herself, then she begged me, "Please don't go. If you go, Tom will go and maybe we'll lose all three of you. Wars are contagious. Pretty soon you'll want to enlist in one of the armies and you'll get yourselves killed over two countries your father and I love, but left for a better life here. It isn't our war!"

I was patient. "It became our war when Susanna disappeared, Mother. You know I'll never be happy without her. Since she's been gone, I can't find meaning in anything I do. Please understand."

"That's the trouble, I do understand, it's just that if something happened to you or Tom too, I don't see how your father and I could bear to go on. Losing Susanna and not knowing if she's dead or alive, tortured or well, is driving us half crazy," and she started crying again.

I had never seen her like this before. My father moved over to the sofa and put his arms around her as she cried. After a moment he motioned for me to leave then offered her his handkerchief and talked to her about letting their two oldest sons run their own lives. As I left he explained, "We need to have faith in them to be careful. Young men were always searching for adventure. If it weren't a war, they would find something equally dangerous to do or would never be satisfied with their lives

Later in the afternoon we all went into town for confession and the evening mass that was being said especially for Susanna. Papa lit a candle every day for her and one for their unborn baby. After having lost his brother, then his first wife in childbirth, and finally his two best friends; he believed much like Susanna that God takes exactly what He wants. He told us he thought if he raised enough heavenly commotion, maybe God would answer his prayers. The priest offered a mass for Susanna often and he hoped by getting other people to pray for his lighted candles and by himself asking for her safety and the good health of his wife and unborn baby several times a day, maybe God would answer his prayers. Once before, when Susanna had measles and pneumonia she had been spared. Why was she given her life then only to have lost it now? Surely she must be hidden away safely somewhere and one day, when the war was over, she would come home.

As we left the church that night, we met Carolyn Smithson on the arm of Jonathan Opiela. She and Jonathan spoke to me, but there was none of the old camaraderie between us now. We probably wouldn't ever be friends again because I had broken the engagement and had broken Carolyn's heart. All the plans had been made for the wedding last fall, but I came close to standing her up at the altar. Jonathan had told me I was the biggest heel he had ever known and Carolyn had said she was never going to ever speak to me. Maybe the two of them would get together since they had a like interest--their dislike for me.

After I got into Tom's car for the ride back to the farm, Tom asked lightheartedly, "Hey, Joseph, do you think maybe you should have gone through with the wedding? You don't look too good right now."

"Marrying Carolyn would have been settling for second best. She's a nice girl and was a good friend, but it wouldn't have been fair to her to get married. I just wish I had never asked her in the first place.

"I wish I hadn't acted the way I did toward Susanna. She probably hates me too."

"She probably adores you now just as much as ever. The thing I can't understand is why hasn't she written to us? She's bound to know we're all worried sick about her. Usually she's so thoughtful. Even if Opa doesn't want her to communicate, as stubborn as she is, I can't imagine her not slipping off on her own to send a note."

"That's the only thing that makes me worry that she isn't alive. What if she was somehow killed in the invasion of Luxembourg? It would have been just like her to lead a revolt and get herself killed."

"We'll find out. I'm going with you in June."

"You can't do that to Mother."

"Look, I never wanted to come back last fall. I haven't accomplished a thing since I got back and I don't want to. I don't love Susanna in the same way you do, but she's my sister and as much as we used to argue and pick at each other, I'm miserable without her. We need to go to Europe and turn over every loose stone till we find her. Somebody has to know where she went."

"Unfortunately, we might have trouble getting into Luxembourg without getting drafted into the German Army. Don't forget we're both German citizens as well as Americans and if we go over there, then go back to France; we could be shot because we're Germans. We may have to get one of Papa's investigators to do some of our leg work for us in Luxembourg. I think we should check out Switzerland too. Opa might have thought it would be safer there."

"I think they already checked that out, but, of course we could be sure they didn't miss anything."

By the time they made the three-and-a-half mile journey home, they had already started to make plans for their search. They had no idea what condition all of Europe had gotten into in the months since they had left. Their search was going to be overwhelming.

On April 24 Mother went into labor in the early morning. She always had hard labors and this one proved to be no different. Papa walked her. He rubbed her back. He promised he would never ever allow it to happen again and he yelled at the doctor to do something when the pain made our mother cry out and finally scream.

At last, after twelve gut wrenching hours, she delivered a 23 inch 8 pound boy they named Paul. He was a very skinny, blue-eyed, blond who seemed only to cry when he was hungry.

The family rejoiced over his birth and none of us seemed to notice what a long-skinny little baby he was. He seemed beautiful to each of us. Papa, who was always terrified for Mother when she was pregnant, had a thanksgiving mass offered as soon as it could be arranged.

"I hope God hadn't given this wonderful little boy as a replacement for our lost little girl," he sighed. "I need to ask that the baby be an addition to our family instead. Nobody can replace Susanna."

On the 14th of June, with the sinking of the Lusitania still clear in everybody's mind, Tom and I left Bayland for France. Mother and Papa hugged us so long and so tightly as we stood outside the train station, that we wondered if we would be able to get loose to board the train, then Grandfather and Grandmother got a hold of us for more. By the time we climbed aboard, everybody was crying. It would be over three years before Tom and I saw them again.

Chapter 2

After Opa died I went from having periods of mild despair to deep depression, always with melodies to match my moods pounding in my head. I tried not thinking of them, but could not push them out of my core. Minnie was my constant companion. She sniffed in the grass and chased the birds, but never strayed far from my side. Without a doubt, I wouldn't be an old woman telling this story if it hadn't been for Minnie.

I spent my days looking out on the serenity of the mountains and wondered how there could possibly be another world with wars and cities and hoards of people bustling down streets. It seemed as if I was the only person living on the earth. I had always loved being alone outdoors. At home I had been strictly forbid to ever go to the woods alone. My parents and grandparents worried about hobos and kidnapers and never trusted me not to climb too high in the trees or possibly to fall into the lake or maybe even get hit by a train that was passing through. Now, as Minnie and I sat on a rock overlooking the mountains I thought how upset they would be if they knew about the life I was living. It was July and I hadn't seen any of them for more than a year. I wondered if they had given up looking for me. The thought of it made me begin to grieve for my family and myself all over again.

My thirteenth birthday brought a loneliness I have never felt since. I woke in the morning feeling as if my body was too heavy to move.

The thin air felt heavy and I had trouble breathing. My stomach was filled with butterflies. "Oh God!" I cried, "Have You forgotten me? Please do something!" I cried. "I'm so lonesome I think I'm dying!"

There wasn't a sound in response except for a gentle breeze blowing through the open window. I didn't dare allow myself to think about whether God was real. I had become close to Him. There was nobody else to talk to so I discussed all manners of things with He and Minnie every day. My faith was never shaken. After all, without God who would have been left? That quiet lonely period of time deepened my faith and dependence on God for the rest of my life. Things hurt me after that, but I never experienced fear again even when I was sure I was about to suffer horribly and die.

To occupy my time I made a makeshift bow from the branch of a sapling and some thick cord and whittled points on the straightest sticks I could find to make arrows. I spent hours shooting them at various targets until I could hit anything within my range. I also taught Minnie all sorts of tricks. She could do backward flips and could walk a tightrope. We went through a routine over and over with her playing dead, retrieving sticks that I had pitched for her, and dancing for me on her hind legs. Eventually we started hiding objects from each other playing hide and find. I almost thought of her as human after a while.

Years later my sons loved the toys I invented while I lived in the mountains. One favorite was called a whirligig. It was spring-loaded apparatus made from a small sapling. I made a launching device from another sapling that looked sort of like my bow and I was thrilled by the heights my toy was able to achieve as it whirled round and round up into the air. An active mind with few diversions can be very creative. Eventually I had several different rudimentary whistles of various sizes that allowed me to satisfy some of my musical cravings.

I hadn't seen another human since Opa had died and I was

lonesome. Maybe Rudolph Switzer had died and nobody would ever come for me. Summer would be short and then Minnie and I would be snowed in again for months. After worrying about that for a while, I was starting to panic. Something had to be done to give me hope! Maybe I could write a long letter to my parents and then if anybody ever did come, even if I wasn't alive anymore, they would find the letter and mail it. At least, my family would know what had happened to me. I wasn't sure I could survive another winter, especially since I would be all alone the next time.

Inside the lodge I found paper Mother bought for the purpose of writing to them just before I left Bayland. I took out one of the sharp indelible pencils Mother had told me to use for the long trip a letter would have to make to get to Bayland. The letter started with an explanation of where I had been for the past year and what had happened to Opa, and then I sent my love:

I told them, "I love you both so much and I'm so afraid I'll never see you again. I wish I had minded you better when I had the chance. Please tell my brothers I love them. I love Joseph too, but it would probably be best not to tell him that since he's a married man, probably with a baby on the way by now."

After that thought, I choked up with tears rolling down my cheeks. Suddenly I realized that the world was rolling along as always even though it had completely stopped for me. It occurred to me that it would be best not to dwell on the uncomfortable aspects of my life if this letter would be the last time my family ever heard from me, so I geared the rest of it to the pleasant things I experienced from day to day. I described the beauty of the mountains, what a good cook I had become, how much I had grown, and how womanly I was now. By the time the letter was finished and placed in the stamped envelope provided by my parents, I felt much better.

Throughout the summer I only killed small game for food since there was no way to preserve leftover meat. The air in the mountains was thin. After working and climbing so much, my stamina was remarkable. I took the horses out every day for grass and walked about looking for mint tea and berries. By the end of July I had piles of wood chopped to be ready for the cold months that would be coming soon.

One day in late August, as I bent down to pick up a rabbit I had just shot, somebody grabbed me from behind, picked me up off the ground, and doubled my arms behind me. Minnie had been barking hysterically, but I thought she was just excited about the hunt for a rabbit or something. Now she was biting the man's leg and growling with all her might. Just as he reached down to knock her off; he lost his hold on me, allowing me to land a firm kick backwards into his groin. Joseph had always told me if a boy or a man ever tried to hold me against my will, I should kick them between the legs with all the strength I had and he was right. The man was out on the ground curled up in a ball the minute my foot made contact with his body. Unfortunately, by that time there were two other men on me. One of them kicked Minnie so hard she rolled into the bushes screaming.

I kicked and screamed while the man I kicked between the legs stood hunched over, still trying to get his breath. A number of men had gathered and were standing around me while the two men laughed and cajoled at me and ripped at my dress. Suddenly somebody fired a shot. The next thing that happened was very confusing at first, but it seemed as if the men who had attacked me were fighting with the others. One man pulled two off of me then hit them so hard they both fell to the ground.

The man who rescued me was dressed impressively in a uniform with medals and gold braid everywhere. He was tall and looked to be about Papi's age. He yelled something at me, but I didn't understand. I asked if he could speak French, German, or English. In school I had also learned Spanish, but wasn't as fluent in that and thought it unlikely that anybody on an Italian mountaintop would be speaking Spanish.

He answered me in French in a harsh voice. "Where are your parents, child?"

His eyes looked kind even though his voice was threatening. I told the truth because soon it would be easy to see that there were no adults around. "My parents live in the United States. I was visiting my grandfather last summer in Luxembourg when it was invaded, so he brought me here where I would be safe. He died in early April though." I thought a moment and asked hopefully, "Is the war over?"

"No, the war isn't over. As a matter-of-fact, it has escalated tremendously since then. You are standing in the middle of what will soon be a war zone," he roared, as if I was hard of hearing and ignorant too. "Italy declared war on Austria-Hungry on May 23 so you have to get out of here soon."

"I don't know how to do that. I would like to go home very much. My parents don't even know where I've been for the past year. Do you think you could help me?"

He was matter-of-fact and abrupt. "Little senorina, I can't help you get home, but we're going to a post at the foot of the mountains where you can probably stay until the war is over. You can't stay here."

"If I can't go home, I have to stay here or my grandfather's man won't be able to find me after the war. I'll never get home," I explained as I picked up Minnie who had just limped over to me.

"You won't live to see the end of the war if the enemy soldiers get a hold of you. We'll spend the night here while you pack up your things and then we'll head out early tomorrow morning. Take only what you need, you have no choice." He looked at me kindly and asked, "How old are you?"

"I just turned thirteen a few days ago."

The soldier looked away thoughtfully, "I have children nearly your age. If I were your father, I would want you away from here even if it weren't a war zone. You can't stay up here all winter by yourself."

I knew that was probably true, especially with the food supply dwindling the way it was, so I didn't argue anymore. "I'll go inside and get my things together. If you're interested, I'll share my rabbit with you when it's done. I have some mint tea and a new loaf of bread."

I think he was taken back by my generosity when I had so little to offer and this time he spoke softly to me when he said, "That's very kind of you. I thank you for the invitation," and he smiled.

"Good," I said happily, "It's been a long time since I've had anybody to talk to."

Inside I gathered up what food was left and put it in a bag, and then I bundled up my cold weather gear and what clothes I had brought with me. Everything was tight on me since my body had started developing last fall. As I emptied a small storage chest, I ran across the soft cotton flannel pads Mother had made for me in case I started my periods while I was gone. A stab of sorrow pierced my heart when I thought of her. I remembered our heart to heart discussion about the changes I would experience and the second conversation we had had in the woods the morning before I left Bayland. Papi had seemed embarrassed. Quickly I changed my thoughts to the letter. It was in a little case, put there for safekeeping. Maybe the soldier could mail it for me. Before closing the envelope I added the news of my rescue, though I didn't know where I would be taken.

My hairbrush and the last of my personal items were gathered in a small cotton bag and the last thing I took out was the gold chain leash and small gold collar with Minnie's name on it. If we were going to be going to civilization, she would need her collar and leash again.

Up here I had always worried that my little dog would get hung up somewhere if she wore a collar.

By the time I finished my letter and packed, the meat was ready. I set the table as nicely as I could and put a small bouquet of wild flowers in a small tin can, long ago emptied of its contents, then called the soldier in to join me.

He was kind and the tone of his voice had softened, "If we're going to eat together, I should know your name, senorina. I am Major Altoviti and you are?"

"I'm Susanna Gertrude Theresa Strashoffer Von Helldorf."

"But you are American?"

"Yes, I was born there, but my family is European."

"You are related to the Strashoffers of Luxembourg? The steel manufacturer?"

"He was my grandfather and his son was my father, but when my father and mother both died, I was adopted by my father's friend Rolf Von Helldorf."

"Your adoptive father is now in America?"

"Yes, he moved there from Germany when he was 20. His wife, my new mother is French. She moved there when she was 22. I wonder what they think now that France and Germany are fighting with each other."

"I would hate to think about it. They must be very worried about you, Susanna."

"I know they are. My brother, Tom, and my grandparents, and my best friend Ilona are probably worried too," I sighed regretfully as I thought about Joseph who probably wasn't at all worried. "Actually, I have written a letter explaining everything. Do you think there is any way you could get it off to them, possibly at a post office or through your army somehow? It would mean everything to them."

He looked softly into my hopeful eyes. "I'll do everything I can, but there is war everywhere, even in the oceans. I don't know if it will ever get through. If you care to entrust it to me, I'll do all I can."

The next morning I took one last look around, and then mounted my horse with Minnie safely popped in the shoulder pouch Opa had made for her before we left the little village for the cabin. Most of my gear was strapped on the packhorses and one of the soldiers rode Opa's horse because his was lame. We wound through the mountain passes until night when we made camp. I stayed close to the Major at all times, never trusting any of the others. I remembered what Opa had said about soldiers of any army being dangerous to young girls and would never forget how they all stood around and watched me be attacked when they had first come to my mountain.

After a week we finally came to a clearing at the base of the mountains. In the compound was a large hospital building with an orphanage across from it. It was an army settlement with a small airstrip, barns for the army horses, and a number of plain, official-looking buildings for the military personnel.

The major took Minnie and me into the orphanage to make arrangements for us almost as soon as we arrived. One of the nuns met us at the door and led us to Sister Macrina's small office. They spoke in French as he introduced us to the old nun who ran the orphanage. The woman made it clear that since I would be one of the older girls in the orphanage, I would be expected to help with the cleaning and the care of the other children. The unsmiling woman warned me that life would not be easy and, of course, that dirty dog would have to go.

Without further comment I stood, excused myself, and left. The major followed me out.

"Child, you have no choice but to stay with the nuns. Be realistic, you have no place to go right now!"

I looked at him with tears in my eyes. "Minnie is all I have left! I'd rather die than lose her and I mean that. I know all about death and

I know what I'm saying." With that I put Minnie back in my carrier bag and mounted my horse. I told him, "I thank you for everything you tried to do for me, but I have to go now. Please, if you can use my grandfather's horse, keep it as a gift from me. It will be easier if I only have to provide grass for three horses this winter instead of four."

After I had ridden a short distance I turned and saw the major still watching me ride toward the mountains. I noticed that he continued to watch until he only looked like a speck in the distance. I knew I would probably die early in the winter, but I hoped he wouldn't feel sad about it. He had tried to help, but some things were just impossible.

I rode all afternoon until I came to a small cave just big enough for me to take my gear inside and make a bed. There was plenty of brush for firewood and it looked as if I could make a good pen and windbreak up against the rocks for the horses. Somehow, I noticed that no matter how bad things got, God did manage to always provide and I was careful to thank Him every night in my prayers. My anger with the Almighty had faded over the months and I realized that I had to depend on Him for my needs.

The days passed quickly as I tried to get ready for cold weather. I chopped firewood just as I had done on my mountain and cut and tore grass wherever I could find it to store it for winter. Game was plentiful, but my ammunition supply was getting low and I was going to have to take care not to let my fire go out very often or I would get to the point where I wouldn't be able to start a new one. It seemed as if calm had come over me now. I never worried about my family anymore and I seemed not to worry about myself. I had told God to do whatever He wanted to with me and I meant it. Dying was the worst thing that could happen and, frankly, that sounded pretty good sometimes even though I was enjoying the outdoors and the quiet time to think of new music to play. If I ever got near a piano again, I thought, I would be able to play forever without playing anything that had ever been heard by anybody but myself.

As the weather changed and winter came blowing in, things got worse every day. By January I had long ago stopped trying to be clean. The weather was bitter cold and the only water I had was snow I melted over the fire that I never allowed to burn out. Game was scarce and so was ammunition and I hadn't had anything but meat to eat in months. I tried to get out every day to gather food for the horses and to exercise, but my body was weakening and it took great effort to leave my cave to do anything now.

In January I wondered if it would be all right to just lie down and not get up. It would be such a relief. I was so weak and I had little desire to live anymore. Then one day when the sun was shining, I looked into Minnie's sad little brown eyes. Her little brow was wrinkled as she stared at me trustingly and I realized that I had to do something to survive. What would Minnie do without me? A dog so small could never live up here alone. It seemed to give me energy just to come to that realization. After much thought, I decided to move my camp closer to the compound below. Maybe they would sell me some food since money wasn't a problem. I had saved Opa's wallet just as he had instructed me to do. Why hadn't I thought of it sooner?

That same day I packed everything up, put Minnie in her pouch, and put my carefully tended fire out. It was time to move on. As I got closer to the compound I felt a flutter in my stomach. What if things didn't work out?

It was early evening when I tied the horses outside a building that looked and smelled like a kitchen. I could hear many people talking and thought it must be about dinnertime. The smell of food cooking made my stomach growl and it caused a wave of weakness to pass over me. I sat down outside the back door with my head between my knees for a few minutes. When I thought I could handle my negotiations I knocked on the door.

A heavyset nun came to the door and glared down at me. "What do you want?" she demanded in Italian.

"Please, Sister, do you speak French?" I asked.

The nun nodded in the affirmative then again wanted to know, "Why are you bothering me at this busy time of my day? What do you want?"

"I am very hungry. I want to know, could you sell me some food? My body is in great need."

"I'm afraid not! There's barely enough for the people I have to serve now let alone I should start selling it to outsiders. This is not a cafe. You go on now, go back to wherever you came from," she yelled as she slammed the door in my face.

I sat back down in the shadows near the horses with my head resting on my knees and for a minute thought of nothing. Off in the distance I could hear laughing and over the mountain ridge to the north and east I could see fire flaring up in the sky sort of like the fireworks they used to have in Bayland on the Fourth of July. I felt peaceful as if nothing mattered and just rested.

About 30 minutes after I had sat down, the door to the kitchen opened and a man threw a large tub of food into a trashcan. Suddenly I had an idea. It would have been sickening in any other circumstance, but I knew it would keep Minnie and me alive for a while longer so I scampered over to the can and opened the lid. By the moonlight I could see half-eaten biscuits and little bits of potato and vegetables. There were a few segments of orange. Everything had been covered with cooking grease they had also thrown out, but I didn't care. I was so hungry I stood and stuffed myself with both hands. Nothing had ever tasted so good! Every few minutes I threw something down for Minnie who ate so vigorously that she made little snort noises and acted half drunk. We were full for the first time since last summer. After that, I led the horses off to look for a place to spend the night. I felt sick. It had been so long since I had been able to eat my fill.

As we walked through the compound I saw a number of military personnel, nurses, and nuns looking at us. They probably all wondered who the young, unkempt girl with the three horses and dog could be, but none of them stopped me.

On the edge of the compound was a large white building with an electric light bulb hanging from the ceiling that glowed brightly. It was empty, but when I looked in, I saw a piano! A piano! I shouted, "Oh God can I play one more time before I die? Thank you God, you truly are good!" as I tied the horses and ran inside. I looked at the big old instrument with amazement, then touched it lightly, then played a few notes with one hand. My heart was beating so fast I wondered if I would be able to see it from outside my clothes. The next thing I did was sit down on the little stool in front of it and start playing. After that I was lost to my music. I played all the music I had thought about during those lonely months in the mountains. Sometime in the night as my heart lifted, I changed to the music I had known and played all my life and was filled with joy. I guess people could hear me playing in the distance because I was aware of a few who ventured out into the night to sit in the back of the hall to listen. I was so intoxicated by my music that I hardly noticed them and Minnie never did more than prick her ears up and look at them wisely as she stood guard over me.

Dr. Alessandro Adami listened to me play all night, captivated by my music. Of course I didn't know his name then, but I was aware of him from the moment he entered the room. When the sun started to shine in the windows and I came out of my trance-like night of playing, I heard him get up and go outside. In a few minutes when I went out, I saw him staring at me as he stood by the corner of the building. I pretended I didn't notice and took my horses by the reins and pulled them over to the kitchen. I looked to see if he was still watching and when I was sure that he had gone, I opened the trash can and started to eat again while I threw scraps to my little dog and talked softly to her in German.

When we had eaten our fill, I led the horses over to a pen where other horses were eating. I sneaked inside and come out with all the hay I could carry then slipped back inside and came out with two cans of chopped grain. When I had finished caring for my animals, I sat down with Minnie in my lap and dozed, propped up against a tree trunk while the horses ate.

When the horses had finished eating, I rode to a thick stand of trees about a mile from the compound and made a makeshift sort of camp. My plan was to eat twice a day at the compound and play the piano all night every night. I would sleep during the days. I wouldn't need a fire anymore if I spent my nights inside. I didn't allow myself to think about what I would do if it rained or if the hall was busy so I couldn't spend the night there. The weather was very cold, but much warmer at the base of the mountains than it had been up higher.

I slept all day and when I awoke, I realized that I was hungry again. My body must have been making up for lost time because I hadn't experienced that sensation very much in the last year-and-a-half. I had been weak, but not often hungry. It was hard to wait till the sun was setting to eat again, but I knew it was essential not to be seen rummaging through the trash cans or I might be chased away and I was basing my whole life on those cans and that piano.

As the nights went by I could feel my audience grow larger, even though there usually was no light in the building with the piano. The people came into the dark very quietly and listened, then left just as quietly without speaking to me. Weeks later several of them told me that they felt it would have been wrong to interrupt so they never said a word. I saw Dr. Adami was usually there sitting close by my side whenever there was light enough for me to see, but I still didn't know his name. All I knew was that he was very young and handsome and seemed moved by my music.

One morning when I went to my trashcan to eat, there was a heaping plate of biscuits, and scrambled eggs sitting on the lid along with a clean fork. I looked at it a moment, wondering if I dared eat it, then looked around to see if anybody was watching. Finally I looked up in the sky and crossed myself before taking the plate and carrying it around to the cover of my horses to eat.

Just as I was getting started, Dr. Alessandro Adami came around from behind the horses and sat down in front of me. He said, "You know, that's my breakfast."

I jumped, clutching the plate of food tightly. I didn't understand what he had said and asked, "Do you speak French, German, or English?"

He smiled and said, "I was educated in Austria before all this started so I speak German. I said that's my breakfast you're eating. By the way, I'm Dr. Alessandro Adami, one of the doctors here at the hospital"

"I'm sorry. I didn't know it belonged to anybody, sitting out here like it was. Do you want it back since I've touched it?"

"I put it there for you. It's the least I can do to pay for the fabulous entertainment you've provided for me all these miserable cold nights here on the compound. How did you ever learn to play like that?"

Words seemed to just tumble from me and I couldn't seem to stop their flow. "I've always just naturally known how to play, but I started attending the Cleveland Conservatory of Music in the States when I was five years old. I haven't had a chance to play for more than a year and I was afraid my fingers would be stiff. At first they were, but they're improving every night."

"You're American?" he asked with a smile on his face and a note of surprise in his voice. "You speak German like a German!"

"I also speak French as if I am French. French and German were my first two languages because my first mother was German and those were her only languages. I only learned English after she and my father were killed in an accident when I was five. My adoptive parents are German and French, both naturalized Americans."

"How on earth did you end up living like this, eating out of garbage cans and homeless?"

Now I was at a loss for words, embarrassed, wondering what he must think of me for living so poorly and what I must look like after all these months of living in a cave. To excuse myself, I told him the whole story of the invasion, the lodge, the orphanage, and the cave. It had been a tale of steady decline. It had been so long since I had really talked to anybody, that I talked and talked.

"Are you telling me the truth about all this? I can't imagine a girl your age living on her own all these months."

"Why would I lie?" I asked. "I have nothing to gain or lose by making you believe a lie."

He looked at me straight in the eyes and then I think he somehow did believe me. After studying me for what seemed like a long time he said, "Well, for sure you can't continue living outdoors anymore. You need a room or something and some decent food. Though the food here can hardly be called decent, you won't starve eating it. I know somebody who can probably help us. Will you wait right here for me to come back? Promise to wait?"

"I have no place to go," I answered dully.

Dr. Adami left me sitting behind the kitchen with the horses.

I was sleeping with Minnie curled up on my lap by the time they returned. I'm sure I looked like a ragamuffin with my tattered, dirty coat and the holes in my gloves. Stringy curls had fallen out of my hat and my boots were falling apart.

A large older nun with a round face, brown eyes, and a mouth that looked like it was accustomed to laughing a lot crouched down close to me and shook me gently, "Wake up child. I need to talk to you."

"I forgot to tell you, she doesn't speak Italian." I heard Dr. Adami say. "Talk to her in French or German."

"This is Italy. She's going to have to learn the language!" She protested.

I was quickly awake and on alert. I looked up at the nun, not hopeful or afraid, but wondering what would happen next.

"Come along child, you need a bath and some food," the nun said without introducing herself.

"Dr. Adami gave me his breakfast, but my horses haven't eaten today. What shall I do about them?"

"You won't need them anymore. You're going to be staying here. May I give them to the army? They always need good horses, though I would say these beasts look like they could also use a few good meals."

"Grass is scarce in the mountains and they haven't had grain in a long time. I already gave one of them away last summer." I said wistfully once again embarrassed, feeling that I had been deralect in caring for them. "It's probably best for the soldiers to have them. It's so hard to keep them fed everyday." Then I thought of Minnie and pulled my dog close to me. "I'll never give up Minnie. I won't!"

"How long have you had her?" the nun asked.

"Two years. She came over with me from home." I answered with glassy eyes.

"Well, this is a hospital and I never allow animals here, but you seem like a very responsible girl. If you keep her very clean and out of everybody's way, I don't think she should be a problem, providing she is well-trained and doesn't bark all the time." She turned to Dr. Adami and gently ordered him to take my things over to the hospital and then take the horses to the stable.

The old nun, Morther Maria Elizabeth, didn't give me any choices. She just took over. They left my belongings outside since everything was so dirty. "We'll wash it all before we bring it inside. Do you have a hairbrush and some clean clothes in any of that?" she asked as she pointed to my grubby bags.

I nodded that I did and took one bag inside with me. Mother Maria Elizabeth took the bag from me and carried it around to her private quarters with me following closely behind.

"What's your name child?" Mother asked gently.

"All of it?"

"Yes all of it and then I'll decide what to call you."

"Susanna Gertrude Theresa Strashoffer Von Helldorf."

"Are you sure you're not a German?" her eyes narrowed.

"No, I'm American and I'm Catholic too," I added, thinking that the nun would look more forgivingly at me with that information.

"Well good. That will make things much easier for us both. Do you know your prayers?"

"Yes," I answered nervously, "I had religion class daily through the school year, and we went to mass every day as long as I can remember." I wondered if possibly this kind lady might think I was some kind of a heathen.

Interestingly, Mother didn't seem to regard what I had just said as important or unimportant. She just went on with the matters at hand. "The first thing we need to do is get you out of these clothes and get you a bath," she said in an authoritative voice.

"I'd like that. I'm usually a clean person," I explained, "but it was so hard living in the mountains in the cold and with so little water. I'm ashamed," I admitted, hanging my head.

"Nonsense. There's nothing to be ashamed of. I can't think of another child who would have survived up there a week in such cold weather let alone for months." Mother poured hot water from her small oil stove into a galvanized foot tub she had pulled out from under her sink, and then she added some cool water. Noticing my matted hair and the smell, both conditions that she commented upon, she told me it was going to take several tubs of water to get me clean as she put another kettle of water on to heat.

She helped me pull off my tattered clothing and I soon found myself standing before her naked. For some reason I didn't feel embarrassed, I guess because the whole situation had been approached in such a matter-of-fact manner. My body was badly emaciated, but I noticed that my hip bones were curved like those of a woman, and somehow I had grown small round breasts, and I had a small, thin patch of curly black pubic hair. I hadn't removed my clothes in such a long time that I never realized the changes. Mother commented with a sigh on just how odd nature was that even with my lack of nutrition, I had managed to begin to develop into a woman.

"Have you started to menstruate yet?" she asked kindly.

I felt my face reddened, but answered directly. "No, Mama thought I would start that last year before I left, but I never did. Do you think I should have?" I worried.

"No, it will happen soon enough. There's plenty of time for that. Come get in the tub before the water gets cold. Here's some soap. It's harsh, but will get you good and clean."

By the time we finished bathing me and washed my louse-ridden hair, Mother had emptied the water four times. My hair was so curly that we couldn't get the matted tangles out. She used alcohol to kill the lice and tried to use a fine comb to remove the nits, but finally had to resort to bobbing it.

"I hope it grows out before your mother and father see you or they may kill me," she exclaimed, "but I don't see any way we could have ever gotten rid of these lice with all that hair. I never have seen so many curls!"

"My biological father and his father both had hair like mine too," I volunteered. "I used to go to the beauty parlor every month to get it thinned because my father couldn't do a thing with it and neither could my mother." I wished I could see myself in a mirror, but knew a nun would never have one so I didn't even ask.

Mother looked me over carefully then told me, "Most girls your age would have reacted differently to having their hair cut, but after having such a hard life, maybe you're just grateful for anything you can get." When she was satisfied that I was clean and free of lice she asked, "Why don't you unwrap that towel and get dressed now? We'll see how your dresses fit. I don't suppose you've worn any of them for a long time."

"It's been a while."

I was embarrassed to note that everything from my drawers out was in shreds. The sleeves on my dresses were too short and the skirt lengths were indecently short. I was so horribly thin that everything hung on me. In spite of my lack of nutrition and my loss of weight, I must have grown at least four inches in the nearly two years I had been away from home!

Mother put her fingers to her lips and thought as she looked at me, trying to decide how to clothe me. "This will never do! Let me think. The nurse's here are grown women and I don't want you around an encampment of soldiers dressed like a woman. The orphanage never has any extra clothes. Would it bother you terribly to dress like a nun?" she asked. "We could tie your hair back in a small scarf to make you look like a postulant and we'll call you Sister Theresa. That should protect you from the men and we'll be able to keep you clothed too. How would you feel about that?"

"I don't mind. I'm just glad to have a place for Minnie and me to stay."

"You're a good girl, Sister," she said with a half smile on her face. "Now let's use your leftover bath water and wash your little friend here, then we'll go to the kitchen for some lunch. After that, you need to nap. We're all going to want to hear you play tonight."

Mother Maria Elizabeth put me to bed in her own small iron cot that afternoon, then set about cleaning a large utility closet out to make a small place for me to sleep that night close to her own room and the cubicles of the other nuns. On the bulletin boards she put up notices announcing that Sister Theresa would be giving a musical program for anybody who wanted to come to the hall. It would begin at 7:00 that night after vespers.

"Are you at all nervous about playing in front of some people tonight, child?" she asked belatedly.

"No," I told her with confidence. "I'm used to playing for an audience. Until this happened, I played for people all the time."

As I entered the little chapel for vespers that night, I felt at peace. I wondered how I could have ever felt tired of going to mass all the time when Papi had required me to go every day back home. The service was so much the same as the ones at St. Joseph's Church in Bayland that when I closed my eyes, I could almost believe I was there, sitting beside my parents, Joseph, and Tom and my little brothers. If things continued to get better for me, I thought, I would need to try to write another letter to them. Right now it would only upset them to hear about how things had been. I didn't think I would ever tell them about staying in the cave or the men who had attacked me up in the mountains. They might think less of me if they ever found out about things like that and I knew they always expected me to be perfect.

By the time vespers were over and we entered the hall, it was packed. Mother led me to the front and introduced me as Sister

Theresa who had just arrived. She gave no further explanation, though many of the people had already seen me when I played in the night dressed in rags. At the end of the first number, the Ave Maria, the applause started. It was like turning on a light for me. Suddenly I felt happy, as if I didn't have a care in the world!

"I've been asked to help make your stay here a little more fun!" I told them in French. They all laughed. Things were as bad as they could be. They applauded again. "We can do this several different ways. I can just play what I think you might want me to play, or you can tell me what you want to hear, or I can play whatever you want and you can sing along. What shall it be?" I asked, once again speaking in French with Mother interpreting in Italian this time.

The mood was getting high. The people there had been desperate for something to lighten their burdens so that almost any break from the day-to-day horrors of war was a relief. They all knew I could play classical music because many of them had heard me playing in the night, but I don't think they knew I could be an entertainer. One soldier called out the name of a tune he wanted to hear.

"I don't know that one. Come up here and sing a little of it for me!"

He was embarrassed and didn't move so I walked close to where I had heard the voice and coaxed him. "Come on, don't be shy!"

The other men lifted him up and pushed him forward. I grabbed his hand and pulled him over to the piano. "Come on, hum a little of it. You can do it. They'll never hear you!"

Finally he did sing a little and I was surprised to discover that he had a beautiful tenor voice. Instantly I caught the tune and started to play. Everyone in the audience seemed to know the tune and soon they were all singing. Now that the ice was broken, it seemed as if each person wanted me to play something special for him or her. Mother stood right beside the piano and Minnie sat under the stool throughout the program.

At 11:00 the crowd broke up and everybody reluctantly went back to their barracks. Mother Maria Elizabeth was so pleased she couldn't stop smiling. "You're just what this place has needed! Tonight you made people sing who haven't had a happy moment in months!"

When we got back to the hospital, Mother showed me where Minnie and I could sleep in the small cubicle made out of the utility closet that was next to her room. That night I slept in a bed with sheets, though only a small cot, for the first time since I had left the lodge. For once I was warm enough and I wasn't hungry. There were no dreams for me, but only the peaceful sleep of an exhausted child with very few worries.

LINDA STEELE

Friedrich

*I*n October a tattered letter arrived at the Bayland Post Office all the way from Italy. It was so damaged that it was hard to tell who the addressee was, even though it definitely said Bayland, Ohio on the front of it. Mr. Helman, the postmaster, looked at it with a magnifying glass and finally decided that it might say Von Helldorf on it. After getting the opinion of several of the workers, he decided to call Von Helldorf Textiles to see if possibly my son or I might want to come down to look at it.

He left a message with the secretary. It was such a pretty day that he had taken a little extra time to sit on the court house lawn to look at the beautiful orange and yellow leaves on the trees. I'm sure he never expected such a fuss when he arrived back at the post office! Both of us were pacing at the door with red faces, looking like two ferocious giants.

"Where have you been?" I growled.

"I thought the post office was supposed to open at 1:00!" My son, Rolf, added in a loud voice.

We were men of power and wealth in this part of the country and actually all over the world and Mr. Helman was intimidated. "I am sorry gentlemen. It was such a beautiful day that I took a little extra time to enjoy it. I didn't know I had anything urgent pending. Please excuse me."

Rolf looked as if he had all he could do to keep from throttling him as he took a deep breath and explained, "I'm sorry, but my daughter has been missing for more than a year and we are hoping that letter might have some information about her. My secretary said the address on the envelope was hand-written. We never thought of looking in Italy. Please let us see it, quickly, man!"

As Mr. Helman hurried to his desk to retrieve the letter he reminded them that it might not even be their letter because the envelop was badly *damaged. He had just thought it looked like it might have said Von Helldorf on the front.*

We snatched the envelope out of his hand the minute he picked it up off his desk. Both of them looked at it by the window in the light. "I'm sure that's Susanna's handwriting!" Rolf verified in a loud voice as he tore the envelope open to find the letter in perfect condition. "Mein Gott, it is from her!" he shouted in German. "Mein Gott, she's alive in Italy!"

We embraced, laughed, cried, and then laughed again. Even Mr. Helman had tears glistening in his eyes. When we finally calmed down enough, we read Susanna's long letter, then we read it again, but this time we read between the lines and realized that things had not been at all good for her and might not be getting any better. If Opa was dead, that meant she was 13 years old and all by herself in Italy during a war! We both knew what country to look in, but were hardly comforted by the thought of her alone with no adult to care for her.

Rolf gave Mr. Helman a handsome tip then went straight to Western Union to send a cable to Tom and Joseph to tell them to start looking in Italy, and then we went home to spread the news to Gabrielle and Trudy, Rolf's mother. The news made Susanna's mother and grandmother cry with relief and yet it was also sobering. How terrible to have had to bury Opa in that cave then spend all those months alone in the mountains. Thank God for Minnie! What was going to happen to her now? Surely she would write more often now that she had been rescued and they would soon know where to find her.

As we had time to absorb the news, all of us started to worry more. Before we knew she was alive there was constant sadness and worry, but things were at a status quo Now that we knew she was alive it was a relief, but now we were worried sick about what might be happening to her. Would there be soldiers abusing her? Would she have enough to eat? What if she got in the crossfire and was shot or maybe bombed? There was hardly a safe place in Europe right now.

Rolf loved his four little boys, but without his three older children he couldn't have a happy day. He kept up with his daily candle lighting and mass was offered for the three several times a week. Most of the time he was withdrawn as if in deep thought, frequently spending hours on a Saturday or Sunday afternoon out in the woods sitting on a log just thinking and bargaining with God. I was helpless to do anything to make the situation better.

He hired a second nurse to take care of the children and Gabrielle started to go out in the community to make calls to shut-ins and women who needed her help in labor. Dr. Barnes had counted on Joseph and his friend Jacob, who had graduated from medical school with him to come into the practice to help with his growing patient loads. As it turned out, only Jacob had come and right now he was nursing a broken leg. The doctor was elated to have Gabrielle to depend on several times a week and it helped her keep her mind off her troubles. She was an excellent nurse and midwife.

Chapter 3

The compound was unnaturally quiet the first few days after I arrived. Mother Maria Elizabeth demanded nothing of me except my little musical performances. Together we made up a schedule of shows for each night with one night classical, one for singing, Sunday for religious music, one for nothing but requests, and one for popular music that Dr. Adami helped me to learn.

I ate three meals a day and while the nurses and soldiers complained incessantly about the bad food, I never did. Before every meal I thanked God for Dr. Adami and Mother Maria Elizabeth, knowing they had saved my life. In the afternoons Mother insisted that I sleep in order to get my body built up and though I wasn't tired, I did exactly as I was told without argument.

In just a few days my life had gotten into a routine. All the nuns traveled in two's and I was no different. I was not to go anywhere without another nun. Each morning I was up for mass and every evening before my performances I went to vespers. At times I thought of home and my family, but most of the time I tried not to think about them. Right now I wasn't ready to think of anything that could make me sad. I still didn't understand about the horrors of war even though Mother had tried to tell me that they were having an unusually quiet time of it right now and that things would often be very bad. One of the youngest sisters, Sister Olga, told me, "The flashes of light you see over the mountains are from artillery fire and bombs exploding. Those flashes usually mean that some young men have either been hurt or died."

I had no comment to that, but wondered whether there were battles being fought on my mountain and whether my cabin was still there.

So far I had no contact with anybody but the nuns. Mother seemed to discourage any mixing between the sisters and anybody else, though she did allow Dr. Adami to come by to see me every day and occasionally allowed me and whoever my companion was to join him for a meal in the kitchen. He had wanted to have me examined, but I absolutely refused to be looked at by a man and Mother assured him that she had checked me over completely and except for being dangerously thin, I seemed in excellent health.

I think it pleased her that I was modest about my body because on the first day when I hadn't seemed at all concerned about undressing in front of her she warned me several times that modesty was very important to all sisters, especially on a military compound. I think she thought I was immodest. The truth was I had been just too worn out to care about anything.

On the fifth night, during one of my performances, the sirens started to blare and there was instant commotion. The hall was evacuated, except for the recovering soldiers who were slower to leave than the able-bodied hospital staff. None of them expected help getting back to the hospital and they refused my assistance. They all understood, but I still didn't.

"Come on Sister!" Sister Olga ordered. "You can help too!"

Over the years I had begged Papi to let me spend time at Dr. Barnes office watching him stitch wounds and set broken arms, but he flatly refused. I had repeatedly asked my mother to allow me to watch some deliveries, but she said, "There's plenty of time for you to know about that when you are grown. Just enjoy being a child for now."

Though I had always wanted to be a doctor, I wasn't prepared for what I was going to experience on this night.

As we stepped out of the hall, we could see the commotion in front of the hospital as soldiers were being taken out of ambulances, trucks, and horse-drawn wagons. Everybody in the compound was out on the lawn along with the soldiers who had brought the men in. There were men screaming with pain and moaning loudly. Doctor's were swearing and ordering people around.

Mother said, "Sister Theresa, I know you're just a child, but do what you can if it isn't any more than holding somebody's hand. Some of these soldiers aren't much older than you and they're scared. Help them."

"Which ones should I go to? There are so many," I asked, horrified.

"They're triaging now. The hopeless cases, the ones who are going to die, will be put over there." She pointed to the left of us. "The ones who might not die but are hurt too badly to go back into the battlefield go in the middle, and the ones on the right can be treated and sent back to their units to fight again. They'll get all the attention from the doctors. The hopeless will get nothing and the ones in the middle may not get any care except what we nurses can do until a couple of days from now. I hate to leave you with it, but I have to get busy now. They're getting them sorted out already. Do as much as you can!"

I walked over to the area with the dying men. Some were screaming with pain. One was burned so badly that, even though I could see him breathing, he hardly looked like a person. He was barely moving. One boy, who looked to be about my age, was begging somebody to help him. I could see he had been shot in the belly as blood poured out of him in a slow, steady stream. One arm was missing. I sat down on the grass beside him and took his remaining hand. I spoke to him in French, hoping he could understand some of what I said.

"I'm Susanna. I'll stay with you until you move to the better side of life."

"Please don't let me die!" he screamed. "I don't want to die!"

"It's interesting," I told him. "You don't want to die, and so many times I have wanted that so much. I've been to heaven. It's a wonderful place! There are big trees with the warmest sunshine pouring down through them and as the wind blows ever so gently, you can hear singing--the most beautiful music you ever heard anywhere. Flowers of all colors bloom everywhere and the smells are more wonderful than anything you have ever smelled before."

The boy relaxed. His voice was calm now. "I wish you could go with me, Susanna," he answered in French.

"I do too. When I was there, they told me I could come back another time. They said it wasn't my time yet, but you won't be alone. There will be a nice lady, like your mother, who will take you by the hand and help you find your family and there will be the warmest light you ever felt and you'll be glad you're there."

I had been looking away, not really seeing anything as I talked. When I looked down at the young soldier, I could see that he was gone. I crossed myself, kissed him on the cheek, and said a prayer to the virgin asking her to meet him on the other side.

Suddenly I heard a coarse man's voice, "That was a great story you told the boy. It helped him, but only a kid would believe something like that."

I turned to see who was talking. It was another soldier lying on the next cot. Both legs were gone and tourniquets were tied tightly around the stumps. He was burned and skin on his arms and fingers hung in shreds off his body.

"I told him the truth. I have been to heaven."

"Then how are you here? Are you an angel?"

"No, I'm not an angel, but I was there once when I was a child and I know about it."

"I wish I could believe you. I'd like to think something good was going to happen, but I believe when you're dead you're dead. You just rot in the ground if you're lucky enough to be buried."

"When I was small, my parents were both killed in an accident. Later, I got sick with the measles and pneumonia. I was unconscious for days. During that time I saw myself laying in the bed with needles in my back and some tubes here and there and then I just walked off from myself with a beautiful lady and that's when I went to the woods. It all happened just like I said. My mother and father were both there, but then they made me go back because they said it wasn't my time. Even though I was very small, I remember it as if it was yesterday."

"I've been a monster of a person all my life. I don't deserve anything, but would you stay with me? You're so strong. Please hold my hand," he begged.

"I held his hand for over an hour and told him he would be forgiven for everything wrong he had ever done if he was truly sorry. By the time he finally took his last breath and relaxed, he seemed to believe everything I had told him and asked Jesus to forgive him and look for the good things he had done in life."

Throughout the night I moved from one dying man to another. Some were so far gone that their glazed stares made me know there was no use stopping at their sides. I only went to the ones I knew I could help. By sunup I was standing in a field of dead bodies. I sat down and put my head on my knees and shut my eyes and tried to collect myself. Right now I couldn't think of anything.

After a while a soft voice said, "Come along Sister, you can't help them anymore. You were wonderful." It was Mother Maria Elizabeth. "I have been watching you off and on all night. Though I don't know what you have said to the dying soldiers, I could tell that whatever it was, it seemed to give them great comfort. It is my job during a crisis to oversee everything and I was especially interested in seeing how you would handle the chaos of incoming casualties. You did very well."

The men who were first in line for care were still being treated in the surgeries and most of the men who were hurt too badly to return to the war had been moved inside to the halls. As I looked over at the moaning and crying group of soldiers who had still not received treatment, I said, "I need to go to those other men. Maybe I can help them."

You need to come with me to the kitchen and then go to bed."

"I'm not hungry or tired, Mother. I'll stay and see what I can do inside, please." I begged.

"If you still have the nerves left for this, we can use you, but you do have to eat. I've never seen a child thinner than you and I won't allow you to skip any meals until we get your weight up to something safe."

"All right, I'll try to eat, but it's hard to think about food when there's such tragedy all around."

"Everybody here needs to be strong to meet up with it." She was firm.

After breakfast, when we went inside the hospital, there were men everywhere. Still they moaned and begged for help. Nurses sat on the floor beside them with basins of water and rags bathing them, and bandaging their wounds. Some of the nurses sutured the deeper lacerations even though nurses would have never taken such responsibility under normal circumstances, even in Italy. Other nurses pulled dead pieces of skin off the soldiers with burns. I knew as brutal as it looked that if you didn't remove all the dead skin from a burn, bacteria would grow where it was dark, warm, and moist and then the patient would die of infection. What I didn't know was whether I could debride such wounds as the patient lay there screaming from the pain.

Mother pointed her finger at the hallway in front of us where men were laying so close together that it would be hard to walk past them. "Pick a patient and get started. Anything you can do is more than is being done now. Do whatever you can and when you finish, somebody will pick up wherever you leave off."

I had read about managing trauma in my books, but had no experience. As I looked over the men, I decided to choose the one I could talk to. "Who speaks French?"

One man spoke up, "I do. Please help me." He was more alert than the dying men the night before. When he looked at me, his face showed disbelief. "You're just a child. You can't do anything for me. Go away."

My temper flared at the thought of being declared useless just because I was young. I shouted, "Fine, I was all you were going to get, maybe for days and I only chose to help you because you speak my language. I'm sure there's somebody else around here who can use my help."

As I turned to leave, he begged, "No! Wait! I'm sorry. Please help me."

I borrowed scissors from one of the nuns and cut his clothes off so I could see his injuries better and so I could cleanse his wounds. He had a deep laceration on his right upper arm and another one on his hip and thigh just about in the same place I had gotten mine in the accident that claimed the lives of my parents when I was small. His right hand was missing. They were right, he would probably live, but what would he do without his right hand? He couldn't pull a trigger.

"Are you right handed?" I asked.

After a deep breath to make him tough he answered in the affirmative.

I bathed him, scrubbed the lacerations and the stump at his right wrist, and then shaved the hair around his cuts. The tourniquet was released long enough to allow circulation into the wrist. The stump would have to be moved farther up the arm because of damaged tissue from the tourniquet. One of the nurses pointed me to the suture kits and to some sterile clamps, assuming I was getting them for one of the doctors. The truth was, Mother had said, "Do all you can," and I intended to do just that.

I released the tourniquet again and clamped the bleeding vessels rather than allow the tourniquet to do more damage. The dead tissue was removed then I tied off the clamped vessels with heavy silk suture and put a moist bandage on the stump. Next I sutured the lacerations to the best of my ability, using small, neat stitches. The man, Paolo, was quiet while I worked on him though I knew he was in severe pain. Even though I was still a child and he had not trusted me at first, he trusted me now. I guess because I had never acted afraid or unsure of myself and probably because he was convinced that I wasn't human. I didn't realize it at the time, but later discovered that many of the patients I saw that day were positive that I was an angel, not just an ordinary young girl.

When it was time to bandage his lacerations, I left him to look for more gauze and tape. In the distance I could hear some commotion, but there had been so much in the past few hours that I paid no attention until I reached my patient's stretcher.

A giant doctor with an angry look on his face was shouting, "I want to know what doctor wasted valuable time on this man! He should have been taking care of our soldiers who will be serving our country and saving us from the tyranny of our enemies in the future!" He was pointing at my patient!

I asked Sister Olga, "Who is that man?"

She had her hand over her mouth and a frightened look on her face when she told me, "That is Dr. Andretti, the head surgeon. Everybody is scared of him, but they say he is the best surgeon in Italy."

One passing nurse claimed ignorance when he challenged her to give him an answer. The patient had insisted that it had been a child dressed like a nun, or probably it was an angel.

"She looked like an angel," the man insisted.

He decided the patient was delirious and stomped off still angry, mumbling. "The next meeting I have with those stupid young men who called themselves doctors, I'll certainly tell them about this!"

When he had gone and I thought it was safe, I went back to my patient and bandaged him properly. Olga told me that later the same day when he was taken to surgery for revision of his stump, the same doctor found the bleeders I had tied off and he fussed again. "It is about time these doctors around here got their priorities straight," he complained.

According to Sister Olga, one of the doctors suggested that maybe a nurse had done it, but after seeing the neat suturing and the way the tissue on the wrist had been debrided and covered with a moist dressing, he knew only a doctor could have done that.

I didn't know exactly what the doctor had been upset about. I wondered if I had broken some sort of Italian law by practicing medicine or if I just hadn't done a good enough job. Because I had been an excellent student of Latin in school, it gave me some understanding of the Italian language I was hearing all the time and consequently I was learning it quickly. As I reflected on it later, I had no doubt that his anger was about the care I had given to my patient. I thought I had done a good job, but apparently not.

The day after we had been bombarded with casualties, when things had calmed down, I went to see how Paolo was doing. When he saw me he started shouting in Italian, "Here she is! This is the child--the angel who took care of me! See, I told you it was a child!"

Dr. Adami, Dr. Andretti, and Mother Maria Elizabeth all looked at me in surprise. I'm sure all the color drained out of my face as they stared at me. Tears started running down my cheeks as I braced myself for their reprimands. "I'm sorry!" I cried. "Mother Maria Elizabeth said I should do all that I could, but I guess I went too far. I did my best."

Dr. Adami was the only person on the compound except for Mother Maria Elizabeth who knew my real name. He walked toward me talking all the time. "Come on, Susanna it's all right. You did such an excellent job that Dr. Andretti thought one of us wasted time doing it when we should have been working on the priority patients." He put his arms around me and held me close making me cry harder. Nobody had held me in almost a year and I had been through so much. He went on, "Not many of us could have done such a beautiful job of suturing. You're going to have to tell me how you know so much sometime soon."

News of what Dr. Andretti and Dr. Adami called my "excellent emergency care" spread throughout the compound quickly. Some children would have been elated by such talk, but I knew my abilities were limited due to lack of experience. I also remembered the nurses tearing skin off the men who had been hit with mustard gas and firebombs. Their screams still haunted me. Maybe I didn't have the heart to be a doctor after all, I thought to myself. In the past I had always been sure that I could do anything. Now I wasn't so sure.

Every day I went to the hospital to help change beds and feed patients who couldn't feed themselves. After I had demonstrated the ability to correctly change a dressing, they had me doing that too. The one thing Mother would not allow was for me to go near any patient with a contagious disease. She said I was still way too frail to be exposed to any diseases. As a matter-of-fact, she was concerned that my weight was not picking up very well. At that time I was 5'5" tall and only weighed 85 pounds. She wondered if it was due to stress or lack of rest.

When casualties came in, I was now assigned to the second priority group with the hope that soon I could be trusted with the top priority men. Dr. Andretti took me under his wing and made me his special apprentice. With the pride of a loving father he marveled over my quick mind and incredible talents. Sometimes the soldiers found it worrisome to have such a young girl take care of them, though it no longer made me angry. There were many times when I wished I was still a child, but now my childhood was gone forever.

I tried never to think about my family. It was just too much of a burden with everything else that was going on in my life. Sometimes I couldn't help thinking about them. Tom's birthday on March 5 was one of those times. I couldn't help but think of him all day. He would be 21. They were probably having a big party with a cake and all his friends helping him celebrate. Maybe he was married by now. I was weepy throughout the day no matter how hard I tried to block it out of my mind. When I could stand no more, I went over to the hall and played the saddest music I knew. After being lost in it for several hours one of the sisters came for me.

That evening when I entered the kitchen alone, Mother looked at me with a hard expression. "Where have you been all day and where is your companion?"

"I had to be alone for a while so I went into the hall to play," I explained as the tears appeared again.

Nothing more was said, though normally that wouldn't have been the end of it. She must have realized my state by looking at me. I'm sure I was looking pretty pathetic after a day of weeping every few minutes.

She looked at me tenderly and said, "After supper, we will go walking, Sister Theresa."

"What about vespers?"

"Tonight I think a walk would be more appropriate."

We were quiet for the first few minutes of our walk that evening. The sun was low in the March sky and the air was cold and damp as the wind blew at our faces. Finally Mother asked, "What made you so unhappy today? Do you know?"

Another wave of sadness moved over me at the thought of it. "I know it isn't very grown up of me," I hiccoughed. "I'm trying to stop it, but today is my brother's birthday. He's 21 and I started thinking about him and my parents and the party they must be having...." I couldn't go on.

Mother held me in her arms. My whole body was shaking. She asked, "Have you written to them?"

"Not since last summer. What would I write about? My father would be so alarmed if he had any idea how things are or if he knew of the things I'm seeing. I can't put him and my Mother through that. The best thing I can do is to wait until after the war to contact them and when I see them, I'll have to be careful never to talk about it ever."

"You have it all figured out, don't you? You mentioned your biological father that first day after you came here. What's your family situation? Do you have more than one father? I never have understood exactly how you happened to be in Luxembourg without your parents."

"My parents were killed in an automobile accident when I was five years old. I went to live with my father's best friend and his two sons, Joseph and Tom, who were a lot older than me. When Papi got married he and his wife adopted me. My new parents never wanted me to visit my grandfather in Luxembourg alone, but it was a condition of the adoption that I spend my summers alone with him starting the summer I turned 12. My mother had her parents in France who checked on me by telephone long distance every few days. I grinned as I remembered Opa's outrage over it. My father sent my brother Tom to see me twice that summer too. When the war broke out, my grandfather brought me here to Italy, up in the mountains. He died after that." I wondered if I had given more information than Mother had asked for. I apologized. "I'm sorry; you don't want to know all of that."

Mother smiled, "Actually I want to know all about you, how it is that you can play the piano so well, handle emergencies so well, and how did the rumor ever get started that you are an angel posing as a child. You aren't an angel, Susanna, but I truly believe that it surely must have been God's will for you to come here to take care of our soldiers. With your music lightening their hearts and your medical skills caring for their bodies, you have already touched hundreds of lives. You are very blessed by God to be able to do so many things at such a young age." She looked into my eyes with a twinkle in her own as she asked, "How did your parents and teachers react to everything that you can do?"

"My tutors loved teaching me and the people at the conservatory did too, but Papi said it was a challenge every day to keep one step ahead of me. He said my life would be easier if I could just be average. My religion teachers never liked me because I couldn't conform. They didn't like my questions either. I've always seen things so clearly when other people never seem to understand. Mama said that was part of my gifts, but I had to have patience with others because everybody didn't have them the same as me. Sometimes I got in a lot of trouble for taking things into my own hands and when I went too far, both of my parents were real good at reminding me that I wasn't grown up yet. My father was very strict." Tears had started to flow again. "I guess I'm going to cry all day. I miss them so much!"

"You need to write to them. Maybe your letters will never get through and maybe once in a while one will, but it will make you feel close to talk through your letters. Tomorrow after breakfast you will visit them on paper and the first time somebody comes through on his way to one of the cities, we'll send it out with the rest of the mail."

The talk helped so much that, even though no musical program had been planned for that night, Mother and I went into the hall to entertain ourselves. People came and went as they heard me playing a light-hearted selection of pieces from my past and music I had learned from the young soldiers and the nurses. By the time I decided that I was tired and needed to quit, I felt better.

The next morning I wrote the letter telling what had happened in the most positive way I could. I described the beautiful trees around the cave I had lived in for so long and told them what an excellent shot I had become. I told all about Alessandro Adami and Mother Maria Elizabeth and my musical programs. Nothing was said about the dying soldiers, the screaming young men who were burned beyond recognition, or the boys who were forever mutilated. By the time I finished it sounded like a good and happy life even though I assured them that I missed each one of them, even Joseph. It never occurred to me to say exactly where I was because I was afraid that it would sound as if I was in a dangerous place. I put a return address on the outside of the envelope, thinking that possibly it would come back if there were problems getting it through to Bayland, though I never mentioned that I was known of only as the little sister or Sister Theresa. It might sound negative not to have any clothes but a nun's habit, and for sure it would sound bad to think of me pretending to be a nun so the soldiers wouldn't take advantage of me, as Mother had put it. The last thing I wanted was for anybody to worry about me.

When I finished, I let Mother read it, then rummaged through my bag for a pre-posted envelope that my mother had prepared for me so long ago.

"You painted a very pretty picture of your life here. Do you think they might believe you? Most grownups know about war."

"They'll never know for sure if I don't say. My father is a worrier and Mama isn't much better. I'd like them to live till I finally get home someday and not die of worry about me."

"Maybe you're wise," she agreed slowly. "I'll put your letter in the mailroom to go out whenever we have a pickup for personal mail. It may be a while."

"It doesn't matter. As you said, it may never get there."

Writing the letter had helped even if it never made it to Bayland, Ohio. Mother had been right about that, but also, ever since the night before when Mother had said that it might not be an accident for me to be where I was, I had felt a little better. From now on, the least I could do was try to make a difference.

After that day, there was little time for thinking about anything but the war effort. Casualties were heavy and morale among the soldiers was low. Living conditions out on the battlefields were horrible. Most of the soldiers came in with lice, malnutrition, and uncontrollable problems with a foot fungus called trench foot along with their injuries. They seemed grateful for anything anybody did for them. When they were able to be up and about, they were regular visitors at the orphanage. It seemed as if all of them loved me for some reason and they seemed to have special affection for Minnie who was starting to get fat from all the treats they saved for her. I noticed that they seemed to cling to the innocents during this war, befriending stray cats, the orphans across the compound from us, and whatever else gave normalcy to their chaotic lives.

I guess I was no different. Before I had been on the compound very long I befriended a six-year-old boy named Niccolo at the orphanage. On quiet afternoons I played school with him and was delighted when he started reading and writing and learning French very quickly. He taught me Italian with his childish dialogue and accepted my grammatical errors without judgment. Sometimes with permission from the sister at the orphanage, I was allowed to take him to the hall to play the piano. Though he had almost no musical talent, I made up little duets to play with him and taught him some of the same little songs I had taught to my little brothers at home. He was a great comfort to me. When I went to the orphanage, Mother didn't require me to have a companion, though she always warned me not to go anywhere else alone and I obeyed because I was so grateful to her for all she had done to help me.

The war had escalated by June and it looked like Italy would soon be declaring war on Germany. The shelling could be heard at all hours of the day and night and sometimes it seemed as if there was no end to the procession of wounded men coming into the hospital. There were never enough doctors or nurses or beds or supplies to take care of everybody and it was a well-known fact that many soldiers died for lack of facilities.

I had worked my way up to caring for first priority men when casualties came in. It was rare for me to have time to comfort a dying man from the hopeless group anymore. Dr. Andretti adored me and did all he could to teach me about surgery and trauma care. He said I was a true genius and that my solutions to orthopedic or surgical problems often demonstrated that fact. I could tell that some of the staff was jealous of me, but most of the time I was oblivious to it. Once I had discussed their behavior with Mother and she told me the best way to get around such problems was to be especially nice to people who were unkind. She told me that their lives were lacking and love and kindness would warm them. After that, I tried to always be quick with a hug and a compliment. Since I was only a child, not quite 14, I had the advantage of being able to even give a hug to a doctor at times when he needed one, though Mother told me one day that I needed to be careful about having physical contact with men. Dr. Andretti could be ruthless to the young doctors and there were many times when they felt defeated as they tried their best to save the lives of the young soldiers coming in every day.

One night a blond, blue-eyed young soldier came in with a minor head injury. He had a concussion and a large scalp laceration, but was in good enough shape to be in the priority one group. I got an orderly to help me remove his clothing and examined him while he was still unconscious. I couldn't find anything major, no obvious fractures, no bleeding in the retina or blood in the ear canals. There was no evident spinal fluid in the nose or other suspicious nasal drainage.

I removed the pressure bandage from his head and cleansed the wound. After I shaved it, he started to arouse. He spoke in German and I answered. As he spoke in his confused state, he talked about posing as a telephone man to get through enemy lines. It seemed as if he thought he was reporting to his superior. His thought patterns were disjointed, but I was thinking that he might be an enemy soldier.

He was still talking by the time I finished suturing his scalp and had applied a dressing. I was sure that even though he had worn an Italian uniform, he was an Austrian soldier. Something about him reminded me of Joseph and Tom as we talked in German. It was very dangerous for him to be talking like this. I had heard of spies being shot, but he seemed just like an ordinary young man who could have been one of my brothers. I knew about the violence of the war, but had little knowledge of the politics of it. When I was finished caring for him, I warned him to stop talking. "Can you speak French or Italian? It is very dangerous for you to be talking this way. You must stop it!"

He rambled on until I finally gave him a shot of Morphine even though Dr. Andretti had told me never to give Morphine or any other kind of sedation to a head injury patient. I didn't dare mark it on his chart or Dr. Andretti would be very angry with me, but I decided it would be more kind to risk killing the boy with the shot than for him to go before a firing squad if he were found out.

Once he was sleeping I moved on to other patients. Dr. Andretti must have noticed me taking too much time with him and he must have seen me giving him a shot of something. It must have looked suspicious to him for some reason. I didn't see him go to the man to examine him and review the records soon after I left because I went straight to another soldier and started suturing his facial lacerations. Quite often, lately, I was given the job of suturing facial wounds. Dr. Andretti said that my small, even stitches made nice scars. That night I had spent much of my time doing facial wounds and debriding superficial burns.

I fell into bed after breakfast late in the morning, exhausted, but early in the afternoon was awakened by the feeling of a presence. When I opened my eyes, Mother and Dr. Andretti were both standing beside my bed looking down at me. Two soldiers were standing at my doorway.

I sat up, still exhausted. "Is something wrong?" I asked innocently.

"Something is very wrong, Sister Theresa," Dr. Andretti said with an angry tone in his voice and a mean look on his face. "There will be no use denying what I am about to accuse you of."

I couldn't think of anything I had done wrong, but my heart was pumping loudly as I looked at him. "What did I do?"

"You aided a spy. Do you deny that you knew that young man with the head injury last night was a spy? I saw you give him a shot to shut him up. Some medical personnel are stupid enough to give a shot to a patient with a head injury, but I know you better than that. You might as well give us the straight story because it's going to come out one way or the other."

Mother looked pale and worried, but Dr. Andretti was violently angry. With tears in my eyes I told them truthfully exactly what had happened. I explained that he looked just like everybody else and he didn't seem bad to me. If I had told on him, maybe he would have gotten into trouble."

That seemed to soften Dr. Andretti. Looking back on it, I must have sounded like the child I still was. People seemed to forget that I wasn't a seasoned adult physician and they expected more from me. Sadly, with tears suddenly appearing in his eyes he quietly said, "Well now you're in trouble. The worst you'll ever have."

I looked at him and felt sad and wondered what was going to happen. Would I be shot like the deserters were shot out on the center of the compound? I said as bravely as I could, "I'm not afraid to die. I've been on the edge of it all my life. All I can say to defend myself is that I thought it was the right thing to do."

"Well, it wasn't. These spies find out where we plan to attack and how we plan to do it, and then our men go out and get slaughtered because the enemy is waiting for them!" As he turned to leave he said, "You'd better get dressed, the police are waiting to take you away."

He seemed devastated, with his shoulders slumped, shaking his head as he turned to leave. Mother was crying.

The military police were gentle with me as they escorted me to headquarters. I was immediately taken before a major who was abrupt and called me a traitor. He didn't give me a chance to say anything, but only motioned to the police who took me to a cell and locked the door. There were no other people around and everything was quiet. I still wasn't sorry for what I had done. I knew I could never turn anybody in to be executed. I was a nurturer. The job of executioner had to belong to someone else.

Once a soldier came in and brought a flask of water, otherwise I saw no one the rest of the afternoon or all evening. It was cold and damp in the cell and I longed for a blanket or a coat to warm me. There was a pot in the corner to urinate in. I wondered if I was going to be shot and I wondered if it would be painful or if I would just fall through the tunnel and find the light and my family again. If it was going to be my last day on earth, I decided I had better say a few prayers. In my prayers I discussed what I had done with God and asked if I had made a mistake. Judging from the feeling of peace that had come over me, I assumed I had done the right thing and I wasn't afraid. It was as if God's arms were wrapped around me giving me comfort.

I tried to understand that Dr. Andretti had been angry with me because he was so weary of seeing the young men of his country mutilated every day. The officers coming in from the field had been saying that lately the Austrians had seemed to know every move they made ahead of time. After he had calmed down, I knew he was sorry for turning me in.

The next morning at 6:00 the Austrian soldier and I were brought before the Colonel and several other officers for a hearing. The trial was over for the soldier quickly. He would be shot at sunrise the next morning. Dr. Andretti and Dr. Adami helped to plead my case, and did their best to see that my life was spared and that I wouldn't be put in prison. Dr.Andretti stated that I was just a child and that I didn't understand what I had done. He suggested a good whipping to make amends for my poor judgment and even offered to do it himself. His arguments were very effective, and though the sentence came from men who had children at home my age and wanted to give me leneincy, they also knew they must deal with my offense severely to satisfy those who were critical of my actions. Normally they were merciless in cases of treason, but they couldn't quite send a 13 year-old girl to a firing squad or a prison for adults. They finally decided not on a whipping as Dr. Andretti had suggested, but rather, a good beating and banishment from the military compound. The punishment would take place the next morning after I witnessed the execution of the soldier. I would leave the compound as soon as I could walk.

I hoped I would die. That night I was awake all night. I was sick and cold and scared. Not scared of dying, but scared of the pain I was about to endure. In a way, I wished I were being executed because I didn't think it would be as painful as being beaten and if I died my troubles would be over. At least then I would finally never be afraid or hurt again.

At 6:00 they came in and took me out to the middle of the compound to watch the execution. Normally executions were not carried out in that exact place, but this time Colonel Giuardi wanted everybody to see what happens when they aid the other side and what happens to the traitor.

The soldier's hands were ceremoniously bound behind him and once he walked to the spot where he was to be shot, they bound his feet. His face was pale and once again, to me, he still looked like Joseph and Tom with his blond hair blowing slightly in the breeze. They asked him if he had any final words, but he shook his head "no". He stood bravely, waiting to be executed. He looked into my eyes and I saw fear just before they put a black hood over his head. My heart was thumping so loud I wondered if anybody else could hear it. My mouth was dry and my legs were weak. The morning sky seemed to glare on the ground. As the soldiers aimed and got ready to fire, I screamed, "Please, don't do it!" They all fired at once and the boy fell to the ground with the hood falling off. Blood ran out of his nose, head, and chest. I screamed again, and then cried uncontrollably.

One of the soldiers sneered, "You had better cry for yourself, girl," but I felt nothing for myself. The horror of what I had just witnessed had me so upset that I could think of nothing else.

The soldiers took me inside to remove my habit and scarf saying that it would be blasphemous to beat a woman clothed in a nun's habit and besides I needed to learn humiliation and I was given just a wrap to put around my breasts while they looked at me and commented on my skinny ugly body. After that, wearing only my tattered old underdrawers and that wrap around my breasts, I was dragged outside and tied to a post where everybody could see. I got sick and threw up on the ground. Then the order was given by the Colonel to begin the beating and a man with a whip struck me hard across the shoulders. By the time I could scream, he was hitting me again and again and again. It was as if my body was on fire and then I seemed to faint or collapse, but could still hear the commotion of the crowd observing, cheering, and crying, "Kill her! Kill her!" Until, blessedly, I finally fainted.

One time when I was discussing it with Sister Olga years later, as old women, she told me, "The beating had gotten out of hand and continued as many in the crowd who were caught up in the violence encouraged the man who was carrying out the sentence to continue. The man whipped your limp body from your shoulders to your ankles, front and back, looking like a mad man as he continued. The flesh erupted into ragged bloody strips hanging loosely off of your body. At last, the Colonel ordered them to cut you down and leave you lying in the middle of the compound as an example to others who would be tempted to aid the enemy. By then you were practically naked as your drawers hung in shreds and the wrap on your breasts lay several feet away."

She told me that when they cut the rope that was holding me up; my limp body fell to the ground with a quiet thud. She said I didn't move as blood trickled out of my wounds onto the dusty ground. The crowd gathered closely around me to look. Though some had cheered during my punishment and others screamed and sobbed, now there wasn't a sound except for a gasp now and then.

Alessandro, Mother Maria, and even Dr. Andretti, who could be heard telling Mother that he wished he had never reported me, were among those who were crying quietly. She said it had been a curiosity to her for the rest of her life to see people who had loved me so much turn on me so quickly. As a matter-of-fact, she said, "It isn't any wonder, after witnessing such a terrible act with my own eyes to believe that our Lord had been treated in much the same heartless way with no one standing up to defend Him. He was also loved one day and then was tortured and finally murdered the next by some of the same people who had loved Him.

Alessandro told me once that I lost several days after the beating, but that isn't true. Those days were the warmest, most peaceful I have had. As I hovered between heaven and earth I was free of all pain, loneliness, or sorrow. It was warm and sunny with the most wonderful smells and the most beautiful music I had heard since I had been in a similar state as a small child with the measles. I met the babies my parents had lost before I was born and I visited my mother, Frieda and my father, Heinrick. I even saw my beautiful nurse, Mrs. Brownson. She encouraged me to go back and wait for my time, but it seemed to me that the people I loved most were there. Papi had never troubled himself to come for me after the war had started and Joseph was married to someone else. My Mother, Gabrielle, had her own babies and Tom would have a life of his own by now.

During the end of my unconscious state it seemed as if I was floating above everybody, looking down at them. I could see Alessandro changing my bandages and Mother sponging my wounds. As I looked at the lacerations all over my body, I thought, in a detached way, what a mutilated state it was in, but I felt no remorse. Several times I fell into the tunnel. As I fell deeper and deeper, the light at the end became brighter and I would be back in heaven again. I think the light might have been God.

The last time I was there I begged the light, which seemed to have life, "Please let me stay! Life is too hard and it is too lonely!" But the light told me, "You must go back." Immediately I ascended through the tunnel and this time I slammed back into my broken body. When that happened I experienced an agony that only the last moment before giving birth could begin to compare to! I heard myself groan loudly.

Alessandro said, "Shhh, my dear beautiful Susanna, you must be very quiet. I'll give you something for the pain."

All I could do was cry. I tried to open my eyes, but I couldn't. He kissed my hand then I felt him put his cheek next to mine. "Cara Mia, you'll live. I'll take you to safety. It will be all right. You will never be alone again."

I was all mixed up. I couldn't think. The next thing I knew, Mother Maria Elizabeth was talking softly to me, trying to feed me broth. I choked, but she gently continued trying. "You must take some nourishment, child. Very soon it will be time to move you to safety and you will need your strength."

After that I seemed to be in a wake sleep pattern, barely conscious, then Alessandro wrapped me in a blanket and picked me up in his arms as if I was a baby. "We must leave now," he whispered. "Sister Olga is bringing Minnie and your belongings."

Outside I became more lucid than I had been anytime since the beating. The air was fresh and cool. The stars were bright and the moon only a sliver. They made a bed for me in the area behind the seats of a military truck and added plenty of cushions. When I was tucked in, Mother Maria Elizabeth said, "I won't see you again, my child, go with God and make the most of the life He has given back to you." She hugged me gently then climbed out of the truck to finish loading it.

The drive, about 75 miles south to Verona, was miserable. I still wasn't clear about what we were doing and I didn't care. All I did care about was my excruciating pain as we bumped over ruts and rocks along the way. Olga and Alessandro sitting in front talked, but I couldn't hear from the back of the rattley old truck and I didn't care to listen anyway. I didn't want to think and for once there were no songs in my heart or on my mind.

It was still dark when we stopped. Olga waited with me while Alessandro got out of the truck and went to the door to deliver a letter from Mother Maria Elizabeth. I was in so much pain that I couldn't help but cry. Olga leaned over me and tried to give comfort.

"We're here at the convent, Susanna. I'm going to take care of you. We'll be safe here. I'll help you get well. Please don't cry," she begged.

A stab of guilt closed over me, "I'm sorry to make such a fuss, it's just that I hurt so badly and I'm so mixed up. I can't remember what happened."

"It is best that you don't remember for a while," she told me. "God is helping you to heal."

Alessandro carried me through the open door of the convent where a tiny elderly nun waited for me. "Senor, you may carry the child up the stairs for us. Sister Theresa will sleep in a cell next to Sister Olga so she can easily tend to her needs."

I was placed in a hard, narrow bed in a room about the size of the broom closet Mother Maria Elizabeth had fixed for me. I couldn't help but groan when my body touched the thin mattress. The pain took my breath away.

The nuns came into the cubicle one by one to observe my wounds as was requested by Mother Angelica who was in charge of the convent. Some looked and me and genuflected, some put a hand over their mouths and shook their heads. I knew I was in bad condition, but their response to me made me cry. Dr. Adami took my hand and told me I was going to be just fine. "Music will be back in your heart one day and you will live out your days in happiness, I promise, Susanna."

Mother Angelica looked kindly at me and said, "I would have probably done the same thing you did for that young enemy soldier. You followed your heart and tried to save a young boy. God will shine on you for trying to help another human being. We don't have much space here, but I have put you in here, in a cubicle next to your friend, Sister Olga. We'll take care of you till you're healthy and we can find a way to get you out of the country."

She looked at Alessandro, giving him a sign that he had overstayed his welcome in that restricted part of the convent. He looked at her and said, "I understand. You need for me to leave. Would it be acceptable for me to return whenever possible? The child has no one left but me."

"You are welcome anytime you can come, doctor," she told him.

He bent down slightly and kissed my hand then my cheek and promised to come back the next time he had a chance. I cried when he left, but was exhausted from the trip and soon fell into a deep sleep.

The next day Mother Angelica helped Sister Olga cleanse my wounds. Most of them were scabbed over except for the deeper ones that had been sutured and they were somewhat crusted along the suture lines and where the suture needle had punctured the tissue along the line. When they were finished Mother Angelica stood back to look at my naked body, gasped and crossed herself. When she had regained her composure, she helped Sister apply clean dressings to the wounds that still needed to be covered.

I tried not to cry during the painful procedure and apologized for being so much trouble. I promised to be up and about to help in the convent soon.

Mother Angelica said, "The letter that came with you says you are quite a musician. Maybe when you get well you can entertain us some evening."

"I don't seem to have music in me anymore. I don't know if I can ever play again. I think my heart is dead." I was in a state of deep depression and it was hard for me to believe that I would ever feel like playing again. I didn't seem to want to do anything. My thoughts were blank and I didn't want to go on with my life.

That evening while Olga was caring for me she told me that Mother had stood at the dinner table that day and said, "This is Sister Olga. She comes from the front lines to be part of our community under unusual circumstances. You see, she brought a young patient with her who will be known as Sister Theresa. This child was punished for treason for failing to report a young Austrian spy to the authorities. She has nearly been beaten to death as punishment for her indiscretion." Mother went on, "Sister Olga will start helping in the hospital as soon as her young patient can do without her for a few hours. I don't know if it would be safe for the little one to ever help lest somebody recognize her, but I understand that she has great knowledge of medicine for a child. Maybe in the future we can find a way for God to use her for good, but for now we are going to concentrate on getting her well and nothing more. She will stay here in complete anonymity until eventually we'll look for a way to send her to France.

I got stronger every day in spite of the depression that constantly hung over me. Sister Olga was bright and happy, telling me about the convent and the local talk. She tried to draw me out of my shell and get me to look at the future. Everyday she insisted that I get up and walk around in the convent a little more. When I started to get restless, she helped me downstairs to the piano in the parlor. The first time I sat in front of the instrument staring, unable to put my hands on the keys, she accepted that. She told me, "It will be all right. I will bring you here every day and one day you will touch the keys and music will come out and you will remember. For now it is enough that you have come down the steps and sat here in front of it. God will heal your heart through the music He gave you in the beginning, while you were still in heaven as an infant."

Olga always understood me and seemed to think in an abstract way much the same way my own mind worked. We operated on the same level and in a quick instant I thought of my old friend Ilona from the conservatory and hoped that nothing so bad ever happened to her to make her lose her music.

The nuns were the only nurses in Verona. The convent was run by Mother Angelica, the elderly nun I had first met when I arrived and who was a regular presence at my bedside from that day forward. She had very few dealings with the hospital. A young sister named Sister St. Monica ran that and Mother Angelica concentrated on the needs of people in the neighborhood.

The convent food was measured out for each sister with nobody ever getting enough except for me. They knew I was a growing girl and some, who had seen my wounds being dressed when I had first come, knew I was skin and bones. Every time one of them found a delicacy at the hospital such as an orange or some sweets, it made its way to me. They made great sacrifices for me and somehow I wanted to repay their kindness. I started thinking about what could be done about the lack of food. Surely there was a way to generate more food if we were to save the seeds from their sparse supply of fruits and vegetables. At home Grandfather Von Helldorf and I had always saved the seeds of our best produce so we could grow more like it the next season. The family always teased me about having a green thumb. It was those thoughts that crept into my mind as I lay in bed or quietly sat in a chair with a blanket over my legs that started to make me look at the future.

With the good care and light spirits of the sisters and the peace and quiet within the walls of the convent, my mental condition continued to improve every day. My body had healed and I now weighed 100 pounds. Mother Angelica had somehow come up with a mirror and placed it in my cubicle so I could see that my face was unscarred. It was vain of me, but I couldn't help but think to myself that my face had become lovely.

My music came back to me all at once. One day when I was sitting in a chair in the large walled garden, one that had a few trees and a small amount of grass, but no other vegetation, the music in my head started to play again. It was a very sweet melody that I couldn't help but hum to myself. As if in a trance I got up and went inside to sit in front of the piano with Olga and Minnie following close behind me. First I put just one finger on a key and then I had to let the music come out. I played until I was exhausted and had to curl up on the floor to rest before going to my cubical. The music was part of the beginning of my healing, truly a gift from God.

It was October and I had turned 14 in August, though I never mentioned my age to anybody. The birthdays that had once been so important to me meant nothing now. Very little mattered except for the love I had for all of my new friends and for Olga and Dr. Adami and Mother Maria Elizabeth, who had done so much to help me. Dr. Adami visited whenever he could. I never thought of grown up love until Mother Angelica saw the adoring look he had in his eyes when he looked at me and said, "Dr. Adami, it is not appropriate for you to have such an eye for our young sister. She is only a child."

His response to Mother's criticism was, "I am not ashamed of my love for Susanna. She is indeed a child, but she will not always be and I will love her forever. I am prepared to wait until she is grown, but make no mistake; she will not always be a sister."

With that Mother Angelica said, "You should not even be thinking such things. The child has been ravished. She doesn't know her own mind. Do not put ideas into her that she may mistake because of her gratitude for your acts of kindness."

"She will love me and one day I will make her my bride and it will have nothing to do with gratitude, I assure you."

I listened in shock, but said nothing, not prepared for any kind of dissention between them. Emotionally I was still crippled and couldn't stand any kind of turmoil. The truth was, I loved everybody in the convent for their kindnesses, but Sister Olga and Alessandro were like a lifeline to me and I loved both of them dearly. I didn't know about grown up love and couldn't begin to think of marriage, but I accepted anything that Alessandro or Olga said as absolute truth and knew from that moment on that one day I would marry him.

In November my weight had finally gotten up to 105 pounds and when it was announced at the dinner table, the nuns cheered and tapped their forks on their tin cups. It was time for the little sister to start making her way here. Italy had declared war on Germany and even though the hospital was farther from the front than the compound where I had been before, it was busy all the time.

When casualties came in and things were in complete chaos, I slipped into the hospital and worked on the men. I never told any of the soldiers or doctors my name and tried to avoid all conversation with anybody but the patient and then it was always about him. I was using all the knowledge I had from my books and everything I had learned from Dr. Andretti. Sometimes I cut bone and smoothed it to make a better stump on an amputated leg or arm while one of the nuns gave ether. Other times I sutured huge lacerations or debrided burns. I did whatever I could do tirelessly.

One morning Mother Angelica sent me and one of the sisters out into the neighborhood for the delivery of a baby. I had read all about it, but had never seen a delivery. It was the most fascinating thing I had ever experienced! The miracle of the birth made my spirits soar. I wondered why Papi had always objected so strongly to having me see one. Mother Angelica said she would send me out for deliveries regularly with one of the other nuns if I would like that. I could work with the townsfolk without being recognized by any of the military. The only time it was safe to work in the hospital was when there was enough chaos to keep people from being curious about me, but I could work in the town every day.

Friedrich

*I*n *June, at about the same time Susanna was being tried as a traitor to Italy, her letter arrived at the Bayland Post Office in about the same shape the other one had. The postmaster knew it must be from the little Von Helldorf girl so this time he called Von Helldorf Textiles and insisted on talking to Friedrich Von Helldorf himself. He was told that Mr. Von Helldorf was in a meeting, but he insisted that he talk with him immediately about an urgent matter.*

The secretary came to me with the information and I think she was surprised when I practically knocked her over in my rush to reach the phone. I shouted, "This is Friedrich Von Helldorf. Mr. Helman, is it another letter?"

"Yes, I'm sure it's from your granddaughter. It's a little torn up, but the contents are probably all right. Do you want me to have somebody bring it over?"

"No, my son and I will come right away."

I wrote a note for my son and handed it to the secretary. "Take this to Mr. Von Helldorf, please."

When the secretary delivered the note to my son, he rose from his chair and without a word to the men in the meeting he left the office and we sped to the post office. The envelope was pale gray, just like the ones Gabrielle had packed in Susanna's bag before she left two years before. This time there was a return address on the envelope. Hungry for news of his daughter, Rolf snatched it up and tore it open as he walked to a large-paned window to get all the light he could. She had wisely chosen to write in pencil again, which had kept her letter from being washed away when it had obviously been soaked one time or other.

I looked over his shoulder. We read it and cried. She was obviously trying to protect us from knowing how bad things were going for her. How I wished there was some way to find her. Joseph had enlisted in the French Army to act as a physician. In his letters he described conditions in the field hospitals and the horrors he was seeing. Susanna must be going through the same things in Italy only she was still just a child.

This time he didn't send a telegram to France. Rolf called and left a message to cancel his meeting due to a family emergency, then we went home. He and my daughter-in-law cried together, and then they saddled their horses and rode to the woods Susanna had loved so much. All of us felt close to her when we went to her little grotto and felt the spirits circling around us.

In the morning Rolf sent a telegram to Rouen to notify the grandparents and the boys of Susanna's letter and approximate location. He asked Guillaume, Gabrielle's father, to get the investigators on the case again and not to give up until they found our Susanna. Surely she could be found now. How many field hospital/orphanages could there be at the foot of the mountains in Northern Italy? Now we had the name of Dr. Adami and Mother Maria Elizabeth and of the post where they were located. Surely they could be found without much trouble.

It seemed as if there was so much to worry about these days. The boys had been gone for a year now and Susanna for two years. We had begged Tom and Joseph not to enlist in any army unless The United States got into it. How could they fight against Germany when their roots were in Germany? It should only happen if it was necessary to defend their own country, The United States of America. Even with our protests, Joseph had enlisted in the French Army, saying that he couldn't stand by and know what suffering was going on and not do something to help. He hoped we would understand. Rolf was sure Tom was doing something dangerous for the French, but he never could pin anybody down to find out exactly what.

As a young man Rolf had told me, "If you have a good wife, lots of healthy children, and plenty of money, happiness will follow." He had the best wife anybody could ever have, he had six sons and a daughter and almost more business than he could handle with government contracts for coats, uniforms, and canvas. Unfortunately, it had been a long time since he had been anywhere close to happy.

Chapter 4

I had turned into a very serious girl. The only time there was a hint of the girl who had left Bayland in 1914 was when I played the piano. After I was finally able to find happiness in my music again, I entertained the sisters daily. Sometimes, when I was playing something light and fun, I would bubble up and behave almost like the child I was. Mother Angelica noticed this and wondered how she could get me to play for an audience without being recognized. "It seems a shame not to share such talent with the citizens of Verona. There was so much tragedy because of the war that a small glimmer of happiness could do so much for the people." she told me. "Christmas is coming and it would be wonderful to put on a musical concert that every person in Verona could enjoy." She consulted Alessandro, Sister Olga, and me a week later when we were all together.

"I could find Susanna a very grown up dress and she could wear her hair up like a woman and we could introduce her as simply Luciana. Nobody in Italy has ever seen her dressed in anything but a habit so they would never suspect it was our little sister."

Alessandro didn't like it. "The people don't need her help. I saw how quickly they all turned on her when she innocently got into trouble out at the compound. You should have heard them cheering and hollering for them to kill her when she was being beaten. These were all people who had just loved her when she was giving her programs," he said, bitterly.

At the remembrance of it tears streamed down my cheeks. Alessandro, realizing that he had brought back devastating memories, put his hands on my shoulders and kneaded them. He bent over and whispered to me, "I'm sorry. I didn't mean to make you sad. Don't worry because you don't ever have to do another concert. We'll protect you always."

Mother Angelica hadn't finished having her say yet as she argued, "Our Lord went through something like Sister Theresa's torture once, but he didn't turn his back on mankind because of it and I don't think He would want our little sister to either."

Sister Olga was unsure. "Her programs made me happy too, but I'd hate to see her hurt again. I couldn't stand it if anyone ever hurt her." She had become my devoted friend since coming to Verona and the look on her face just at the thought of something else happening to me seemed to devastate her.

They looked at me for my opinion. I thought about it then said very seriously, "I would like to play and make people happy again." But I had to gulp back a sob before I could continue. "Surely there must have been a few people who didn't hate me, but who were afraid to speak out. You tried to stop them, Sandro, and you see what good it did. I will play and try to give a little cheer to the people of Verona. I only ask that you put a bullet through me if it looks like something is going to happen again, because I couldn't stand any more torture." I quickly added, "You could get absolution for it."

Alessandro jumped up from the table in a rage. "That settles it; we're not going to do it! I love her too much to let anything happen."

"Dr. Adami, must I remind you again that the child is only 14 years old!" Mother reminded him.

"I can't help my love for her. It's a fact and it's highly respectable."

I thought of Joseph for just an instant, but quickly remembered that he had been married for two years. I did love Alesandro more than anyone in the world. He truly had my heart. Life wouldn't be worth living without him. He had saved my life on two or possibly three different occasions. I thought of doing a show. It would be fun, but Alessandro had become very protective and for good reason. If anyone recognized me, the charges for treason could be brought up all over again. At the moment everyone thought I was dead so I was relatively safe. Still it was a God-given gift to be able to play so well and I knew I should share my gift with others.

As we moved into the parlor once again I said, "I'll do it. We'll do the concert together and you can try to keep me out of trouble."

A worried look crossed Alessandro's face. "Please don't," he begged, looking at me with his deep-dark eyes.

"I want to do it. If you can get away, will you come?"

"You know I will."

"Then it's settled."

The date planned for the concert and party was December 23, a Saturday night.

The next day after our discussion I had a headache when I woke up. I wondered if I was afraid to do the performance and wanted to be sick to get out of it. Later that morning I started cramping in my lower pelvis and lower back. I thought I must be coming down with dysentery. When Sister Olga came in I mentioned it to her. Olga thought maybe it was influenza, but since I didn't have a fever, she doubted it.

In the afternoon when I went to the bathroom I discovered at the age of 14 years, I had finally started menstruating. Suddenly I remembered my mother complaining of not feeling well because of a "woman's problem". There had been worse things in my life, that was certain, but I couldn't say that I felt exactly well today. I couldn't believe how much blood was involved and never thought it would be anything like this when my mother had told me about it a few days before I left Bayland.

That evening I told Sister Olga what had happened. Olga hugged me and told me it was the beginning of my womanhood. She confided in me that she had been doing that since the age of twelve. Later that evening, after Olga talked to Mother Angelica, she reminded me that I could bear a child now and that it was a mortal sin to engage in the love act before marriage. It occurred to Mother that possibly I had never been told about the love act. She knew that I hadn't been quite 12 years old the last time I had seen my mother so Mother Angelica asked Olga to speak to me the same way her mother had spoken to her when she had ventured into womanhood.

"Do you know what the love act is?" Olga asked shyly.

"Yes, Joseph, he was my betrothed when I was a child, told me about it. He said it was a sin if done out of marriage."

"Well, never let anybody coax you into it no matter what they say or you're both doomed for hell."

"It never sounded like anything I would want to do anyway," I confessed innocently.

"Well, my mother told me that sometimes a man can make a woman feel like it would be worth it for him to love her more."

"Oh. well, I want to get married some day, but I would never let my husband do that even in marriage!" I protested. "Joseph told me it isn't a sin if you're married, but I still wouldn't want to do it, not even for Joseph or Alessandro."

Olga agreed that it was best never to partake in it. After all, the Virgin Mary had never done anything like that and it would best if all women followed her example.

That night as I stood at a little sink in the back of the convent washing out my soiled pads in the cold cistern water, I wondered what other miseries were in the plans for me. No wonder my mother had told me some girls called it the curse. I could hardly imagine that I had to look forward to it every month for the rest of my life. For a moment I thought of Joseph and how I would have told him about turning into a woman today. Then I remembered I could never confide in him again. He was married to someone else and, even if I ever got home, I would be unsuitable for marriage. Scars from the brutal beating last summer still covered my body and always would. I almost looked as if I had been severely burned. Nobody would ever want to marry me, except for my beautiful Alessandro.

The sisters in the convent were always busy taking care of the citizens of Verona much like my mother had taken care of the people of Bayland County, Ohio. There were major differences though. First, there usually was no doctor to help if problems arose here. People often had to die if the sisters couldn't do enough to help. The doctors were busy with the soldiers who were top priority. On top of that, medical supplies were impossible to get and even food was scarce. I dealt with malnutrition and families with lack of shelter and with people who had horrific memories of the devastation of war every day.

As I walked the streets of the city with the sisters who were making their calls, I saw half-starved children everywhere I went. Husbands had been faced with going to war or being shot so there were no men left anywhere except the elderly and those so badly mutilated that they could no longer fight. All able-bodied men were in uniform. The war had been hard on me, but it had affected everybody. It was like a plague that would never end.

It would have seemed that being so far south, there wouldn't have been heavy trauma coming in, but that was not the case. Men came in with tourniquets still on, unsutured wounds, unbandaged burns, in worse shape many times than they had been on the front because they had gone so long without care. Though I had hardened to the sounds and the smells of war, sometimes I stood in the middle of the chaos and thought to myself that hell must be exactly like this, and then I worked on, undaunted by it.

Many times the soldiers managed to touch my heart when they begged me not to leave them. Each time I took care of a patient who wanted me to promise to come back to him, I told him I would not see him again, explaining that I was only there to help until the emergency was over. After a while the sisters told me that I had became a legend. Men wondered who the child was who had set their broken limbs, or had so carefully sewn up their cuts, and gently bandaged their burns. Even the doctors couldn't say. They had all seen me moving about doing my work during times of greatest need, yet nobody knew my name or anything about me. They wondered who I was, but I was always gone when things began to settle down. They asked the other nuns, but always got an evasive explanation that told them nothing. Even Sister St. Monica who ran the hospital told the doctors she didn't really know who I was, but that I came highly recommended by another sister and two doctors from the front lines, Dr. Antonio Andretti and Dr. Alessandro Adami. Even though Dr. Andretti thought I was dead and nobody had ever heard of Dr. Adami, Dr. Andretti had such a good reputation all over Italy that they dropped the subject and never questioned my credentials again.

The women and children in the area were the only people who thought they knew who I was. To them I was Sister Theresa. The children seemed love me and their mothers trusted me to take care of them all. Though so young, I was like everybody's mother. I was constantly coming up with home remedies for the children's coughs and fevers, and scrounging for things to help them stay well. Mothers asked my advice about the children and Sister Genevieve said they thought there was something special, almost mythical about me. They tried to get me to talk about myself. They asked where I had come from, but I was careful to see that they never got any information. For self-preservation I always turned the talk back to the women and their children.

In the spring I planted an enormous garden behind the convent. Finding seeds was no easy task, but I still had the money my grandfather had left in his wallet and I had been able to buy whatever I could find. Grandfather Von Helldorf and I had kept a garden since I had been five years old and now, as always, it seemed as if anything I touched grew. I showed the sisters that it wasn't hard to grow food with care for the plants, plenty of water and sunshine, and God's help.

My shows had been taking place weekly ever since December 23. Mother Angelica kept me in lovely, but modest dresses she borrowed from various women. When I performed, there was a nun stationed on either side of the stage, just out of sight of the audience. I played under the name of 'Luciana' and nobody ever suspected that I was Sister Theresa just as nobody ever suspected Luciana or Sister Theresa was the brilliant little sister who gave such good care to the soldiers so anonymously at the hospital.

I loved dressing up in nice dresses. My breasts had grown. My waist was tiny and I thought my hips flared just enough to be pretty. I was still 5'5" tall and had never gained more than up to the 105 pounds I had achieved last fall. It was good that my face had not been damaged in the beating. With clothes on and long sleeves, nobody would ever know how deformed I was. Mother Angelica had allowed Sister Olga to bring the mirror to me so I could do my hair and sometimes I just enjoyed looking at myself. I thought I looked like I was finally grown up and had turned out to look pretty decent even if my hair was too curly. The sisters never commented on my looks, but when I came out into the streets after my concerts I often heard the men and even some of the women call me beautiful. I didn't see it because with all the scars under my dress, I could never feel truly beautiful. Still, it did make me feel nice to fool other people into thinking that I was pretty.

The Americans were in the war now. It was fun talking to them in English. At first I had to hesitate to think of how to speak again, but as time went on, it was as if I had never left the United States. During my shows and in the hospital it didn't go unnoticed that I could speak without an accent in English, Italian, and French. I had never spoken a word of German since the beating even though there was no punishment for doing it. Many Italians spoke German. I just didn't want to seem in any way sympathetic to the Germans or Austrians, though I still worried about which side of the war my family might be on. Since my parents loved the United States so much, I thought they were probably on the side of the French, British, and Americans, but I wasn't sure.

Alessandro had never been able to transfer away from the compound, but he came to visit whenever he had enough time to make the trip. Sometimes, after making heroic efforts to borrow a truck and after making a long drive on bad roads, he would come only for a few hours, before he had to leave again. There was no doubt that, even though I wouldn't be 15 until August, the doctor was in love with me.

Once after Mother Angelica saw him put an arm around me to walk out in the garden, she had a talk with me. "You once mentioned being betrothed to someone named Joseph." She started.

Surprised, I said, "I was betrothed at birth, but he was nine years older than me. When I left, he had decided not to wait for me to grow up." I hesitated thoughtfully before continuing. "I still can't believe it, but it's true. Even when I was little he treated me like a lady by opening doors for me and helping me into the car or the sleigh." I sighed and went on, "By now he's been married for years." It still hurt to think of it.

She tried another approach, "You are very young. It wouldn't be good to get involved with a man at such a young age. These are troubled times. Sometimes your heart can fool you into thinking you are in love when it is simply loneliness and need for attention."

"What are you telling me, Mother?" I asked as I looked at the old woman sharply.

"Dr. Adami loves you. I can see it with my own eyes. Don't be foolish enough to give him your heart. Let him just be a friend, at least until you are much older."

I couldn't understand the harm in loving Alessandro. I waited for an explanation, but when none was forthcoming I felt the need to explain my feelings. "He is a friend. I love him too. Is that wrong?"

"It would be wrong to love him as more that just a friend. He is all grown up and you are still a child."

"I don't feel like a child. I feel like I've always been grown up."

"I'm just asking you not to fall in love in a husband and wife way at such a tender age."

"I won't," I answered with a smile of relief on my face. "I just love him like the very best friend I could ever have."

During my shows I often talked to my audience. In the beginning I always talked to them in Italian, but now I spoke in English too. The soldiers loved my shows and they seemed to love me too. I was the darling of Northern Italy it seemed. The soldiers painted my picture on all sorts of things. Dressed as I always was, I looked 20 years old and with the assurance I had in front of an audience, nobody would have dreamed I was so young. Men were forever sending me notes asking me out or waiting outside for me after a show just to get a better look. When Alessandro was there, he hated the way the men hung around and he always escorted me back to the convent in a roundabout way so we wouldn't be followed.

One night before we got to the convent, he pulled off behind a tree near the park. The first thing he did was put an arm around my shoulders. At first we were both quiet, and then he said, "Ten soldiers were executed in the middle of the compound yesterday for trying to desert. They didn't want to go back into battle. Conditions are bad out there and it's no wonder they're leaving. The executions reminded me of what happened to you last summer. We never know what's going to happen anymore. Our lives are so unpredictable. A person is about as likely to be killed by his own as by the enemy. The reason I'm telling you this is because I have something I want to tell you even though under normal circumstances I would have waited a couple more years to say it." He put his other arm around me. "I love you, Susanna. I've loved you and have known you were special ever since I first laid eyes on you. I'm so sorry life has been so hard," then he kissed me in a way I had only seen my parents kiss.

When it was over I was breathless. I had never experienced anything close to it. "I'm scared," I said honestly.

"You're scared? Can you say you don't love me too?"

"If I love you because I want to cry every time you leave and if I love you because I care so much deep inside that I lose my appetite when I think of you, then I do love you." I answered, reassuring him that my age was not a problem. "I've almost always felt grown up and I'll be 15 pretty soon."

He looked at me in a way that seemed almost sad. As an old woman looking back, I suppose I looked so innocent and vulnerable. He almost whispered when he said, "My heart aches for you. I promise I'll never hurt you." After that he kissed me again. I wanted it to last forever.

We sat there in the old army truck in the moonlit shade of the bushes with our arms wrapped around each other till we knew Mother Angelica would be worrying, then reluctantly we left. At the convent he kissed me again, then sadly drove back to the field hospital.

I was miserable after he left. I wondered if this had been how Joseph had felt about Carolyn Smithson, but decided that nobody had ever loved anybody as much as I loved Alessandro. As I moped around for the next few days the sisters noticed the change. Normally I was reserved, and I tried to be kind to everyone, reaching out to help in any way I could. Now I stayed to myself. It must have seemed as if I was unhappy, but I wasn't. I simply wanted to be alone with my thoughts of Alessandro and our future together.

By July of 1917, my garden was thriving. There were fresh vegetables enough for the sisters to share with the women and children in the area. Everyday when I packed my bags to make my rounds to the sick, I carried a heavy bag with food to help my patients get well. I told them how to save the seeds so they could grow their own food the next spring, though many of them had no place to plant a garden.

I had become a confidant midwife and hadn't lost a patient until one day in early August. The woman's mother had been planning to attend the delivery, but after her daughter had suffered hours of hard labor, she sent for the sisters. Sister Genevieve and I went out together. An examination revealed that the baby was lying transverse in the womb. There was no way it could be delivered unless we could turn it. The mother was exhausted.

I had seen the pain of labor, but fortunately in the seven months I had been in the neighborhoods, I had never seen a delivery like this. Because the bag of waters was still intact, I knew we had a chance of turning it. Together we pushed deeply on the woman's belly until she screamed in pain, but we couldn't make it move.

"What if we rupture the membranes, stretch open the cervix and reach up and pull the baby out?" I whispered.

"It's not that easy," she assured me. "The mouth of the uterus, the cervix, hasn't opened up any and as thick as it is, it's pure muscle. We won't be able to just stretch it open. If the pain doesn't kill her, the bleeding we cause will."

"What can we do? I've read about cesarean sections. Do you think we could find a doctor to do one?" I asked.

"No, I don't. Too bad your friend, Dr. Adami isn't here."

"It wouldn't be that difficult," I coaxed.

"Without any facilities, it would be impossible! You know better than that," the sister said impatiently.

"I don't mean here. What about if we would take her to the field hospital?"

"We cannot take her to the hospital, but if you insist, I will go and seek a physician to assist us." Even though Sister Genevieve believed there was no hope, she left for the hospital to see if any doctor would take pity on the laboring woman and offer to do the needed operation.

Genevieve had been gone about two hours when the young woman got a strange look on her face, then her eyes rolled back in her head and she started convulsing from head to toe. Suddenly her body became limp and she stopped breathing. I checked for a pulse, but there was none. The woman was dead. Her head and chest were purple by the time she stopped convulsing. Quickly I talked to the grandmother. "Your daughter is dead," I told her. "Do you want me to open her up and try to get the baby out before it dies?"

"Yes, do what you can for it!" she answered sobbing. "Please hurry!"

I had nothing but one knife, a few clamps and some suture for repairing tears in the vagina and for stitching up children who had accidents in the neighborhood. Thank goodness a dead woman wouldn't bleed, I thought to myself as I quickly made an incision from the belly button down to the pubic bone. The uterus was unmistakable as it lay there enlarged, dusky pink and shiny. I quickly cut it open as clear amniotic fluid rushed everywhere. Without gloves,

I reached inside the warm cavity of the uterus and scooped out the baby. It was blue, its arms were limp, there wasn't a sign of life. The grandmother let out a cry and a scream of sorrow. My own heart was pounding as I held the baby upside down and stroked its back. It made a little gasping sound, and then seemed to choke and cough. Finally after what seemed like eternity, it let out a weak cry and took its first shallow breaths.

'The grandmother crossed herself and said, "Thank God."

I cut the cord, wrapped the screaming baby in a soft blanket, and gave the new little boy to his grandmother; quickly I busied myself, crudely sewing the mother back together so the body would be intact for the funeral. Even though there was the noise of the baby, the room seemed cold and quiet. I had never worked on a dead body before. I had always wondered when I lost my first pregnant mother if the family would blame me, but this woman had seen that there was nothing that could have been done and was only grateful that at least the baby had been saved.

Just as I was finishing, Sister Genevieve and one of the older doctors showed up. At first the doctor had looked at me skeptically, thinking I had killed the patient with my surgery, but the grandmother was quick to tell him what had happened, then he looked at me with obvious admiration.

"Even most doctors wouldn't have done a c-section on a dead woman to save the baby. They would have considered it a lost cause. Maybe if I had gotten here sooner, I could have turned the baby, but if she died of a convulsion, there would have been nothing I could have done. I have many years experience delivering babies, but I needed to be working at the hospital anyway," he said thoughtfully. "My first responsibilities are to care for the soldiers, as you well know. Even a dying woman in labor couldn't take priority over caring for the men who are defending their country."

Before he left, he looked me over. "You're an odd child. People all over the hospital wonder about you. Who are you? How do you know what to do? You couldn't have more than 14 or 15 years. Where do you come from?"

I shrugged my shoulders and answered without giving an answer. "I'm from here and there. It isn't important." I was very troubled as my eyes darted into his and then quickly darted away.

"If that's the way you want it, I'll ask no more questions," the short, chunky, bald-headed doctor answered curtly.

"That's the way I want it," I answered.

After he left, Sister Genevieve and I washed the woman and brushed her hair. We wrapped her in a clean blanket and went to look for the grandmother's other daughter. I felt inadequate for not having been able to do the c-section before it was too late for the mother. Sister Genevieve tried to comfort me, but only time and a few successes would help me get over the first maternal death of my career.

That evening the hospital sisters told me that the doctor had asked around over the hospital to see if anybody knew who I was, but everybody claimed ignorance. He even went so far as to ask the patients he had seen me caring for what I had said to them. Had I told them my name?

According to Sister Olga, one of the American men said, "She spoke English like an American with a midwestern accent," but he told the doctor, "When I asked her about it, she told me it wasn't important for me to be thinking about her."

The sisters agreed that I always handled such intrusions into my personal life very well and they were glad of it.

On my 15th birthday Alessandro surprised me with a visit. He got special permission from Mother Angelica for me to wear a street dress to go on a picnic in the little park in Verona. The grass was uncut and the shrubs needed trimming, but it was still beautiful and a treat to be in a quiet place without chaos.

He seemed thoughtful as he spread a blanket out on the ground for us to sit on, then he said, "I wish I could take you to Rome for a vacation. The war hasn't really been such a problem there. We could see the sights and eat some good food for a change. You could meet my father," he said with his dark eyes shining.

"He lives in Rome?"

"Close. Just a few miles north."

I sat back on the blanket and really looked at the man I loved. He was light skinned with dark, concerned eyes. His hair was wavy and jet black, his smile earnest with slight dimples in either cheek. He was slender and tall like Papi and Tom and Joseph, but the men in my family were all blond and blue-eyed. He made me feel so good and I loved him so much. The only times I had ever been completely happy since I had left Bayland were the times I spent with him. Though he and Joseph looked nothing alike, there was something about the way he treated me that made me feel warm and good just like it had always been with Joseph.

We sat close on the thick wool army blanket. Mother had made him promise to remember that I was a child, but he didn't seem to see me that way. He leaned down and kissed me, then put his arms around me and kissed me again. I responded by putting my arms around him, hoping to make the moment last forever. It was as we clung to each other that I remembered Joseph and wondered if things had been different, had I never gotten on that train to leave Bayland, would he really have married Carolyn? Of course the answer was "yes". It never could have been real love like this because he had never been sincere, probably didn't know the meaning of the word. As my mind wandered and I continued to think with my arms around Alessandro, he seemed suddenly to realize the need for restraint when he gently pulled away and started opening the box he had brought for the picnic. He started talking rather breathlessly, "We need to get this picnic started. I've brought some treasures!"

It was hard to believe during a war when everybody was going hungry, even the soldiers that he could have found such delicacies for us to eat. There was fresh bread, yellow cheese, oranges, and even two small white cakes!

"How did you ever find such food as this? Did you hold up a general?"

"Almost," he answered with an almost childlike grin. "Ask no more questions."

I told him about the c-section and the baby as we ate. The pain of it had nearly passed now that I had come to the full realization that I had done more to save the baby's life than was ever expected of me. Alessandro assured me that I had probably done more than he would have, but then clarified that he would have done the c-section before she died if there had been facilities available for an operation.

"When this war is over, you should consider becoming a doctor," he told me. "We could get married and find a good medical school that accepts women. I'll practice medicine there while you go to school, then we'll practice together after that."

"What if we have children?"

"Didn't you have a nurse when you were small?"

"Only after my first mother died, but after that I did and she was wonderful," I answered dreamily as I thought back of Mrs. Bronson, who I had loved so much.

Alessandro could see that he had hit a nerve. I guess he didn't want me thinking about my family and my country today. To go home would be to leave him and he couldn't allow that to ever happen, he had told me many times.

Then he pursued his thoughts. "Would you consider marrying

me in a year, when you're sixteen?"

"Yes," I answered quickly as I looked straight into his eyes, though knowing it would mean never going home again. By now I had been gone so long and so many things had happened that I was sure I would never fit in back home. My family would never understand me anymore. I would be a guest, an oddity, no longer a member of the family. Joseph was married and my parents had all their little boys. They probably rarely even thought of me anymore. Tom might miss me some, but he might have a wife and children by now too. Even Ilona would have continued at the conservatory and in my absence would have made new friends.

Alessandro must have read my thoughts because he asked, "What's troubling you my darling? Are you thinking about your family?"

"Yes. I'm thinking it probably wouldn't be good to ever go home. All that's behind me now. They probably gave up on me years ago anyway. I did love them so much," I said with tears in my eyes. "I try not to think about them, but sometimes I just can't help it."

He put his arms around me and gently stroked my hair. Maybe when the war is over we could go to Ameerica for a visit. Then you could talk to them and see, but we'll have to be married first. I wouldn't want to get you over there and have you refuse to come back with me."

"I'd never do that!"

"Well, just in case, I don't want to take any chances."

For my birthday Alessandro gave me a ring with a magnificent marquise-shaped diamond mounted in lacy antique silver. "This ring means you are promised to me," he said as he gently slipped it onto my left ring finger. "It belonged to my mother. Next year we will be married."

I looked at the ring and cried, not really knowing why.

"You are sure you love me?" he asked, bewildered by my crying.

"Yes, I love you. My life belongs to you. I don't know why I'm crying. I guess because I'm so happy that something so good could happen. Are you sure you remember my scars? I don't look very good most places."

"They just make me love you more. They'll always remind me of what a strong girl you are."

When the sun went down, we went for a drive just outside of the town where we parked to look at the moon and the stars.

"I used to love the outdoors," I said as I looked up into the sky. "Lately I've been so busy I haven't had time to even sit in the garden unless I'm working in it."

"Someday we'll have a home with a big garden. Our children will play in the trees and chase butterflies. The little girls will bring us flowers."

"...And the boys will play baseball!"

"Baseball?" he looked surprised.

"Yes, in my country almost all little boys play baseball. My brother, Tom, is an excellent player."

"Well, we'll see about that," he chided as he took me back into his arms again. As he kissed me I felt breathless and his breathing became heavy. Suddenly he pulled away. "We need to get you back to the convent."

"Why did you stop kissing me?" I asked, feeling dejected.

"Because you're not my wife yet and I don't want to bring you any more pain than you've already had." He hesitated then continued, "I'm working only miles from the battlefields. What if you were with child and I should be killed? Your family would disown you and here you would be with a child to raise all alone. To say nothing of the fact that I would be bringing sin to us both that we can never afford to commit it these terrible times." He was silent, his breathing returning to normal before he spoke again. Finally he added, "From now on we'll not get in this position until we're married. No more sitting in the car or any other place alone. I love you too much."

Not understanding the problem I said, "I'm not afraid of you. I love you and I don't see what kissing you has to do with babies."

He smiled a slow smile and said, "That is the problem...you are an innocent and I want you to stay that way. You are the brightest most innocent person I have ever known."

LINDA STEELE

Mother

*I*lived in a household of men after Susanna left for Luxembourg. At
first I didn't mind because I knew Susanna would be returning in a
little while and I was used to her short absences while she attended the
conservatory. How I missed the stories about her adventures with Ilona
and her classmates! They were a group of the most unusual children in the
United States. All of them were gifted beyond exceptional and most of them
would have been misfits in any other setting.

The letters from Susanna had been encouraging and at the same time
frightening. We were glad she was still alive, but wondered what atrocities
she had survived. It was obvious that she was avoiding any subject that
might upset us.

I lite a candle for my beautiful daughter every time I had an opportunity
to go to the church and I kept a candle burning in the house at all times.
I asked God to bring her back and to protect her from harm, but as much
as I tried to place her care into His hands, I couldn't stop feeling sick every
time I thought of her.

Paul hadn't been born when Susanna left and the twins were small.
Only Henry could remember her. His recollections seemed to be faint and
it irritated him to hear the adults discuss her fate. Sometimes I thought
maybe he was jealous of her, but then, after thinking about it, I decided
that he was probably as sorry as we were to have lost her. Maybe he felt that
she had abandoned him. After the twins had been born, Susanna had gone
through some serious behavior problems. Her disobedience to her father and
to me had forced us to deal severely with her on several occasions. We were
sure she was feeling displaced by the new members of our family who were
occupying so much of our time, and it was at about that time that young
Joseph had announced his engagement to the Smithson girl. We thought

that we had to discipline her, whatever the reason. I wonder if we were wrong about that. We knew she was feeling berift so eventually she turned to Henry, her small brother, and had showered all her love and attention on him and seemed to shut everybody else out. We had hoped that a trip to see her grandfather, her last living relative by blood, would help her to feel better about her place in this world. I never dreamed when we put her on that train that we might never see her again.

Our household was bleak with Joseph, Tom, and Susanna all gone. Only our smallest children, the twins and the baby Paul, could be happy and we all tried to keep up a good front so they could have a decent childhood. None of them remembered our three older children and that was probably best. They could become acquainted if they ever met. We celebrated Christmas, Easter, birthdays, and Thanksgiving as if we hadn't a care in the world. I'm sure we made happy memories for them and that they never suffered.

Chapter 5

I noticed Dr. Bonfiglio, the one who had come to help with the delivery when I had done the cesarean section, watching me when I helped in the hospital. The thought crossed my mind that I might need to stop helping out for a while. He seemed important and I didn't need to be identified as a traitor again. If I were thrown out of Verona I would have no place left to go and certainly didn't need to have anybody trying to cause me trouble. I would have to be careful to try to stay out of his way, I decided.

One day as I was suturing an American soldier's face with my tiny overcast sutures using the thinnest suturing silk I could find, I felt a presence behind me, but paid no attention. I had been talking to the American in English, telling him if he could stand the pain, I would make him the most handsome man in Indiana. We teased back and forth as we discussed the Midwest.

The man asked, "Have you been there? You talk like you know all about it."

I broke a cardinal rule I had set for myself by answering, "Yes, on several occasions. When I was younger."

"Are you American?"

I was careful not to answer. Instead I said, "I'm just about finished and it looks good!"

From behind me an unfriendly Italian voice started firing questions at me. "Well, are you an American? Why did you use an overcast stitch? Why such flimsy suture?"

I turned to see who was questioning me. Nobody ever questioned my judgment or cared what I did. It was that same doctor again. I ignored his question about my being an American and about my choice of suture and instead said, "Sir, if you would prefer that I not be here, I'll do as you wish."

"You don't have to be so defensive. I just want to know how much you know and then I want to know how you know it."

I teared up. The American asked, "Is that guy giving you a hard time? I don't speak Italian, but he sounds like a real jerk to me."

"It doesn't matter. I'm finished. Somebody else can bandage it for you. I have to go."

"Will you come back?"

"No."

I turned and walked out of the hospital with the doctor right behind me. "Wait!" he demanded in English.

I kept walking until he caught up with me and grabbed my arm. I was shaking.

"I'm the chief surgeon of this hospital and I have a right to know who's working in my hospital."

"I thought the sisters were wanted at your hospital!"

"They are. You are, but I have to know about you. I don't even know your name for sure. I know the other sisters, but you? You're different. Even the other sisters refuse to tell me your name. I've gone to the convent and had them tell me you weren't available when I could see you playing the piano. --You're quite good as a matter-of-fact."

"I have to go!" I shook his hand loose and ran for the convent. When I got there, I ran to my garden and tried to calm myself with deep breaths, I thought to myself that I had better be sure I never saw him again.

That night I talked to the sisters about what had happened and they decided it would be best for me not to return to the hospital anymore. There was enough work to do in the community to stay busy and I still had my musical programs and my garden that seemed to be supporting most of the neighborhood. They decided that I definitely had enough to do without helping in the hospital.

After the discussion I played for them as I did most nights when we weren't busy at the hospital or when I wasn't doing a show.

Alessandro hadn't been able to get back since my birthday and it was now late September. Letters arrived almost daily addressed to Sister Olga who gave them to me unopened. I wrote to him every day, but signed them Sister O. He knew whom they were from. Often their messages were cryptic in nature because there was always the possibility of them being read by someone else. The sisters knew of the engagement and Sister Margaret had even given me a sturdy silver chain to use around my neck for my ring while I was working. She said it could be close to my heart at all times. They could see how right it was for Alessandro and me to be together, though Mother worried that Alessandro would take advantage of me. After all, he was a man of 24 years and I was still practically a child, she reminded me frequently.

I kept busy with my garden, the neighborhood, and my shows. I loved attending mass and often remembered the times Papi and I had gone to church early in the mornings through the snow and rain to "give our day a good start" as he always said. Back then I loved him so much that I wanted to be perfect for him so he would be glad he had adopted me. He always told me I was everything and more than he could have ever dreamed of for a daughter. He wouldn't think so now, I thought. Whenever the thoughts of my family came, I tried to push them away before I could start being unhappy. I had already decided that I could never go home again. They could never understand what life had been like and would certainly condemn the way I had been living for years. Papi hadn't even wanted me to see a baby delivered and now I was caring for men who used swear words that were sometimes directed at me, I delivered babies, discussed male problems with the soldiers from time to time, and knew things about low life living that most women never dreamed of.

Monday, October 1, Alessandro finally came. I thought by his letters that he might be coming, but so much depended on the casualties that we never knew for sure. I was so happy to see him I couldn't stop hugging him, and then I laughed at myself. It was only when I was with him or when I was doing a show that a little flicker of my old Bayland self showed through. It became easy to smile and sometimes I felt as if I was a 15 year-old girl for a while. Alessandro said he loved seeing the child in me.

Dressed in my dark red print dress again, I left with him to go for a walk. There was never much to do in Verona except enjoy each other's company. We discussed the war and the curious doctor. More American casualties were starting to show up now. Alessandro found them a different breed from the Europeans, but also unlike the Australians who were so boisterous. They were better equipped than the Italian soldiers and their officers treated them much better. Their food was good compared to the practically nonexistent rations of the Italians.

"They even carry a roll of what they call toilet paper! Imagine!" Alessandro claimed in amazement. "People over there must have everything!"

"They do," I agreed. "My father always kept a firm hand on us to keep us from being too spoiled."

That sparked a bit of curiosity in Alessandro. "Did he ever beat you?" he asked.

"I wouldn't say he beat us, but he was very strict. If we disobeyed him, he was quick to give is a good spanking. Though he loved us so much that everybody said he was the most overly protective father they had ever seen, we had to behave because he meant business. Tom and I were punished pretty often, but he never beat us. Afterwards we were always crying, but it was the strangest thing because he almost always had tears in his own eyes. Did you ever hear of a father crying over a child he has just given a spanking to? He was the best father anybody ever had. My mother was pretty perfect too. She had been in a convent for three years before she married my father."

"She was a nun?" he asked, obviously surprised.

"Well, she never took her final vows in all that time so she probably wasn't ever cut out to be anything but my father's wife and our mother...oh yes and a real good nurse and midwife. We were always proud of her because she was so good. What about your parents, were they good to you?"

"My parents were well educated. My father was a professor of art in Rome. Mother had studied in the university. They loved each other and all of us. Mama died in childbirth when I was eleven, but Papa always took good care of us. Like your father, he'd give us a good threshing if we needed it, but it always seemed to bother him too."

"I'm never going to strike our children. I don't care if they do turn out to be spoiled, I just couldn't."

"I can understand why, but children have to be threshed every so often or they don't turn out to be any good. Besides, they have to mind or they might kill themselves!"

"I still couldn't."

"Then I would have to always be the mean parent who did it."

I changed the subject. "How many children should we have?"

"Six would be a good number. After six the pregnancies are hard on a woman, but I would be satisfied with six. Does that sound good to you?"

"Six sounds like a lot, but I guess that would be all right."

We laughed at each other as we ate in the cafe. The only things on the menu were soup, bread, and cheese. We each had a small glass of wine, then left. Whenever we could find a little privacy we kissed, but true to his word, Alessandro never became passionate with me at any time during his three-day visit.

When he left, I must have asked him to be careful at least a half dozen times. I always worried that he would say something wrong or do something to look suspicious and would be executed. I even worried that he would be associated with me somehow and would throw suspicion on himself. After a few days I worried less, but the thought of something happening to him was always there.

I never went to the hospital anymore, but the good doctor hadn't stopped his investigation. Obviously there was something about me that made him curious.

He tried to get into the convent on numerous occasions, but the sisters wouldn't let him in. They tried to make it look as if I had disappeared. He told them that he missed seeing me around and wished he hadn't pushed so hard. He said my work had been excellent and they should tell me to come back.

He was seen attending my concerts regularly. The first time I saw him in the audience sitting close to the front in the center row, I almost ran off the stage. Somehow I managed to keep my cool and act exactly the opposite of the little sister he had seen in the hospital. I swished around on the stage and played the gayest most popular tunes I knew and had the audience singing and dancing. I thought I had disguised myself well enough that he would never figure out who I was. What I didn't know at the time was that I hadn't fooled him one little bit.

In November several German planes circled over the compound

in Northern Italy where Dr. Adami, Dr. Andretti, and Mother Maria Elizabeth had been stationed for so long. Enemy planes always sent everybody at the compound inside the buildings as fast as they could get there. This time instead of diving down and shooting everything that moved below them, the enemy dropped bombs on the hospital, the orphanage, and the officer's quarters. Casualties were heavy. Most of the children in the orphanage were killed and most of the hospital personnel who were in the building at the time were also killed. A few managed to escape, but with serious burns and other injuries. The nearest hospital was in Verona. All injured, including the children, would be coming in. The evacuation started almost as soon as those who had managed to survive could collect the other survivors.

When word came that so many casualties would be coming in, Dr. Bonfiglio headed for the convent. He stood at the steps of the convent and demanded to see me. He told the sisters he would break the door down if they didn't let him in and he had two military police with him to prove it. Mother Angelica went to me and told me about the bombing. I was dressed for a concert and could hardly be seen like that, but when Mother went back to talk to him without me, the three men forced their way in. When he saw me with my hair pulled up into a loose chignon, wearing a deep blue silk dress that accented my tiny waist and my round breasts, he said, "I don't care if you are a nun or Luciana or whatever and at the moment I don't care about your problems either. We need you at the hospital. One of the field hospitals up on the front has been bombed and we need everybody we can find. We're expecting the heaviest casualties we've ever had. The personnel from the field hospital who are uninjured will be coming to help."

I immediately worried that it might be the hospital where I had been and that Alessandro might be among the dead or injured. I felt weak and cried out, "Oh God!" and sat down.

"Excuse me for being so brusque Luciana or whoever you are, but get up and get yourself get over to the hospital!" I don't care about your games and your secrets. You are going to help."

"Let me change my clothes. It wouldn't be good to be seen dressed like this."

"There's no time for that. Come immediately!"

He noticed me slip the engagement ring off my finger and put it on the chain around my neck, but said nothing. I guess that was the moment that he realized that I wasn't a nun.

Everybody in the convent including Mother Angelica went to the hospital. Mother squeezed my hand and whispered, "Be brave child. I'll be praying that it wasn't Dr. Adami's hospital."

Some children had already arrived, most in a state of panic. I recognized them and knew it had to have been the compound where I had lived. Niccolo never showed up so I assumed he hadn't survived. I panicked as I wondered about Alessandro and Mother Maria Elizabeth. As the trucks rolled in, they put the moaning, crying people out on the lawn and in the street for lack of any other place to put them. A chill ran down my spine when I recognized Dr. Andretti standing by a truck that was unloading more casualties. He was unhurt and triaging patients. It was hard to decide what to do first in such disorder, but with Dr. Andretti and Dr. Bonfiglio both working at it, things were quickly being pulled together. I considered running, but concern for Alessandro kept me there. Dr. Bonfiglio had ordered a young soldier to watch me and make sure I didn't leave the scene, but I figured in the chaos I could probably escape him without much trouble if I had a mind to.

When Dr. Andretti saw me he didn't bat an eye, "Susanna, come over here and get on the priority team. Take Dr. Adami first."

Dr. Bonfiglio looked shocked that the famous Dr. Antonio

Andretti would want me on his team and I guess he was more shocked when I screamed, "Alessandro!" as I ran for the man lying at his feet.

"My God Sandro, can you hear me?" I cried as I looked at the burns on most of his body.

"Susanna, calm down and get busy or do you plan to let him die?" Dr. Andretti asked in a gruff voice.

I was devastated when I saw my Alessandro lying on the lawn. I ran for water to scrub and debride the burns and as I worked he screamed in pain only half-noticing who was with him and I cried. He screamed, "Susanna" once, but it seemed as if only Dr. Bonfiglio noticed.

The debridement was brutal, but when it was finished, I gently wrapped him with moist bandages, added another I.V. bottle of salt water, and gave him another shot of Morphine.

I kissed him before he was taken inside the hospital and I didn't care who saw me. Mother Angelica promised to stay with him so I could go back to work.

My next patient was a child I knew. I asked him about Niccolo, but he said he didn't know. I set his broken arm as he screamed in pain, but he never moved. When I finished I kissed him too. It was obvious to anyone watching that we knew each other very well. As a matter-of-fact, anybody watching could tell that I knew almost everybody there. Even the ones who had wanted me put to death acted like I was their best friend now.

I never knew which people were which so I treated them all with compassion, certain when this was all over, I was going to either lose my life or have to leave Verona in the middle of the night for some other place.

Every few hours I ran to see Alessandro. The Morphine was helping his pain, but he was so heavily sedated that his speech was slurred. In the early hours of the morning, long before dawn, in a moment of lucidity, he told me, "My darling, I'm not going to make it. You must promise to go home to your family as soon as possible. I could never bear to think of you over here alone. Find a good man, somebody who's been here who understands and marry him. You have so much love to give. ...Promise."

"I could never promise to marry anybody but you, Sandro. There could be nobody else ever!"

"You have to promise to try!" he begged. "I'll love you forever, but I can never rest if I have to think of you alone. Please promise."

Crying as hard as I ever had, I promised as Mother Angelica looked on.

I didn't return to the lawn again. I just couldn't leave Alessandro. I stood on one side of the bed and Mother stood on the other side, waiting to comfort me, I knew, when the inevitable happened.

He died slowly and painfully three hours later. I'm sure my screams of sorrow could be heard all over the hospital outside to the lawn, but I didn't care what anybody thought or what anybody did to me. Life had been too hard for too long and I just couldn't take any more.

Of all people there, it was Dr. Andretti who finally came to take me away. Dr. Bonfiglio watched him lead me gently out to the back garden, away from everybody. He saw us sit down together on a bench while he took my shaking body into his arms.

"My dear child. I'm so sorry for everything that's happened to you. God will surely punish me for all that I have done to make your life such hell."

He never left me as I cried and cried. During that time he told me that I was the most brilliant person he had ever known. He offered to help me find my parents and told me about my father's investigators who had visited the compound and how, thinking that I must be dead, he had sent them away with no information. Most of all he asked that some time I consider trying to forgive him for the angry outburst of temper that had caused me to take such a severe beating.

Between sobs I told him, "I never held that against you. I could see that you were sorry when you came to my trial with Alessandro." I held my breath and tried to suppress a sob. "Back then I was such a child. I couldn't understand what I had done that was so wrong because that soldier looked so much like my brother Tom and like his brother Joseph. I wouldn't have wanted anybody to tell on them if they were in trouble, but I guess I was thinking like a child who was keeping something from her father instead of as an adult in a time of war. I was stupid."

"You were just a child, but for a moment I forgot it because you were so grown up in other ways. It was the worst mistake in my life."

"Don't punish yourself by thinking about it. I forgive you and still think you're the best doctor I know," I declared as I looked into his eyes remembering what a hero he had been to me. "Alessandro wanted to be just like you." I grew quiet, trying to collect my emotions and keep them under tight wraps then continued, "We were going to get married and then find a medical school for me. He was going to get more training at the same time. I wanted to be like you too." I gulped.

"Alessandro was a promising young doctor and so are you. When this is over, I'll help you get into whatever medical school you want. You just name it, even in the States, if you decide to go back."

"I wasn't going to go back. So much has happened that I don't think my family could ever accept me. Alessandro made me promise to go just before he...left. I don't want to even think about it. Maybe some of my enemies will just kill me so I can go peacefully to Sandro."

"I think most of them will, like me, spend the rest of their lives regretting what happened that day. It was probably the cruelest exhibition of human nature since the crucifixion."

"It's all in the past...like everything else in my life."

Dr. Andretti must have known he should be doing something in the hospital, but I suppose his conscious wouldn't allow him to pull himself away from me. He just held me in his arms, as a father would comfort his child.

Mother Angelica interrupted when she felt that I had spent enough time with my grief. She put a hand on my shoulder and coaxed, "Come child, there's a lot of misery inside that hospital besides out here. You must put your grieving aside until later. I'll be close at your side to help you be strong while you give your talents to your poor friends from the compound. Please come."

When we got up, the doctor put his arm around my shoulders and Mother held my hand.

"We'll work together. We always did make a good team," Dr. Andretti added.

We worked tirelessly all day, through the night, and through the next day with Mother close at hand at all times. The doctor and I operated on open fractures, a broken jaw, an open gut wound where a piece of wood was lodged into the belly of one of the sisters. It went on and on from one thing to another. We did still make an excellent team even though we hadn't seen each other in over a year. Dr. Bonfiglio looked dumbfounded as he walked slowly past us every 30 minutes or so.

When we finally called it quits, Dr. Andretti gave me a fatherly hug and told me to sleep. He gently ordered me not to think about anything yet. "The time is not right," he warned.

As we walked back to the convent, Mother asked, "Was he the one?"

"Yes," I answered simply.

"Can you forgive him?"

"I never really blamed him. He has a hot temper and often says things he doesn't mean. I knew at the trial that he regretted ever getting me in so much trouble, but by then it was too late."

I cried off and on all day upstairs in my cubicle. I knew nobody could help me and so did Mother Angelica, who kept everybody away from me. I asked God to give me peace so I could go on with my life.

After that day, I never wore a habit again. Everybody knew I wasn't a nun. They didn't know if I was Luciana or Theresa. Only a few people knew I was Susanna and they weren't talking. The hospital people and the people I visited in the neighborhood called me Theresa and when I did my concerts, I was still Luciana, though of course, many knew me by both names. Only Dr. Andretti called me Susanna.

Dr. Andretti and the rest of the staff and the sisters who were left from the bombing stayed to help with the swell of patients, knowing they would soon be getting orders to be sent somewhere else.

Olga heard Dr. Bonfiglio as he quizzed Dr. Andretti about me.

"Why are you so interested?" he asked.

"She is a very interesting girl."

"I have nothing to say. Some things are better left alone."

I was so withdrawn by now that I never talked to anybody unless they asked me a question. The only exceptions were when I became Luciana or when I was working with patients. Then it was as if I had never had a problem in my life. I became an actress, a puppet, but deep inside me my sorrow was inconsolable.

One day I started to write a letter home, but when I read it, it sounded so depressing that I tore it up. Without Alessandro I didn't see how I could ever go on. It bothered me that I had promised to go home, but the only reason I had made the promise was to help him relax and feel better. I just couldn't ever return to a family who had never known any pain except for the death of an occasional family member. They knew nothing of beatings, executions, and screaming pain. When I could no longer stand my thoughts, I invited Mother to go with me for a walk. At first we practically ran as I tried to get a hold on myself, then when I realized that Mother was probably exhausted, I slowed the pace. It reminded me of the walk I had taken so long ago with Mother Maria Elizabeth at the compound. When I glanced at Mother Angelica I realized that the elderly little nun with a stooped little back and weathered old face was truly out of breath from trying to keep up with me. "I'm sorry Mother," I said. "I was walking way too fast. Sometimes I'm not very thoughtful."

Mother Angelica said, "Think nothing of it." Gently she went on, "I know you're having a hard time with Alessandro's death. You may have trouble believing this, but I honestly believe that God takes, and then gives back seven-fold. Dr. Adami came when you lost your grandfather and needed someone so badly. He was there for you through it all. When you finally didn't need him so much, God called your beloved doctor home. One day someone will come along who is even better suited to be your husband. Trust in the Lord, child. All the gifts He bestowed on you prove you are one of his most loved children. He won't forget you."

"It seems to me He forgot all about me years ago."

"Oh no, child! He sent you to us special. We needed you here so much. Think how things would have been without you. Your music has brought pleasure to so many of us where there was no pleasure before. Look how the people in the town love you. Now that they know you're not a nun, they're all trying to find ways to get brothers and uncles home to meet you. How many babies have you delivered and how many bones have you set and what about the soldiers? Most of them are in love with you and besides that, how many of them would be dead if you hadn't saved their lives? How many would have entered heaven without a hand to hold? Most of all, what about Alessandro? He had you to love him for over two years. How lonesome he would have been if you had been at home being pampered by your family. Your brothers are probably fighting in this war. Would you have been happy over there with them here?"

"Mother Maria Elizabeth said some of what you just said once, but I never thought about some the other things that way."

Well, you should. God couldn't give you all those gifts then let you stay home and keep them to yourself. They were given to share with the needy."

The weight on my heart seemed to temporarily lift. I looked at Mother with a smile. You always know what to say to help me. Maybe I am going to live through this. Sometimes I feel so sad and empty inside."

"You will feel sad and empty for the rest of your life when you think of these times but as the years pass, you will not think of it as often. Still, the thought of it will always cause you to have a heavy heart."

From that day on I think I started to lift myself out of that dark depression I had lived in for so long. I still had my bad times, but nobody had ever heard me sing before and now, I hummed a little song as I dressed in the mornings and when I helped with the cleaning. Dr. Andretti noticed the change right away and wondered what had happened. The patients even seemed relieved. I didn't worry about being identified as a traitor anymore. God was going to do whatever He wanted with me so there was no use worrying about it. The one thing I was sure I would never understand was why I had to be beaten so severely while serving Him. Did He want to be sure that I would remain unmarried forever? Now that Alessandro was gone, He had made it clear that I could never go back to my family or get married either. I guessed I would just serve Him and not ask questions. I was not on this earth to belong, only to serve.

RANDOM ACTS

ANGEL CHILD OF VERONA

Child of Verona, are you an angel or are you real?
I wonder as you sit by my bedside wiping my forehead, concern written
on your face.
Sewing me back together so perfectly only God could match your skill.
Talking softly to me in whatever language I speak.
What child are you?
A child of God

So very young, green eyes shining, dark curls wild around your face,
like a child
Dear Luciana, are you a child or an angel?
Thrilling us with your music.
Making us laugh with your jokes.
Who taught you to do that?
It had to be God!

Joseph

*A*s the American soldiers I treated made their way back through Europe and home, they talked about a young girl who took such special care to gently help them. This was a girl who could speak English like an American and could play the piano like nobody they had ever heard. One man had even written a poem about her that was published in military newspapers all over Europe, then made it all the way back to the newspapers in the United States.

Though I had started in the French Army, I later transferred to the United States Army after the Americans had entered the war. Jacob, who had been Tom's and my chaperone when we started college at the tender ages of 12 and 14 was stationed in France with me. He was sure when he read the poem that it was about Susanna even though it said Luciana. The first opportunity he had to get to me, he brought me the clipping.

"What do you think? Do you think it could be Susanna?"He asked excitedly.

I told him, "I don't know. Our people have combed Verona and they never had the slightest break, not a clue. It would be a miracle if there is anything left of her after being all alone in such a hellacious war. A few weeks ago I had a man come through with a facial laceration that was beautifully repaired. Whoever did it used tiny overcast sutures with fine silk and told him to be sure and get them removed in exactly five days. He said it was a young woman with dark hair--the most beautiful woman he had ever seen. He said she spoke English like she was American, but she was definitely Italian because he had heard her talking in Italian and there was no doubt. I'm beginning to think everybody is Susanna and sometimes I'm afraid she's gone forever. I have to admit, though that I haven't given up hope and nobody in the family had given up the possibility of finding her either.

Chapter 6

I composed a light, happy Christmas arrangement for the last number I played at my show Saturday, December 22. I told my audience it was my gift to them. They enjoyed it so much that they begged for an encore. As an encore, I played a medley of Christmas songs that would be commonly heard in the United States. The crowd stood up and cheered. Some sang along. The Italians were in the spirit too. When it was over, the auditorium roared with applause. My second Christmas program was even more successful than the first one I had given the year before.

When the sisters and I got ready to leave through the back door, it was crowded with men, mostly Americans, wanting to see me up close. Many missed their wives and girl friends and they said that I seemed like such a hometown girl that they just wanted to experience me for a few more minutes. I knew how alone they must have been feeling this Christmas because I had felt that way so many times and often still did. Then I impulsively said, "I know what it's like to be so far from home. I was the same way when I got stranded here three-and-a-half years ago, but the people of Italy are good and they're very glad to have you. Learn to make your life wherever you are and know that I will be praying for each of you till this war is over."

I looked off to my side and saw Dr. Bonfiglio and knew that he had heard what I said. He told me one day that he had suspected for a long time that I was probably was an American, but now he knew for sure. The sisters were sick of his constant questions about me and Dr. Andretti could hardly tolerate being in the same room with him.

In March of 1918, Dr. Andretti told me he was being transferred closer to the battle zone again. "I'm going to give you my home address. After the war, if you need a place to stay or if you need a letter of recommendation, or help finding your family, write to me. My wife and I will always welcome you."

The day in April when he left, I felt empty and depleted of every emotion. This man who had caused me so much misery had turned out to be a true friend. Before he left, just as Alessandro had done, he advised me to write home.

Though I missed the doctor, I went on with my daily life quite well. Ever since my talk with Mother Angelica that day, I had put my life in God's hands and never had another worrisome day. There still were periods of depression when I would play heavy, sad music for hours, then go to the far corner of the garden to be alone in my misery, sometimes for most of the night. Those times occurred about once a month and when they came, the sisters stayed away until I returned to them cheery and smiling as if nothing had ever happened.

One day, after I had bathed, I really looked at my body objectively. It was still badly scarred from my shoulders to my ankles. One thing about it, I thought to myself, only Alessandro could have loved anybody this badly mutilated. My body was shaped well and my breasts had developed to be round and firm. My stomach was flat from my breasts to my pubic bone, but a man would have to shut his eyes and use a lot of imagination to ever find me attractive.

I wondered what I should do after the war. Of course I would go to medical school and with the reputation Dr. Andretti had in Italy, it might be wise to try to get into an Italian school where his recommendation would mean something. I would need money, but possibly could earn enough for school by giving concerts as Luciana. I wouldn't need to contact Papi to have him send me money. It would be best for my family to think I was dead. After school I would establish a clinic for the poor. No other woman or child would die for lack of medical attention if I were around.

Dr. Andretti told me this story one day and Tom confirmed it:

In June of 1918 a young blond American soldier came through the field hospital Dr. Andretti was working in near Trento. He was Major Thomas Von Helldorf, an American who had been working as a spy in Austria. His leg had been badly mutilated by a gunshot wound as his comrades had rushed the enemy compound where he was facing a firing squad. They had managed to save him, but the leg would have to be amputated.

The doctor wondered if this could possibly be my brother, but said nothing at first. The young man was in obvious excruciating pain even though he joked about it as he talked to the doctor in fluent German. Dr. Andretti remembered that I used to speak in German when he had first known me. This young man did look unbelievably like the young man who had been executed at the compound that horrible day three years ago.

Though tears streamed down his cheeks, the soldier continued to make jokes, trying not to show his pain. The doctor finally found a nurse to give him some ether while he amputated the leg and formed a stump just above the knee.

The next day when Dr. Andretti visited, Tom said with a grin, "I know you did the best you could. My brother's a doctor and my mother is a nurse and I know how much they hate complaining patients, but how am I ever going to chase the pretty girls around with only one leg?"

Dr. Andretti remembered me telling him that my betrothed, Joseph, was a doctor. He also remembered that my mother was a trained nurse and midwife. It would be too much of a coincidence to ever think this young man could be my brother, but everything he said pointed to it. Finally, as the young man continued to talk, there was no doubt. This was definitely my brother. It had to be an act of God!

Dr. Andretti answered him cryptically in his usual brusque way, "It seems that the people in your family are all so good-looking the opposite sex chases them. Now the girls can finally catch you."

"How do you know about my family?" Tom looked slightly irritated.

"Because I've known your sister, Susanna, for a number of years. She often talks about you and Joseph. It's too bad your brother married somebody else. Susanna is the most unusual girl I've ever known. She'll be a great doctor someday," he answered casually, knowing what he had just said was going to cause a stir.

The young man was already deathly pale, but the doctor thought he became even whiter. He propped himself up off the bed and looked him straight in the eye and said, "Nobody has seen her since the war broke out and it's been almost two years since we've even heard from her. Reading between the lines from the two letters we received, it didn't seem as if things were very good back then and we've looked everywhere for her. Tell me what you know?" There was a look of desperation in his eyes and Dr. Andretti suddenly wished he had handled it in another way.

"I not only know where she is, I know everything about her and along with half the people in Italy I love her. She lives in a convent in Verona."

Tom stared at him in disbelief. "You love my sister?"

"Not in the way you're thinking, but just the same, I do love her."

"What makes you think she's my sister?"

"Now that's a stupid question...it must be the effects of the Morphine. You are Tom Von Helldorf and you have a brother who ended a betrothal with Susanna Strashoffer Von Helldorf so he could marry someone closer to his own age. She talks about her brother Tom and his brother Joseph. To this day she refuses to call your brother her brother. Could there be another Tom or Joseph Von Helldorf in the United States?"

Tom had tears in his eyes, "No, it has to be Susanna. Why hasn't she tried to contact us? None of us have ever had a happy day since she came up missing. Dear God, how we've missed her!"

"I don't have time to tell you her story now, but I'll come back this evening and tell you everything. When I finish you'll either let me take you to her or you'll kill me and I wouldn't blame you if you did. She has deep scars inside and out and thinks she doesn't need anybody, but I know how wrong she is."

"Please, could you send a telegram to my brother? You can't imagine how relieved he'd be to know! This is so wonderful!"

"Wait till I explain and until you've seen her. You may react differently then."

"What are you saying?" he asked with worry written all over his face.

"I'm saying she has been through hell and you need to know her story and talk to her before your whole family has plans of running over here to save her. She's a very independent lady and it's going to take her some time to be sure you can adjust to her and she to you."

"You just don't know how much we all loved her," he argued.

"No, I don't, but I guarantee you'll love her more now." He stood to go. "I must be on my way, but I'll be back as soon as I can."

"Don't go. I have to know about her," Tom pleaded.

"I can't stay. Don't worry. She's safe and I'll be back.

True to his word at about 7:00 that evening Dr. Andretti was back. Tom was sweating with pain when he sat down, but didn't complain. "Tell me all about my sister, please."

"You look miserable. When have you had a shot?"

"I haven't, but I don't care about that. Tell me about her."

"I first met her when she was 13. It was January and she had been living alone in a cave not too far from the makeshift compound where I was stationed. She had been living up there with her little dog Minnie, she still has her by the way, and three horses. A young doctor named Alessandro

Adami saw her eating out of the trash cans, then going into the hall when nobody was around and playing the piano, sometimes all night. He got the head of the nursing sisters, Mother Maria Elizabeth, interested in her. Of course Mother took her in, got her cleaned up and gave her loving care. Alessandro loved her from the first day he set eyes on her even though she was still just a little girl."

Before long she was working in the field hospital. We were so close to the action that casualties were coming in constantly. She was just sort of let loose to do whatever she could and it seemed there was almost nothing she couldn't do. After a couple of months she was assisting me in surgery, suturing wounds, doing everything. We were all enchanted with her. You know the child's an amazing genius."

"Yes, my father really had to keep hopping to find teachers who could teach her anything and she had read all my brother's text books from medical school...and remembered everything she read!"

"Yes, I know!" he smiled. "She is a joy. Unfortunately though, one day a young man came in with a head injury and some lacerations. He was a spy for the Austrians and she knew it, but didn't turn him in. I was suspicious and when I confirmed my suspicions, I made a scene big enough for her to be arrested. "There were tears in his eyes. "She was only a child, but I was mad and it was no time till the police put her in prison." He couldn't talk as he choked on his words.

"Please go on," Tom coaxed.

"I went to the hearing the next day and so did Alessandro. By that time, I knew I had made a mistake. We tried to tell the board that she was only a child. She explained that the soldier looked like her brother and she didn't want him to get into trouble. She sounded like the child she was when she said it. The soldier was executed while she watched then she was stripped and publicly beaten until long after she was unconscious. Many of the people who watched had loved her, but that day they yelled 'kill her!' It was like the world went mad."

"After they cut her down, Alessandro and Mother went out to where she was laying, wrapped her up in a sheet and carried her away. I figured she was probably dead, but I was wrong. He and Mother hid her and took care of her till he and one of the other nuns could move her to the convent in Verona to recuperate."

"I never asked any questions about her until I saw her at the hospital in Verona over a year later. To tell you the truth I didn't see any way a human being could be beaten like that and still survive. I tried to concentrate on my work and worked night and day so I wouldn't have to think of what I had done." Tears streamed down his cheeks.

Tom broke in. His hostility showed clearly. "I know my father's people have been to Verona. Surely if she's so loved, somebody would have talked to them."

"The sisters were afraid if anybody knew where she was they would kill her for being a traitor so they'd never talk to anybody. When she was well enough, they sent her out to deliver babies and to take care of the sick dressed as one of the sisters. Some people still call her Sister Theresa, though she no longer wears a habit. She only worked in the hospital during the times of crises when nobody had time to ask questions about her. She does a concert every Saturday night in Verona, dressed like a grown woman. Her name is Luciana." He smiled, remembering her performances. "She packs the auditorium every time. The men stand around the back door waiting for her to leave just to get a closer look!"

"Our investigators mentioned an Italian woman who played the piano. I guess Susanna could have been mistaken for an Italian. She always did have all that thick curly hair."

"Yes, well, she and Alessandro became engaged right after she turned 15. Though she was young, nobody could deny they loved each other very much, according to Mother Angelica and the sisters at the convent in Verona. Mother told Alessandro he couldn't marry her till her 16th birthday."

"So she's married?"

"Unfortunately, no. The field hospital where Alessandro and I were both still stationed was bombed, so was the orphanage that was located there, and the officer's quarters went down too. Mother Maria Elizabeth was killed instantly, but Dr. Adami lived until several hours after he reached Verona. That was the first time I had seen Susanna since the beating. In the middle of all the confusion while the casualties were laying everywhere, there she stood looking like an angel, dressed in a purple-colored dress, trying to decide what to do first. I knew what she could do so I called her over to work on the first priority folks. I assigned her to start on my young friend Alessandro, never realizing they had continued seeing each other and were planning marriage. She was hysterical the minute she saw him. I yelled at her and made her settle down. Several hours later everybody heard her screaming when he finally died from those horrible burns. For a few weeks I didn't think she would live. I never saw anybody grieve the way she did, then one day it was as if a curtain lifted off her and she seemed much better. Now she goes in stages where she acts cheerful and all seems well, then I can see it coming. She clouds up and seems to withdraw from everybody. After that she disappears for a day or so, no matter what's happening. When she comes back, she's okay again."

"You said you're friends. How is that possible after what you did to her?"

"I don't know. Your sister is a very unusual person. The night Alessandro died she worked with me for hours in surgery and continued to work with me the next day all day. She said she always knew I was sorry and there was nothing to forgive. There must not be an inch on her body that doesn't have a scar!"

"My God!" he said quietly to himself.

"On his deathbed Sandro asked her to contact her family. He also asked her to try to fall in love with a soldier who would understand, but she says she never wants to love anybody again. She also says her family could never

accept her after the way she has lived and the things she has seen. She seems to think that your parents expect her to be perfect and now she isn't perfect anymore. I don't think she'll ever be able to talk about all that happened to her, but I think you might understand her better if you know. She just couldn't write and tell about her life when it was so bad."

Tom was sick. "We tried to protect her from everything. I used to fight with her, but Papa and Joseph and even our grandfather were scared to let her out of their sight. She was such a little rebel!" He took a deep breath. "My God! I agree with her, our father and Joseph may never get over it. If they had known what was going on, it would have killed them both."

"Do you still think it best to go see her? I wouldn't want her to know that I've told you this."

"Yes, I want to see her as soon as possible and I couldn't let her know what you've told me. Did she really love this Alessandro?"

"As a little girl she idolized him. I never saw them together after she became an adult, but Mother Angelica said they were totally devoted to each other. The child grew up loving him and he was there for her when she needed him most." His voice dropped, "I guess finally she was there for him when he needed her too."

Dr. Andretti continued, "I don't see how there will ever be atonement for what I did, but maybe if I can bring you two together, I'll be able to sleep a little better at night, at least."

Tom was quiet. Though his pain was severe and under normal conditions he would have grieved over the loss of his leg, all he could think of was getting to Susanna as soon as possible. "How soon do you think I can make the trip?"

"A week."

"Why not sooner?"

Because you're going to be in a great deal of pain and I don't want your reunion to be miserable. I also don't want you to bleed to death before you get to her, she'd never forgive me. You've waited a long time for this. Let's make it good. Susanna isn't going anywhere."

"I wish I could go now."

"That just isn't possible," He said firmly and, changing the subject he added, "I'm going to have a nurse bring you a shot and I want you to have one every three hours through the night so you can get some relief from the pain." As he left he squeezed Tom on the shoulder.

If Tom ever mourned for his lost leg, nobody saw it while he was there. He tried to tease the nurses in French, English and German and when they didn't understand, he did his best with his limited Italian. They loved going into his room whenever they could and he met them with a big smile every time. He told one nurse who was able to understand him, that this might actually be the best time in his life. She thought he was crazy, but just like everybody else, sensed that he was a very brave man.

Dr. Andretti came to see him twice a day and always stayed to talk. The nurses wondered who Tom Von Helldorf was that the head surgeon would give him so much attention.

One week from the day he arrived at the hospital, the doctor arranged a transfer to the hospital in Verona. Hopefully he would be able to recuperate a few weeks at the convent hospital before being moved out of Italy...if he could get Dr. Bonfiglio to cooperate with him.

The trip to Verona seemed endless. Tom was obviously in pain though he firmly denied it. They didn't talk much. Tom hated Dr. Andretti for what he had done to his sister. Only she was a nice enough person to be able to forgive him for what he had done. So for most of the trip each of them was wrapped up in his own thoughts, wondering how the meeting would go. It was dark when they drove into town.

Dr. Andretti interrupted the quiet by saying, "Susanna will be starting her Saturday night show, as she calls it. I wish I could have gotten you here sooner. Maybe we should get you checked in to the hospital. I'll bring her over after her concert."

"Oh no, I'm not getting this close to her without seeing her right away.

I've waited too many years for this moment! Take me over there. I promise I won't make a scene. I just want to see her."

"I hope you don't pass out or get sick."

"Come on, doc, I'm just fine!"

When they got to the auditorium there was a large crowd out front. Dr. Andretti had forgotten about the steep steps. There was no way Tom was ready to negotiate something like that.

"Let's go around to the stage entrance. You can sit back stage with Mother Angelica. It's probably better anyway so you can sit in a better chair with your leg propped up."

When they walked in with Tom on crutches, Mother Angelica and Sister Olga met them with smiles on their faces. Minnie dashed to Tom and almost knocked him down. The sisters were surprised to see the little dog befriend him so quickly because she didn't usually like men very much.

Mother turned her attention from Minnie back to Dr. Andretti quickly, "Theresa will be so glad to see you doctor. We didn't know you were coming!" Then she looked at Tom, very tall, good-looking and pale. "How do you do, sir?"

"Very well, Sister."

"I'm sorry, I should have introduced you," Dr. Andretti apologized. "Tom, this is Mother Angelica, and this is Sister Olga. They have both given Susanna their most loving care." Looking at Mother and Sister Olga he said, "This is Theresa, or Susanna's brother Tom. I ran across him when he came through the field hospital. He's very anxious to see his sister, but he probably needs to wait till after the show or half of Verona's going to be disappointed if the concert gets called off."

Both sisters beamed as they looked at him. Yes, he looked exactly the way Susanna had described him except he didn't look like the happy carefree person she had described. He looked deathly ill. They noticed the empty pant leg pinned up and understood. "We'll put him right here in this nice soft chair and Theresa will never even notice him!" Olga said. "Now

I understand why Minnie got so excited. She must have recognized you, Major Von Helldorf."

A few minutes later Susanna walked right past he and the doctor and never even noticed them. She kissed the old nun, and walked on stage. The crowd thundered. The doctor slid Tom's chair over so he could see her as flowers were thrown on stage and she picked them up. She talked to them in Italian and English, welcoming them and telling them she would take requests in the second half of the program. She told them the first thing she would play would be a piece that reminded her of her childhood, a Bach Concerto called "Sheep May Safely Graze".

"She played that for our parent's wedding the day we were all adopted," Tom whispered to the doctor and Olga.

The crowd never made a sound until it was over, then they roared, whistled, and stomped their feet enthusiastically. She played one piece after another, always announcing the title and the composer. Sometimes she walked to the edge of the stage and told them about the music or the composer or related a story about how the music related to something in her childhood, a luxury she enjoyed from time to time nowadays. Many of the pieces were her own compositions, some heavy and some light. She never took a break as she moved from the first half of the concert to the last. The crowd sometimes almost seemed rowdy during the second half of the program as one member of the audience fought to be heard over the others, each screaming out the title of their favorite song. Several times she insisted that the person making the request come up to help her get started. They always acted embarrassed, but seemed to love every minute of it. Susanna was definitely a show person as she teased them and laughed with them. She reminded the Italians of funny things they do then teased the Americans for their peculiar little ways until she had them all laughing. For a while Tom almost forgot that the woman out there was his little baby sister.

When it was over, there was an encore and a demand for a second one, but as she came off the stage the second time she noticed the man sitting in the chair watching her. She stopped in her tracks. She looked, and looked some more, her face blanching. "Tom?" she whispered.

He smiled and answered her in German, "That's me, little sister."

Now I will continue my own story, but I thought you might like to hear the circumstances of my reunion with my brother, Tom, as it was related to me.

I screamed, "Tom! My God it is you!" then I ran to him and put my arms around his neck. We both cried, not for just a minute. We cried and cried. "How did you end up here? I never thought I'd ever see any of you ever again!"

It was so touching that the people watching were crying too. We never heard the chanting for another encore. This was one night when the audience would not come first.

After a while I noticed Tom's missing leg. As I looked down and it registered in my mind that he had lost a leg I shook my head and as my voice trembled I said, "Oh no, not you too! Is there no end to what this war has done to the people I love?" I knelt down and put my arms around my brother and held him.

After a time I asked, "Where's Joseph? Is he still alive?"

"Yes. He joined the French army as soon as he finished medical school then transferred to the American army when we finally got into it. He's been in Paris for most of the war. Things have been better for him since the United States came in. I did the same thing, but worked in intelligence first for the French and now for the U.S. I guess it's good that we all spoke German and French at home."

"I guess, but I think maybe we would have been better off if we had never learned German. You have lost your leg and things would have been better for me too if I had never learned," I said dropping my eyes to the floor. Quickly I changed the subject, "How did you find me?"

"When I went through the field hospital near Trento a friend of yours recognized my name. He brought me," he said as he nodded at the unnoticed Dr. Andretti.

Tears dripped down my cheeks when I looked up and saw the doctor. I kept my shaky voice low as I said, "See? I knew there was some reason why we were such good friends. There you have it." I walked over to him and embraced him. "Thank you, thank you so much!"

"It was a genuine pleasure my dear," he said with a smile of pride in seeing my obvious happiness.

I walked back to Tom and put both hands in his and in English said, "To think the bratty brother who used to make me so mad could turn out to be so wonderful!"

"You always loved me. I was the balance in your life from Papa and Joseph who wouldn't let you do anything because they were so afraid you'd get hurt. Remember when we both got our bottoms whacked for going swimming alone in the lake? Joseph would never have taken you!"

I wrinkled my brow, "I'm not sure either one of us would have ever tried it again after Papi got finished with us!"

Mother Angelica, noticing the pallor of Tom's skin interrupted, "Why don't we go back to the convent. Tom can sleep in the room we have for guests. You can talk all night, but by the looks of him, he could use a rest."

Dr. Andretti agreed. "It's only been a week since his leg came off. Orders are only for him to be transferred to the hospital in Verona. We'll have to report by midnight." He shifted in his chair then went on, "I hate to agree with Mother Angelica, but the truth is, Tom lost a lot of blood and needs some rest."

I immediately started to move when I noticed his weakened condition, but when we got up to leave; it was more obvious that Tom wasn't himself. He became pale and nearly fainted. We put him back down for a few minutes then tried again. By that time he was able to get up on his crutches and move out to the waiting car. The two nuns and I rode in the car with the two men to get Tom checked into the field hospital. Once in bed, he was given a shot and was asleep in minutes. I watched him sleep for a long time until the doctor put an arm around me and guided me out.

"Tomorrow is another day. You need to go to bed now so you can visit him early in the morning. Sometime soon he's going to realize he has lost a leg and then he'll need you very badly. You might consider sending a telegram to your brother in France."

"Yes, I guess I should. I don't know what I'll say."

Rolf

I'll never forget the day. Our family was at the breakfast table when the front door bell rang. Hannah, our housekeeper answered it and seconds later was standing before me with her face white as a sheet. She just stared at me and said not a word.

"What is it?" I asked her.

"Herr Von Helldorf, it is the Western Union man here at the house waiting to give you a telegram!" She was nearly in tears, her voice trembling.

My wife, Gabrielle, and I jumped out of our chairs at the same time, practically running for the door.

She mumbled, "Good news rarely comes from telegrams."

I had to agree.

The old man with the telegram handed it to me as soon as we reached the door.

"Don't leave," I commanded. "I may want to send a response. My heart was pounding so loudly that I had to wonder if anybody else could hear it. My eyes couldn't seem to perceive what they were seeing. The telegram was from Joseph. It read:

TOM HURT LOST LOG RECOVERING VERONA ITALY =
SUSANNA WITH HIM ALIVE AND WELL =
DETAILS LATER =
JOSEPH.

"Do you see that?" I cried. "They've found our little girl!"

Gabrielle started crying, "Our boy has lost his leg! Oh Joseph what shall we do?"

I looked at the Western Union man. "Give me a minute to write a response."

This was my message:

THANK GOD THEY ARE ALIVE=
SEND DETAILS=
WE TAKE WHAT WE HAVE AND BE GLAD=
PAPA.

The day of the telegram Gabrielle contacted the Red Cross to help get more information. The next several days we cried and we thanked God. We placed flowers of thanksgiving in the church.

The following weeks were torture as we waited to hear more. News was slowcoming and we wondered why.

Chapter 7

Iwas at Tom's bedside by 5:00 the next morning. Mother excused me from all my duties as long as my brother was in Verona. Her final words to me that morning before I left the convent for the hospital were that I should send that telegram to my other brother. I winced every time anybody called Joseph my brother. He may be married with three kids by now, and I no longer wanted to marry anybody now that Alessandro was gone, but I could never see Joseph as a brother.

Tom was having severe phantom pains that morning. He never complained, but it was obvious as I watched him restlessly moving from the bed to the chair with sweat pouring off his face. I said with an air of authority, "Big brother, your chart shows that you've refused your pain shots all night. I don't suppose I can convince you to take one because I'm probably the last person you'll ever want to give you advice on the subject of pain, but just in case, I have to try. Please let me give you a shot, you could feel much better in 30 minutes. I hate seeing you hurt so badly."

"I have to learn to live with it. We both know it could last for years." With his eyes teary he went on, "It's not my stump that hurts; it's my toes and my foot!"

"Oh, Tom." I cried as I went to him and put my arms around him. "This war has swept a path of destruction across every battle field for thousands and thousands of miles. I'm so sorry. I can't even say if it will ever be better. When the pain leaves, the nightmares will come, sometimes when you're not even asleep. For that, I wish I could go home with you to help you get through it, but I can't. Is there any way you might stay here after the war?"

"I don't know. I never thought about it. Papa and Grandfather are going to need me to help with the businesses eventually. Right now I don't know what I want. I can see Papa running around trying to do everything for me and Mama and Grandmother crying their eyes out." Tears ran down his cheeks, "I just want to be normal. I don't want people feeling sorry for me!" He turned his back to me and I knew he was crying.

"I understand," I said soothingly as I sat down on the edge of his bed and rubbed his back. "You couldn't know, but I do understand. It's why I can't even write home or consider ever going back. I had a good friend, he's dead now, who said that he and I needed to go back together, just for a visit, but I know I never could now that he's gone. I'm never going back. My heart wants to see Mama and Papi and even Joseph, but it could never be right after all that's happened. You'll be discharged soon. Why don't you come back to Verona or go to Rome and stay? Nobody has any comforts here, but at least people never ask questions and they understand about things."

"I don't know. Maybe you're right. I'll have to think," he answered.

"You have all the time you need. Dr. Andretti is trying to keep you here for a month. We should be safe and they say the war is winding down. The last reports were that we're finally starting to make some gains along the borders."

I was sitting on the bed rubbing his back when Dr. Bonfiglio came in. When he saw me he cleared his throat loudly. I turned and smiled and so did Tom. "Good morning doctor. Have you met my brother, Tom Von Helldorf, formerly of the intelligence division of the French Army? He is now in intelligence with the United States Army," I said proudly in Italian.

"This girl never stops surprising me," he said in broken English. "I never thought of Luciana having a brother. You are American?"

Tom looked at me for interpretation.

"He wants to know if you are American."

"What else would I be?"

"He doesn't know."

"Yes, I am American he answered in French, hoping the man might understand as he shook his hand."

He did speak French, much to my surprise. "Your sister doesn't look much like you, Mr. Von Helldorf. She is American too?" he asked suspiciously.

"My sister looks like her father, she and I are both adopted, not related by blood, but she is my sister as sure as if we had the same parents," he said crossly then added, "Yes, of course she is American too. We were both born and raised in Bayland, Ohio, U.S.A."

The doctor removed the dressing and cleaned the stump while I assisted. There were no signs of infection.

"Did Dr. Andretti do this, Tom?"

"Yes."

"Well he did a good job. When you get back to the States you'll probably do very well with an artificial limb. Nobody will even be able to tell except for a little limp."

I thought to myself that maybe Dr. Bonfiglio did have a heart. I had never thought of mentioning prosthesis to Tom. Maybe he would do all right back home. It would have been nice to have him stay here with me though.

Late, after Dr. Bonfiglio had gone, Dr. Andretti came in to say good-by before leaving for his post near Trento. After greeting us and checking on his patient he asked me, "Did you send that telegram?"

"No," I answered, looking up in his eyes like a child who might be in trouble. "I can't."

"You can and you should. Your family has a right to know where you are and what happened to Tom. You have to do it!"

I didn't want to argue so I was quiet.

"I can tell by your silence that you aren't going to do it," he said crossly. "Look how well you and Tom are doing together. Why don't you think you can be the same way with your parents?"

Not answering his question I said, "Tom doesn't want them to know he's been hurt. He might not go home either."

Looking at Tom he said, "If this is true, your parents must have made some big mistakes when they raised you two. Children should run to their parents when they have problems, not away from them. I would be very disappointed in my children if they were afraid to come to me."

"Don't worry, Dr. Andretti, I'll take care of Susanna. It's all going to work out in time," Tom answered angrily.

"I hope so." He shook Tom's hand and hugged me, ignoring the hate in Tom's voice and the rigidity of my body. Looking at me he said kindly "I'll be back when I can. Take care of your brother and send that telegram."

Saying good-by always seemed so final to me these days that I ran after him, crying and hugged him again before he could get away. I continued to cry after he left. In an effort to keep Tom from noticing, I looked out the window, but of course he had seen me run after Dr. Andretti as he was leaving and knew how upset I had become over his departure.

He said in a brotherly way as he patted the bed beside him, "Come over here Suzy. You look lonesome standing by that window."

"I always hated that name. You were the only one who ever dared call me that." I shrugged and wiped a tear away with my finger. "I'm sorry, I don't like saying good-by. I always feel like I'll never see the person again. It's silly, I know, but it has happened so many times."

"These days nothing's silly." He turned with his leg dangling over the edge of the bed and patted the spot beside him again. "Sit here so I can put my arm around you." I climbed up beside him and he wiped my tears with the corner of the sheet then put his arm around me. "Ummm, that feels good," he teased.

"You're crazy."

As we sat together quietly I asked, "Do you mind terribly if I don't send that telegram? What would I say, 'Dear Joseph, Tom's been shot. He's fine. Love, Susanna?'"

Tom laughed for the first time since we had been together. "You're right. That's ridiculous."

I suggested, "You could just write him a letter, though I don't think it does much good to write letters from here. Most people say that even if they're mailed in Rome they hardly ever get to their destination."

"How many letters have you written since you've been gone?"

"Two."

"They both got through. Papa had people combing Italy both times, but nobody could ever find a trace of you. Joseph and I even came the first time. Too bad we didn't come upon some of your friends."

"Mother Angelica has helped me realize that it was probably meant to be the way it turned out. There's only one area that I can't understand and never will, but we don't need to talk about that right now. It's past history," I said trying to smile. Then I started putting things Tom had said together. "So you were here in the summer of 1915? You said you and Joseph were both in the French Army before you joined the United States Army. How long have you been over here?"

"We came the summer of 1915 as soon as Joseph graduated and we haven't been home since. Papa's final words when we got on the train to leave were, 'Don't get involved in the war. It doesn't concern us.' He was really worried about all three of us."

"If you two haven't been home in almost three years, what about Joseph's wife? That's a long time to go without seeing your wife."

Tom shook his head in sudden awareness and said, "My God, you've been gone so long you don't even know. Joseph broke the engagement right after you came up missing. Luxembourg was invaded and he and Papa came straight over to get you. When it was apparent that you were hidden away somewhere, we hired a team of investigators and he forced Joseph and I to go home for a year. Right after we got back to the States, Joseph told Carolyn it wouldn't be fair to marry her. He said if he married her he would always regret not waiting for you to grow up because no woman would ever be able to measure up to what you would be some day."

I was shocked. For so long I had accepted the fact that he was married and now he wasn't. I quickly told myself, oh well, that doesn't mean anything to me. I was no longer a candidate for marriage. Quickly I answered with, "Well, the war will be over soon. Maybe when he gets home, if she's still single, she might take him back."

"Do you hate him for hurting your feelings?"

"No!" I protested. "I'll always love him, but I was so young and so much has happened. I could never marry him now. Everything is different." I tried to smile, "Let's talk about something else."

The next week Tom and I were going for short walks over to the convent. He was impressed with my garden. Everything in it was flourishing. I was boastful when I told him of my accomplishments. "My patients are well-fed as long as the weather is nice. I actually get two good growing seasons. Some of the women have copied me this year. I gave them seeds and they have little tomato and potato gardens around their houses with herbs growing down their walks. It helps feed their children a little better. Some of the husbands have been gone so long their children won't recognize them when they come back, but we've managed to keep them from starving."

"You're unbelievable. Maybe Mother Angelica's right, it was meant to be for you to land in Verona, Italy. I can see how right it is, but the war will be over soon. What do you want afterwards?"

"Well, I'll find a medical school that accepts women and I'll become a doctor. I don't want to have an honorary degree in medicine. Dr. Andretti suggested it, but I want the real thing so he has agreed to help me get into a school. When I'm finished I'll set up a clinic around here somewhere and I'll be sure everybody has the best care I can give them."

"You really have no plans to go home or to marry and have children?"

"No. I can't do any of that."

"Can't or won't?" he asked as his blue eyes gleamed into mine. "You would have been an excellent mother."

"I'll probably find some children to take in if I look around. There are always homeless children."

"I guess so."

I could tell that he was troubled by my attitude. There was a wrinkle in his brow and for a little while he said nothing. I didn't know at the time that he had already written to Joseph about me and told him everything, begging him not to notify our parents. The last thing he wanted was for the investigators to come rushing in and get me all upset. His hopes were for Joseph to get to me before he had to leave.

Years later, in an old box of Joseph's things stored in the attic, I found that letter he had written. He said that he looked at me in the garden as I stood by one of my plants inspecting it for bugs. The sun was shining down on me. My hair was as curly as ever, but I wore it rolled under on the sides and twisted up in the back with persistent little curls springing out all around my face, and he said I was beautiful. Even though food was scarce, he told Joseph that my face was clear, without a blemish, and my cheeks were rosy. The blue/green eyes that always showed so much expression still did. He went on to say that any guy but a brother would have gone crazy over my figure. It was very slim with a waist that couldn't have been more than 19 or 20 inches, and then there were those breasts. "My God," he said, "Did Frieda Strasshoffer have breasts like that and I was too young to notice? No wonder this guy Alessandro was so much in love with her!" He wondered if Joseph had a chance competing with a ghost. It was a good thing I never saw the letter until years afterwards or it would have made me blush. He made me sound so beautiful that any man would have been in love with me, but, of course, he didn't have a clue about the mutilation that lay under my clothes. No man could ever love a woman as disfigured as I was.

When Tom finally admitted that he had sent a letter he explained why he hadn't told me at first. "You were so adamant about not making contact with the family that I was worried that you might never forgive me for telling Joseph you were alive, but I do admit to having sent the letter to him." He went on to say, "You need the whole family's attention. I want you to go home after the war. I promise to take care of you. I assure you that the family will love you the same as before you left. They need you as much as you need them. You can't imagine the emptiness of that house without you there."

I said nothing…just stood up and walked away from him. For a long time I pulled weeds furiously from the garden, then I watered plants until I was exhausted. Tom sat silently on the bench at the back of the garden and watched me.

The last week Tom was in Italy we were able to get train tickets to Rome. When we got there, we ate at the cafes and stayed in a hotel with adjoining rooms. I hadn't been able to eat my fill in years. When faced with it, I found, much to my disappointment, that it made me sick.

"How do you like that? All these years I've thought about how I would enjoy some real good food and now that I have a chance to eat anything I want, it's killing me!"

Tom took me to a dress shop and bought me some clothes. I carefully bought all long sleeves and high necks without explaining why. I never told him about my past or about my scars. There wasn't much selection, but still we were both happy with the purchases. Most of the money from Opa's wallet was gone now. It had been spent bit by bit for various things my patients had needed over the months so I was unable to offer to pay for anything."

I was careful never to reveal anything unhappy about the past four years and tried to point out only the good things that had come along. One day, after carefully thinking it over and brooding about it, I asked Tom if he would mind terribly taking me to see Alessandro's father. "You see, I was engaged to a very nice man," I explained. "We were going to get married on my 16th birthday, but he was killed." I tried to fight it, but I teared up. "I wasn't able to get to the funeral since it was so far away, but I need to give the ring back. It belonged to his mother and should stay in the family. It would help to have you with me."

Tom assured me that he would be glad to take me to see Signore Adami

When we got to the Adami residence, I was surprised to see a large stone home with high airy ceilings and deep wood paneling. There was a lavish garden outside that was protected from the outside world by a thick, high rock wall. They had a very fat maid who let us in and sat us in an elegant room with many plants and large windows with a beautiful view of the carefully manicured garden.

I told Tom, "Alessandro said his father was a teacher, but he certainly has a nice home. Teachers in the United States are usually poor.

This is nice," Tom agreed.

Signore Adami came in at exactly 2:00 as had been planned the day before. He was tall like Alesasandro with silver hair and a matching silver beard that was well trimmed. We got through the formalities then I said what I had come to say.

"Signore, Adami, I'm sure you know Alessandro and I were engaged to be married," I choked. There was a silence then I went on, "He gave me this ring. I understand it had been his mother's and I feel I should give it back to you so someone in your family can have it. I would have sent it to you, but with the mail the way it is, I was afraid it would get lost."

It had been nearly a year since Alessandro died, but obviously, the pain hadn't faded from either of our hearts. Sandro's father took the little ring with the big stone from me and looked at it sadly. "What do you know of my son's last days, child?"

"I was living at the convent in Verona. He came to visit whenever he could, about every six weeks or so. I took care of him when they brought him in," I started to cry. At this point I tried holding my breath to keep from sobbing out loud.

"He wrote to me about you many times, Susanna. You're more beautiful than even he was able to describe. He loved you very much," he said gently as tears ran down his cheeks too.

When I was able to talk I said, "He was badly burned and he knew he was dying. I know he couldn't have had a life had he lived, but I miss him terribly."

It was an emotional meeting and when it was over, Signor Adami placed the ring back on my finger. "My dear, you are still mostly a child. You need to go on with your life. Go back to America and find a good man to marry. Sometimes, when you go to your jewelry case and you see this ring, remember my son and how much he loved you."

He kissed me on both cheeks then abruptly bid Tom and me farewell.

I was in tears all the way back to the hotel and on into the evening. Finally, when I came out of my room, I tried to smile and insisted in going out to eat. I told Tom, "I hope I haven't used up all your money this week. I can't remember ever having so much fun as I've had!"

"Are you serious? This was a terrible day!"

"I'm sorry. It was pretty bad for a while, but I've learned that we just have to deal with things then go on, like you always used to do. I guess I thought you were still that way too."

"Well I am still quite a bit like that, but I was worried about you."

"I knew if I ever got close to Rome I would visit Sandro's family and I knew it would be a difficult meeting, but all the rest of the time since we've been here things have been great!"

"You haven't minded seeing the sights of Rome with a one-legged man?"

"Of course not! I hardly think about it unless we come to some steps. You're doing pretty good with crutches. Actually, you've been good for me. Something very bad happened to you and you just seem to go right on even though it hurts deep inside, I know. Your strength rubs off on everybody around you. Other people should be more like you." Then I said, "I can tell that you plan to go home. How are you going to handle our parents and Grandmother when you get there?"

"I guess I'll just let them go through their little stages until they get used to me. Most likely, I'll say I was shot and I'll leave out the part about the firing squad and the guys who rushed me out of there at the last minute. It'll kill me to have them feel sorry for me, but once I get that artificial leg, they won't think about it much. Old Dr. Bonfiglio is nosy, but if you can get past that, he's pretty encouraging. He says eventually I'll be able to walk without even a cane."

"You've always been like a cat. You land on all fours!" I grinned at the pun. "I can remember when we used to get into trouble at home, Joseph and Henry and I would stay upset for a couple days afterwards, but as soon as your bottom stopped stinging, you'd act like nothing had ever happened. I wish I could be more like you.

He looked at me with loving eyes and said, "I don't know why I was so mean to you when we were kids except that we were a lot alike and maybe I resented that. It kills me to remember how I used to call you a pest or a brat. You'd walk away for a while and a few minutes later be back wanting to play or to just hang around. I've regretted those times when you used to say,' I'll just sit over here real quiet if you'll let me stay.' and I'd say 'no.' I'm so sorry about that."

"Those little things are in the past and when I remember you, I never even think about them. I've always thought you were wonderful and so strong. Nothing ever seemed to get you down. You could make me happy when nobody else could." For a minute I was thoughtful and then I added, "Now that you know where I am, if you ever want to write, or better yet, if you want to visit me, you can."

Tom's blue eyes pierced into my heart as he looked seriously at me. "I've hesitated to say this until now, but I think after the war, when the seas are safe, you should come home. When people start asking questions, I'll help you. We'll take care of each other. You can go to Western Reserve for medical school. They take women. Life won't be the same without you and the family could never be complete. Please come home. Think how miserable we'll be without you."

"Nobody has seen me for years. They've learned to live without me. I doubt that Henry and the twins even remember who I am. You'll probably be the only one who will miss me from time to time and I'll miss you too. You mean even more to me now than you did when we were children. Before you came, I swore I'd never allow myself to be close to anybody again but you, big brother, are the most important person in my life now. I'll consider going home some more, but I don't think I can do it. You're stronger than me. You can do it, but I can't, besides, I'm not the same person I was before the war. I'm hardened. I have flaws."

"I'm not stronger than you. I've known you all my life and I know you're ten times the person any of us are. That's why at the age of five you were able to take care of us and give us a reason to live. You patted us and kissed us and brought our parents together. Papa never would have gotten married again if it hadn't been for you."

"That's funny, I always thought of myself as a little trouble maker. It seemed like I just couldn't mind Papi."

"You did have some problems with authority," he agreed, "but no matter, you still did so much for us. You gave us more than we were ever able to give to you."

I looked down at Minnie sitting on the grass in front of us. Her ears were pricked up and her forehead wrinkled. "Poor Minnie, she's taking this conversation all in! In a minute she'll be crying!"

Before we knew it, Tom was getting on the train headed for Southern France. He would eventually wind his way north with a stopover in Paris, then Rouen and would be shipped out of England to the United States. I planned to pray every day that his ship wouldn't be sunk on the way home by one of Germany's famous U-boats.

I asked him not to say anything to Joseph or our grandparents in Rouen about me. "Please just let them think whatever they think. I've been gone so long. It's best that way." When he hugged me and said nothing, I knew he was refusing to promise and I feared that something would happen to him. I was sure it was meant to be that I would never see any of their faces again and if he tried to interfere with God's will, he wouldn't ever make it to Paris, besides, I didn't want anybody else coming around. "Please do as I say, for good luck, insure your safe passage home."

He said nothing, hugged me tight, turned and boarded the train. His seat was by the window and he waved as the train slid past me. Tears poured down my cheeks as I stood on the dock with Mother Angelica's arms wrapped around me looking, I know, very sad.

Later I was told that Tom spent a night with Joseph in Paris. They stayed up all night talking, mostly about me. By morning when Tom's train moved out, both brothers were exhausted. They gave each other a tearful embrace then parted. Tom's next stop would only be for a few hours to visit the family in Rouen. Uncle Pierre, the priest, was waiting for him as were our grandparents; a few of the cousins who were not off fighting at the moment, and whatever aunts and uncles were left. The war had hit the family hard not only economically, but also they had lost Uncle Edouard and several cousins who weren't much older than me.

Evidently it was a tearful meeting. They had all been in the middle of the fighting and had all suffered. Our grandparents and aunts volunteered at the field hospital and did whatever else was needed for the war effort. They were much too thin due to the lack of food in France. It seemed as if everybody Europe was starving. The people back home would never know what was going on over here. Tom told me once that even he had thought nothing had ever happened in Italy, until he got there. It seemed as if all of Europe had been devastated.

Tom told our grandparents all about me. He said it was a heartbreaking visit. He asked them to pray that Joseph could convince me to come to France to stay with them. When they asked if I was all right his only answer was that the war had been very hard on me. Though they didn't know what had happened, they understood about the horrors and understood that I may have suffered tragically.

As he prepared to leave for England, Uncle Pierre comforted him by saying he would escort me home to the United States personally if they were able to convince me to go. "If Joseph isn't successful in bringing her back, I'll go to Italy and try. Maybe if all of us who understand go with her she can handle it better."

"Do you understand, Unc?" Tom asked.

"I don't know exactly what happened, but I've worked for intelligence for years, you know that. I'm very much aware of what happens to people when they're living in the middle of a war zone. I don't have to know the specifics to understand how it must have been for a child so young to grow up in it all alone."

"Thanks Unc. I love you," he told our uncle, his mother's twin brother, our favorite uncle.

After he left, Pierre, against the advice of his nephew, sent a telegram to Mother and Papi telling them that Tom was on his way home, missing a leg. He reassured them that he was handling it well and added, "Susanna spent time with him in Italy. Not sure of her condition." I saw the telegram folded neatly in the bottom of my mother's jewelry box many years ago, just after her death.

According to Papi, he and his father, our other dear grandfather, left the plant the minute the telegram arrived. Grandmother had been called over to Papi's house before the two men left town. When Papi read them the telegram they cried.

Mother asked Papi, "What do you think Pierre meant by saying he didn't know Susanna's condition? If Tom had been with her, surely he knows her condition!"

"Maybe it's hard to explain in a telegram. Maybe she's been starved or maybe..." Rolf got up and walked to the window without saying maybe she's been raped by a bunch of soldiers. He shut his eyes tight and held his breath to keep from sobbing. They all knew what he was thinking. None of them moved toward him.

Grandmother changed the subject with, "I hope our Tom makes it home. The seas are dangerous these days."

"He didn't go through all this just to die at sea. He'll be home. When he gets here we'll have to be careful not to baby him. He'd hate that," Grandfather said looking at his wife and his daughter-in-law.

The family spent the day together quietly encouraged that everybody was still alive, and yet miserable about what condition they might be in.

The day Tom left; I played the piano all day. I didn't allow myself to feel the grief that was just under the surface until in the evening. Just as the sun was setting I went out to the garden. I hadn't eaten or emptied my bladder all day. Finally I went out behind the tree at the farthest corner near the rock wall and sat without moving, staring straight ahead, thinking of nothing in particular, I just sat. Mother couldn't see me from the window, but she knew by now that when the music stopped I would be in that emotionless, trancelike condition until I could handle life again. Nothing could be done for the girl of many sorrows, as she sometimes called me, but let her be. She understood that it was my way of coping so I could go on.

Dr. Bonfiglio came by to talk to me, but Mother said I was sick.

"Well I am a doctor. Let me see her," he argued.

"She doesn't need a doctor for her illness. Her brother left today."

"I'd still like to talk to her."

"I'm afraid that's impossible," she answered firmly.

"I'll be back tomorrow."

"That will be fine," she said, thinking that the next day would be a good day for me to get an early start on some rounds with Sister Genevieve.

Luckily, Sister and I were called out on a breech delivery at about 4:00 in the morning. When the good doctor got there at 7:00 he was told that I had been gone for hours.

"I don't know why you sisters are always so protective of her. I just want to talk to her!" He mumbled as he turned to leave then he added angrily, "It doesn't matter, eventually I will see her."

When Genevieve and I got to the young mother's bedside we found a tiny foot already sticking out of the woman's vagina. The grandmother didn't know what to do. She told her daughter this was what she got for sleeping with a soldier. Genevieve and I ignored it. We quickly rolled up our sleeves and washed our hands. Genevieve nodded at me to go ahead and try to pull the other foot down with my slender hands while she and the grandmother each held the mother's legs apart. I inserted my hand then reached inside the uterus to find the other foot. The woman screamed and I was sweating as I searched in the tight little space for the other foot. When I finally found it, I pulled it hard. My hand slipped off then I had to hunt again. I was merciless as I pulled with all my might on the little foot. After several attempts I finally delivered it.

Both tiny feet were pointing up toward the ceiling. Genevieve and I both knew the baby's chin would get caught on the mother's pubic bone if it weren't turned around. With blood all over my hands and arms, I crossed the baby's legs and turned it so the toes pointed down to the floor. With the mother still screaming I reached back up to check for arms. When I couldn't find them, I assumed they would stretch over the baby's head, like a child sliding down a slide, when I pulled the baby out. With the next contraction I pulled the baby ever so gently from her mother as I gently lifted her feet up until the infant was upside down. I had to do that to get the back of the head to pass down around the pubic bone. Genevieve quickly suctioned the baby's mouth before it could cry. Together we delivered the back part of the head and cut the cord.

The mother was exhausted and so was the baby. Normally babies come out fighting, but this baby was limp. She grunted and tried to breathe, but didn't cry until the grandmother dashed her in a pan of cool water. Against anything I had ever read in a book, it seemed to revive the baby. The tiny baby girl coughed then sputtered then started to cry a weak cry. Her little legs seemed to flail every which way from having been in a squat position for so long. An hour after birth, her palms and soles were still blue, but the rest of her was pink.

The mother bled heavily so Genevieve and I stayed all day to massage the top of her uterus to help it contract. We put the baby to breast to help the bleeding, but she was too tired to nurse and it was no help at all. We never left until after dark that night and were back the early next morning to see how the mother was doing. She seemed better, but the day after that she had a fever. Her bleeding was heavy with a sickening rotten odor and it looked like she had childbirth fever. You just couldn't reach into the uterus without risking such things. The grandmother's friends told her to put the baby to breast. She would pull the poison out of her mother and she would die instead, but by the fifth day the mother died.

Genevieve and I went to the funeral mass. The baby cried all through it. Genevieve assured me that I had done everything perfectly. I knew that was true and told her, "Having babies is dangerous. A lot of women die. It's God's will I guess, part of the punishment to women for original sin, but I have to admit, I don't understand God sometimes. The father of this baby is probably off impregnating some other woman right now with no punishment from God."

"His punishment comes later," Genevieve assured me.

I wondered.

"If we had lived in a more progressive place where there were trained doctors, could they have washed that foot with an antiseptic and done a c-section? Maybe under sterile conditions they could have saved her. When I become a doctor I'm going to try to save women from dying so often. I wonder if God will help me. If He does, then we'll know if it is really God's will that women die having babies or if it is just our ignorance that allows them to die.

I met Dr. Bonfiglio at the door when I went back to the convent that day. Mother had told me that he wanted to talk to me and, of course, I had heard them arguing. At the moment I was drained and angry, though I had long ago stopped being afraid of my past. If somebody wanted to kill me for being a traitor, they could go for it. I didn't care anymore.

"I've been trying to talk to you for days," he said accusingly.

"Sister Genevieve and I have been busy with a footling breech, then hemorrhage, then sepsis. Today we went to the funeral. I feel spent. What do you want?" I was impatient with him.

"Can I come in?"

"I guess so."

We sat down and he looked at me straight in the eye. "Ever since you came here I've been curious about you. It seemed as if a lot of people knew your secret, but nobody would tell. It wasn't until your boyfriend, the young doctor, came in with Dr. Andretti that I started to get somewhere. Slowly, Susanna Strashoffer Von Helldorf, I have figured out who you are. Do you realize your father has investigators looking for you all over Italy? I've talked to them several times, but I never put it all together till your brother came."

"So what do you want of me? If you think I'm a traitor to Italy, I can't fight that. I've already nearly lost my life over my mistake and I'm scarred so badly that I'll be a freak for the rest of my life. There are plenty of people who would enjoy seeing me dead even now. I don't care. There isn't that much left of me anyway. You would do me a favor to kill me."

The shock registered all over his face, "Kill you? I don't want to kill you. I've seen what compassion you have for the people of Italy. In my book you're a saint! I just want to help you get out of here. You need to go home with your parents. I have a leave coming up and I've saved some money. What I thought was maybe I could take you to England and find passage for you to America. The U-boats are pretty dangerous, but a lot of ships are beginning to get through. I see in your eyes the kind of sadness only a family can ease. Your father must love you very much to still be hunting for you."

"You don't understand. It would kill him to know how things have been and I don't see how I could ever go back and pretend none of it ever happened. Alessandro and Dr. Andretti and the sisters know, but even Tom doesn't."

"Alessandro doesn't know. He knew! He is gone forever. He can't help you anymore. You need your family. I've already sent them a telegram telling them you are here and that I will arrange for your passage home as soon as possible."

"Oh no!"

"It's time somebody does something. Everybody claims to care about you, but nobody takes it into their own hands to do anything." He smiled, satisfied with himself and went on, "Well I'm going to do something, by God! You're the most brilliant person I've ever known and I'm going to take care of you! I cannot believe your brother left you here!"

"All this time I thought you were dangerous. I thought you would want to kill me if you found out. Dr. Bonfiglio, I'm sorry I misjudged you, but I'm not ready to go home." Flabergasted I wondered how could I have misjudged this man so much? I was amazed that I could have been so wrong!

He was firm. "You are long overdue to go home. The first day of September you will have your clothes packed because I'm going to see that you go home. I've already got my leave arranged."

"I won't go."

"I have to get back to the hospital, but I will see you later. Do not think of running away because I will find you and then I will take you home. Your father can take it. Do you think he's a weakling?"

"I think he loves me too much. He'll grieve over it if he finds out. He'll be disappointed in me for not doing better."

"Ridiculous! Anybody can see that you are an amazing young woman. If you were a man there are no limits to what you could accomplish in your lifetime. Even as a woman you will go far if you ever get past your grief. Your father will grieve with you and that will be good. You can grieve together, but your father will not be disappointed in you!"

I couldn't imagine anybody just taking over my life like this! He was like a father getting after a wayward child. Just how did he plan to get me on that train? Was he going to drag me? Well, I wasn't about to anywhere!

Joseph

I could hardly wait for my leave to go to get Susann in Italy. Tom had been confident that she wouldn't go anywhere and be lost again. He told me that it seemed that she had made a place for herself in Verona, but still; I worried that something would happen before I could get to her.

The trip to Verona had seemed endless. Before leaving France I had an engagement and wedding ring set made, determined that she would soon be my wife. It didn't matter that she was young. She would be mine for the rest of our lives...no matter what.

At the convent I met Sister Olga, Susanna's friend, and then Mother Maria. They knew me at once and assumed that Tom and I were twins. While they wanted to talk about our resemblance, all I wanted to do was get my hands on Susanna. Language was a problem as they didn't speak any of the languages of my family except for broken French. Finally Mother Maria, perceiving my need ordered Sister Olga to take me to Susanna.

The hospital was crowded. Everybody was busy. It was easy to see that they made do with what they had. The facility was archaic. Still, I guessed, Tom had probably been very grateful for the care he had been given at this makeshift hospital. I had to admit; Dr. Andretti had done a good job on his amputation and had made the stump ready for a prothesis with plenty of soft tissue to cushion the bone.

Olga led me up a flight of stairs to a small area outside the surgical suite. I understood her to tell me to wait there. I wasn't sure why I was waiting outside of the operating room. Surely Susanna wasn't in there!

After a few minutes a short, heavy-set Italian doctor came bursting through the double door. I tried to dodge the doors and ran right into him.

He took one look at me and stopped dead in his tracks. "It's you, the twin! Good! Your girl is closing a gut wound. She'll be out in a few *minutes." His English was excellent.*

Before I could ask him anything, he was gone. I waited close to half an hour and finally could hear happy voices coming toward the double doors. This time I stepped to the side to avoid being hit.

They crashed through the door and Susanna said something in Italian to the nurse on the other end of the gurney and chuckled as she glanced down at her sleeping patient. The young nurse made a comment. Neither of them seemed to notice my presence. I thought they were going to walk right past me.

Just as Susanna prepared to pass me, she glanced my way. I heard her take a gulp of air. She pulled the stretcher to a halt.

"Espereme," she called to her helper and she stared at me, speechless.

"Joseph!" she finally gasped. "Oh Joseph, I never expected to see you again! I never did! Tom said you would come, but I didn't believe him." Tears streamed down her cheeks.

I thought to myself that even with her hair tied up in a white turban and with her bloody surgical gown; she was the most beautiful woman I had ever seen.

I stepped forward and took her into my arms and it was as if we were alone on a desert island. After that, nothing was planned. The guerney with the patient was pulled away by the nurse and the doctor who had returned to the operating room suites and the doors to the hallway outside slammed shut.

"Susanna," I whispered, "We've looked everywhere for you. I don't know what I would have done if we couldn't have ever found you."

After that, I knew everything was going to be all right.

Chapter 8

As the days passed, I kept on with my work and said nothing to anybody, including Dr. Bonfiglio, about going home. I hoped his threat to make me go had been an idle one, but then one day he reminded me that I would be going soon. "I've discussed this at length with my wife. We both agree, if you were one of our daughters we would want somebody to take that extra step for her. I want to assure you that you have no choice if I have to get the military police to accompany you out of Italy with me, you are going."

Now I begged him, "Please don't make me do this. I can't face it. I love everybody here too much to go away."

"You can come back for a visit with your father and mother or when you are grown up or someday you can come back with your husband. Right now your place is at home with your mother and father."

I looked at him, but didn't say anything. He seemed to have just taken charge of me. I could run away, but I didn't really have any place to go. Maybe something would happen before then. Things always seemed to happen.

One night a few weeks later there were heavy casualties. Most of them were from the area around Trento. The hospital there had been overwhelmed so Dr. Andretti had shipped the ones that could stand the move on to Verona. Several had died on the way. We worked all night debriding wounds and suturing. Everybody had been checked when they were triaged, but one man had a belly wound. He had been afraid of being given up for lost so only complained about his other wounds. Nobody had noticed his major injury until much later. One of the younger doctors and I asked Dr. Bonfiglio for his opinion as to whether there was any use to operate. Since everybody else was pretty well patched up, he gave us the option of staying to take care of it or calling it a lost cause. The man would most certainly die of infection after all this time, but he would let us make the decision. The young doctor was tired and wanted to give him up. I was tired and wanted to try to save him.

"All right, Luciana," he said with a smile, "I'll help you, but you will be the surgeon since he will probably die anyway. You can never call anything a lost cause, can you?" he smiled again, a tired smile.

We took the man into surgery at 10:00 that morning and worked on him for three hours, suturing intestine and rinsing out his abdominal cavity over and over to try to wash away the bacteria. Finally, when the doctor was satisfied that all had been done that could be done, he left Sister Olga and me to close the man's belly up.

As he left the operating room suite he pushed open the swinging door to go out, but he hit somebody! He yelled, "Get away from the door! Are you crazy standing right in front of the door?"

He was tired and I didn't think anymore about it. I was only concerned with my patient. Working as carefully as I knew how and at the same time, sending little prayers up for his healing and for protection from infection, I finished the surgery.

The doctor was still standing outside the door when we came out pushing the gurney with our patient wrapped in warm blankets. He was talking to a giant of a man, one he had to look up at, but I wasn't interested in anything but my patient and my tired feet. Sister Olga was on one end of the stretcher and I was on the other end. Just as she got beside the doctor I looked up at him and asked in Italian, "I thought you were going to get some sleep?"

He took his finger and pointed at Joseph. "I've been talking to your brother; I knew it had to be another one of your brothers. You didn't tell me that Tom had a twin."

I stood in a baggy white surgeon's gown with a white cotton turban wrapped high on my head to keep hair out of the patient's belly and I was speechless. I turned from Dr. Bonfiglio to his companion and stared at him in disbelief for a long moment then I felt my face flush as tears welled up in my eyes. Words suddenly came tumbling out that barely made sense. "Oh, Joseph," I cried. I was trembling all over and felt as if I might fall down. "I tried to make Tom promise not to tell that he had seen me. You shouldn't have come! I'm not the same person I used to be. It can never be fixed."

Before I could say more, I was wrapped in his arms. I responded by first trying to pull away, but he was persistent. I only resisted for a few seconds before I put my arms around him and squeezed him tightly. Dr. Bonfiglio helped Olga move the patient out and Joseph kissed me, not like he would kiss his sister, and not the way he would kiss a little girl. He kissed me like a man kisses a woman and I felt butterflies from my stomach to my throat and a cold chill ran down my spine and made me shiver.

Years later he told me that though he knew he had to make time with me fast since he only had a little over two weeks till he had to start back, he didn't want to scare me. Tom had told him that it had been less than a year since Alessandro had been killed and that I had loved him very much so knew he had to be careful not to make me feel rushed. He had decided that he was not about to go back without me. As a matter-of-fact, he had already bought my train ticket.

When we could finally let go of each other, I removed my turban and gown. I was wearing the light blue dress Tom had bought for me. I could feel my face flushing as Joseph stared at me.

"I knew you'd be a beautiful woman, but you're even more beautiful than I ever imagined. Your waist is so small I could reach around it with my hands! He put his arms around me again.

Though I loved the feel of his embrace, I knew it could be dangerous for that to happen too often. We couldn't just start a courtship and get married. I was no longer a candidate for marriage. This time when he let go of me, I explained, "I'm not at all beautiful. You always were silly! Tom told me you broke your engagement with Carolyn, but now that the war is winding down, maybe you'll go home soon and you two can patch things up."

He looked at me with the same piercing blue eyes as his father, my adoptive father and his brother, "I don't want to patch things up with anybody but you. I've loved you since the day you were born and I still do. As a matter-of-fact, if you can ever forgive me for the way I acted before you left, I want to marry you. It's just that simple. We'll wait till you're ready, but if you don't marry me; I'll never marry anybody else.

"You don't understand. I'm the one who's never going to get married. I've changed," I protested.

"No serious talk now. I've stated my position and I'm not going to change it. Let's get out of here and you can tell me about the things you're doing," he said taking my hand and leading me through the halls to the outside."

"There isn't much to tell. I'd rather hear about your life. Are the French soldiers treated any better by their commanders than the Italian soldiers are? Many of our men are executed by their own officers. It should be a crime. When they go out on the battlefield, they know it's only to die, but there's no value to human life anymore. Desertion is an everyday thing and then when they get caught, they go before a firing squad."

Joseph was sympathetic and gentle as he agreed with me. "It's bad with the French and the British too. The Officers are careless about sending men to die. They don't seem to care if they lose most of a battalion. There are units that have lost hundreds of men till they have to join up with another group because only a handful of them are left. I'm not sure anybody connected with this war will ever be the same again."

"I'm sure they won't. It has ruined everybody it's touched. Look at Tom, and he's one of the lucky ones. I had a friend who said he thought things might be better for the American soldiers, but even then, I see them coming in with burns from gas, choking to death from the fumes. After this, I don't think anything in life will ever affect me again."

He stopped and looked into my clouded eyes and looked like he wanted to cry. "I wish you had never had to go through it. Papa wishes he had insisted on staying with you. We should have told Opa we changed our minds. He probably never could have survived a trip to the States and another one back to Luxembourg with you."

"For a long time I felt that way too and I thought Papi should have come for me. I thought that since Papi and Mother had their own family with Henry and the twins, they didn't care enough to come. One of the doctors here says that isn't so that he has been looking for me all over Italy and Tom confirmed what he said. Whatever the reason for my being here, I think I agree with what a good friend of mine said before he was killed. Mother Angelica at the convent where I live says it too that it was meant to be that I ended up here where I could do good and work to my maximum abilities without rules and regulations to hold me back. One of the doctors, the one who recognized Tom when he came through the lines to the field hospital, is going to help me get into medical school and afterwards I'll set up a clinic here in Verona. I'm sick of seeing women and children do without medical care because they don't have money or because there aren't enough doctors."

"Those problems are everywhere. I want a clinic where I can do the same things. You could go to Western Reserve and we can go into practice together."

I looked him straight in the eye, remembering that Alessandro and I had talked about the same thing just a year before and then I said, "That wouldn't be a good idea. Something always happens." Changing the subject I said, "Tomorrow would you like to go on my rounds with me? I have several new mothers to see." With a grin I added, "How our birth rate manages to be so high when all the men are away at war is still a curiosity to me."

When we got to the convent, Minnie was at the door to greet us. She had warmed up to Tom quickly, but this time, when she saw Joseph, she ran around in circles, jumped up past his waist and got so excited she wet on the floor like a puppy.

"I guess she remembers you," I said as I went for a rag to clean up the mess.

"She should remember me. I taught her everything she knows including not wetting on the floor. She seems to have forgotten that lesson. It was tough hiding her from you till Christmas that year." By now he was holding me again. "So good old Minnie has been with you through it all?"

Yes. The truth is I'm not sure I could have made it without her. I hope she lives forever."

He told me that he had met Mother Angelica when he first arrived, but I introduced him anyway. I said, "This is Joseph, Tom's brother."

A strange look crossed Mother Angelica's face I guess she wondered if Joseph was Tom's brother would he not also be my brother. She didn't question it. I guess she had become used to my little oddities and one more didn't make much difference. She might have remembered that this was the Joseph I had been betrothed to when I was a child, but I had said he was married now and that would have been confusing.

Joseph smiled as I said it. I guess maybe he was happy to think that it was still important for him not to be my brother. He probably thought that he might have some chance with me, but I thought to myself, I didn't need his charity or his pity and I knew if he ever married me it would be either charity or pity. I was unlovable now.

To break the ice I asked, "Do you want to see my garden? It's still thriving."

"I would. Tom said you were feeding half of Verona with it."

"This is the second year for it. The sisters help. For once, none of us are hungry and we've eased things for the women and children who have no men to take care of them." Pulling his hand I ordered him to, "Come see!"

The entire area within the stone wall was nothing but vegetable garden with little paths cut here and there to get from one area to another. Joseph's face showed his amazement at the size. "This is beautiful! I guess all those hours you spent with Grandfather and Grandmother in your mother's garden must have taught you a lot!"

"Mother told me one time that she thought I inherited my mother's green thumb."

"You know, I'm sure that's what made me fall in love with you," he said as he looked at me admiringly.

"What, my green thumb?"

"No, that smile of yours. Even when you were a baby your smile made my day."

I ignored him. "Want to sit down? There's a little bench over in the corner on the other side of that tree. I planted a few flowers so when one of us wanted some solitude we could have a pretty place to sit."

I sat down and he sat close to me with his arm around my shoulders. I knew I should move his arm, but it felt so good to be touched and I had such hunger for human contact that I sat there and enjoyed it. The sun was getting low in the sky and everything was quiet. "You'll probably be sorry you came."

"I don't think so. You don't know how much I've wanted to see you."

"After Opa and I fled Luxembourg I used to pray that you or Papi would come and save me. I was sure somehow you would get to Opa's company and Mr. Switzer would tell you how to find me. I knew you were going to marry Carolyn, but I still thought you loved me enough to try to save me and I was sure Papi did. After the snows melted at the end of the first year, I realized that nobody was ever going to come. By then Opa was dead and I was on my own."

"I never loved Carolyn. She was just grown up and I had some physical things mixed up with love. I don't know if you can ever forgive me, but as soon as we heard that Luxembourg was being invaded, Papa and I headed for Europe. Grand-Pere and Tom had already been there to get you, but nobody knew where you were. Papa and I went back and I thought he was going to kill Mr. Switzer when he said he didn't know where you and Opa had gone. By that time Luxembourg was overrun with German soldiers and Papa was afraid both of us would be drafted into the German Army. Since nobody seemed to know anything, we went back to France and hired investigators to look in Switzerland and France. After your letter the next year, Tom and I combed Italy, but we couldn't find you."

"By that time I was living in the cave. The nun at the orphanage on the compound said I had to get rid of Minnie or I couldn't stay. I left. You would never have found me and by then I never dreamed you would be looking."

"The investigators went back to Italy after your next letter, but they still couldn't find you."

"I was known as Sister Theresa at that time and was dressed like a postulant because I had outgrown all my clothes and there wasn't anything else to wear." I shifted in my chair then changed the subject, "Let's talk about the babies. How is Henry and how are the twins? They're still alive and well?"

"Did Tom tell you about Paul?"

"Paul?"

"Our baby brother. Mama had him in April of 1915. We haven't seen him, of course, since right after he was born, but he was a very homely baby, long and skinny. Grandmother fussed her head off about it. Mama says he's very healthy looking now and will probably be the giant of the family."

Tears filled my eyes. Suddenly I felt completely separate from the family I had been raised in. I had a little brother three years old and hadn't even known of his existence. I sighed and said, "I've been gone so long that I have a three-year-old brother I don't even know about." I knew if I tried to talk I would have to let out an uncontrollable sob. Joseph wrapped his arms around me and held me. Later when I regained my composure I said, "I don't suppose our other brothers remember me either. I was five when my parents died and I hardly remember them so I guess the boys would be the same way with me. What a sad thing to not even be remembered."

"You know Mama and Papa have made sure they know all about you and when we get home, they'll fall in love with you right away," he assured me.

"I'm not going home, Joseph. I never can! There's a wall between us that will never come down."

He was gentle, but firm. "When it comes down between us, I'll help you tear it down at home. We're both going home, but not until I can be there with you."

"I don't want to go," I protested. "Dr. Bonfiglio says if I don't leave by the first of September he'll get the military police to force me to go with him to England and then he is going to put me on a ship for the States. I already told him that I won't go!" I thought a minute then asked, "Do you think there's any possibility that he could do that? He did get them to break in here to get me the night Alessandro--the night the compound was bombed when some of my friends were killed. He can't do that can he?"

"This is Italy. They're more ruthless here than other places. If he says he can do it, he probably can," he lied. "If you go with me in two weeks, you can stay with our grandparents in Rouen. They're already planning on you coming. They've been in the middle of the war almost since the beginning so they know about hardship. It'll give you some time to adjust to having people around who love you."

"People love me here, as much as people ever love anybody."

"It's different with family. They're loyal to the point of dying for each other."

"That's a rare quality. The sisters have it too and once in a great while friends will step into the danger zone for each other, but not very often." The thought of Alessandro and Mother Maria carrying me through the compound to rescue me after I had been beaten and the thought of Tom's rescuers storming the spot where he was about to be executed flashed through my mind.

We talked into the wee hours until I, who hadn't slept in two days, fell asleep in Joseph's arms. He didn't wake me. Instead, he slipped off his boots, leaned against the big old tree and dozed to the rhythm of my breathing. I was occasionally aware of it throughout the night, but seemed too tired and too comfortable to move away. As the sun came up, the birds went crazy trying to feed on the fruits of the garden. Unfortunately for them, the plants had been well covered by whatever the sisters and I were able to find to protect the vulnerable fruit from their early morning appetites.

Joseph had unbuttoned the top two buttons of my dress that seemed to be tight on my neck. He must have been able to see one of the repaired lacerations on my chest because I woke to the feeling of his finger gently massaging it. He had a serious look on his face as I stared at him. When I stirred, he kissed me with love and passion. He seemed surprised when I responded to him in the same way. When it was over I whispered with a half smile, "Joseph, you take my breath away, but you know nothing can ever come of this."

"Something's going to come of it," he argued, "Mark my words."

"It can't. You don't understand."

"I don't understand, but I'm willing to listen to your reasons. We'll get married."

"Stop it!" I ordered as I sat up. "You need to listen to me! I'm never getting married and I'm never going home. Now let's change the subject."

He looked astonished when I asked, "Are you hungry? We could go get freshened up then have breakfast. Nothing here is fancy, but when the garden flourishes so do we. I think we might even have some eggs, but maybe not. The patients often give them to the sisters and they bring them back to the convent." Embarrassed I added, "I'm afraid I usually end up giving things like that to the women with children who look like they could use a good meal, so we may just have vegetables to eat. I usually stick to eating things from the garden. You'll find that everything is filling, but it doesn't stay with you very long and for some reason they seem to make you lose weight. Mother doesn't get after me about eating unless my weight gets below 105. She's just like a real mother when it comes to most things," I added. "I have to get on the scales for a weight check every week and if I'm an ounce below 105 she nags at me to eat the eggs and eat whatever meat we have. When I first came here I only weighed 85 pounds so she takes great pride in keeping me nice and fat."

Joseph said nothing.

That day we went out on rounds without another sister. I introduced him as Dr. Von Helldorf. The patients were surprised to have an American doctor and an important looking army officer visiting their humble homes and were proud of all Sister Theresa had done for them as they bragged about me everywhere we went. Since the compliments had been in Italian, I downplayed them, but Joseph understood enough to see that they loved me just as much as Tom had said and he told me how proud he was of me.

It was Thursday, August 15. Joseph had bought me an engagement ring for my birthday, but he could see that I wasn't ready to accept it. Fortunately, he had planned for that possibility. After the rounds were finished and we had eaten a dinner of chicken soup with very little chicken and many vegetables, we went for a walk. At the same park Alessando and I had visited so many times, we sat down on a bench near an empty fountain.

"I know you haven't forgotten what day this is. The people of Bayland haven't forgotten either, I know." He searched in his pocket and brought out a small box. "I have a present for you."

The last present I had received was the engagement ring Alessandro had given me the year before. "I try to forget about birthdays and holidays," I said as I took a big breath to avoid crying. I looked away from him, avoiding his eyes.

"Open your present."

When I opened it I found a delicate silver chain with a small diamond-laden cross hanging from it. As he put it around my neck, he saw the other chain. He pulled it out of my dress and looked at the delicate ring with its stones glittering in the morning sun. He gently said, "I noticed the other chain last night when I loosened the neck of your dress. Tom told me you wore an engagement ring. I assume he's the friend who died." I looked down, still avoiding his eyes, but Joseph went on, "You must have loved him very much."

"He saved my life twice, maybe three times. He was killed last fall when the compound where I first stayed was bombed." I knew my face was red as I tried to control my emotions. "Now I don't know what I'm feeling. I feel guilty to let you kiss me and I feel disloyal to even let you whisper about us having a future. We were going to get married."

Joseph gently took my hand. "He's gone. Staying here and waiting for him isn't going to do any good. I'm sure he'd never want you to stop living for him."

"The night he died he told me to go home. He made me promise, but I just said I would so he would stop being so upset," I volunteered.

"I'm going to take you home, but first we'll get married and stay in France for a while."

"You still want to marry me after I just told you I had loved somebody else and was engaged to him?"

Joseph remained firm. "Of course. The fact that you loved somebody else for a while doesn't mean you ever stopped loving me. I'm glad you had somebody and I wish I had been here to comfort you when you lost him." He kissed me tenderly, then held me close. "Nothing you tell me can change my feelings for you except maybe to make me love you more. I just pray you can forgive me for what I did to you before you left Bayland. I regret it more than I can ever say."

In the early morning hours, long before dawn, all the sisters and I went out for a mass onslaught of casualties. While I was out Joseph and Mother Angelica talked. Joseph told me all about it when he saw me. She told him, "Go to the hospital and make our little sister eat. She won't unless somebody gets firm with her. I often bring her back here to eat in the middle of all the turmoil. Dr. Bonfiglio knows that's the only way I'll allow her to work over there. She's still a child and I'm not about to let anybody forget it, you either," she added pointedly. "She's not ready to add a husband and children to her burdens. Let her have some time. I told Alessandro that when he was still alive, but he insisted that he would marry her on her 16th birthday. He thought a year was plenty of time, but to a child like Theresa, a year is nothing."

Joseph was defensive, "She's grown up for her age and I've loved her since the day she was born. It was always planned that we would marry. We have everything in common. My father adopted her because she needed a home and he loved her, but even then it was planned that she would never be treated like my sister. I always treated her as my betrothed even when she was a small child. I can help her."

"I thought you had married someone else. What about your wife?"

Joseph told me he wondered how many other people were going to throw his short engagement to Carolyn up to him. Did everybody in the world know about it? He was ready with the same defense he always used. "The engagement only lasted a few months and I regretted it almost from the first day. After Susanna came up missing, I broke it and haven't heard from the girl in over three years. I knew I could never love anybody as much as I would love what Susanna was going to grow up to be."

"Then maybe you are perfect for her, but give her time to make her own decisions. Don't push her."

"I'll warn you now; I plan to push as hard as I can to take her back to France with me. She can stay with our grandparents in Rouen until after the war and then I'll take her home. The rest can come naturally, but I will marry her eventually too." He added, thoughtfully, "I am thankful for the way you have taken care of her. She's lucky to have been brought here with you and I'll never forget you or the sisters for what you've done. Whenever you need anything, I'll always help you."

Mother Angelica said no more except to send Joseph off to get me fed.

I could feel Joseph the minute he came into room where I was working. He quietly watched while I attempted to debride an American man with burns to his chest, arms, and back. I had already given him a shot of Morphine, but as I pulled the burned skin from his chest he screamed a string of profanity at me.

I looked at him with fire in my eyes, no longer thinking about Joseph watching in the background, and said "If you talk like that to me one more time, I'll walk away from here and let the skin rot off you. You can die on a stinking heap!"

"Sorry miss," he said shrinking back to the stretcher.

I started the debriding process again. As I pulled the large pieces of skin off the big man's body he moaned loudly. I put a cloth over his eyes and gently told him not to look, but soon he was at it again, screaming obscenities that were as degrading and evil as any I had ever heard. Without saying a word, I turned and walked away, so angry I could feel every part of my body pulsating.

"Come back here!" he demanded.

I took two steps more and bumped into Joseph.

"You're pretty sandy these days!" he chuckled.

"It's a matter of survival. I'm sorry for you to have seen me like that," I answered embarrassed and unsmiling. "I'm afraid I'm not a very good person anymore."

"Yes you are. All of us have had to get tough. I wouldn't dare tell you what I would have said to him, but it would have rivaled his words quite well." He put an arm around my shoulder, "Let's get out of here. Mother says you get lunch no matter what's going on."

Smiling I said, "I've said it before and I'll say it again, she's like a real mother or a very loving grandmother."

"We need to get away from here. We don't have much time till we have to leave for France and before then I want us to get to know each other again." With a grin he said, "I have to get you to fall in love with me."

"Maybe you won't love me when you get to know me again. I love you now, as I always have, but what good will it do for us to love each other when we can never do anything about it except break each other's hearts?"

"I guarantee, the only way my love for you is going to change will be that I'll love you more as every day goes by. I'm praying that you won't break my heart." He squeezed my hand as if to change the subject to a more positive note, "Tom told me Rome was nice. Let's go there."

"What will the accommodations be when we get there?" I asked suspiciously.

Joseph looked surprised that I would ask. "We'll get a suite with adjoining rooms," and suddenly a new name I had never heard before was used. "Honey, I'd never force you to do anything you didn't want to do and I'll never hurt you."

I could see that he was hurt that I would think he would take advantage of me. "I'm sorry; I guess I've gotten defensive over the years. I forgot who I was talking to. If I can't trust you, I guess there isn't anybody I can trust. I'm not sure Mother Angelica will approve, though. She knows our relationship is different than Tom's and mine."

At lunch we told her about our plans to go to Rome. She shot a dark look at Joseph and said, "When she went to Rome with Tom, I didn't have a worry about it, but with you, I think it could be very dangerous. I don't trust you Joseph Von Helldorf. I'm not sure she should go."

Ignoring the real reason for her concern he attempted to reassure her, "I'll take good care of her. I swear she'll be safe with me." He looked earnestly into the elderly woman's eyes and added, "I will never hurt her."

In the afternoon he helped out in the hospital. The care they had to offer wasn't nearly as good as in the American and French field hospitals. Supplies were makeshift at best. Later he asked me, "How have you been able to stand this place?

I was surprised by his question. "Had I been anywhere else, they never would have allowed me to practice as a physician like I have been doing so I have been happy for so many opportunities to practice my skills and have enjoyed taking care of my many patients."

We operated together on a leg wound hoping to avoid amputating. It was bad, but the circulation to the toes was still intact so we decided to try to save it. He said, "I'm impressed at how well you function."

I felt proud as I assisted, clamping off bleeders and anticipating in advance every move he made. He said, "I always knew you were gifted but I didn't realize you were so good that you could teach yourself to be a surgeon."

"I have Dr. Andretti and Alessandro to thank for many hours of practical training they have given to me."

"Remember how Papa, filled with pride in your accomplishments, had half complained about a girl being too smart while we were growing up?" Joseph asked. "I always knew you were something special and unusual and so did he, but I have never been more aware of it than I am right now."

"There's nothing special," I protested. "Anybody with the opportunities I have had could do everything I do." I believed it when I said it, but now, so many years later, I realize that God had given me blessings that other people didn't have.

"You were magnificent today. It's hard to believe you're not already a doctor," he said.

"You were good too. I always thought Dr. Andretti was the best, but you're just as good. Alessandro was educated in Austria. He always said the war was good for him because he needed experience and it's true that I always thought he was a little unsure of himself when things were going bad. He was going to try to get some more training when I went to medical school." Wistfully I went on to say, "Even though he lacked confidence, he saved so many lives."

"How did he save yours?"

"The two times he saved me were pretty sad. Some things are better left alone and hopefully are never thought about even by those who can remember. They most certainly should never be talked about to anybody lucky enough not to remember."

Joseph sat back stage during my show on Saturday night. As usual, there was standing room only. Over the months word of my shows had spread over Northern Italy and people traveled miles to hear me play. I turned on the charm, laughed, and teased during my show, like always. I felt like a young girl and a woman at the same time. Maybe in time I would get back to being my old self again when I wasn't on stage as well as when I was on. It was one of those great nights when I was able to bring the house down after every number. The crowd was enthusiastic as they all sang together with the leadership of a woman from the crowd who had a strong clear voice. They called for an encore twice, until finally the show was over. Outside the auditorium, as usual, men lined the stairs and stood close just to call out my name, to ask me out, or to tell me of their love for me. I smiled at them, shook their hands, and thanked them for helping me make the show so much fun. I held Joseph's hand as we headed for the convent.

"Alessandro just hated that!" I told him.

"I hated every one of the bastards who were ogling over you. You looked like you were enjoying every minute of it. I like that they love you, but I hate it too. It makes me jealous to think that every one of them wishes he could steal you from me."

I was unaffected by his words and reassured him by saying, "I've been playing for them for a long time, but I've never desired to get to know any of them better."

"I can't wait till tomorrow morning when we leave for Rome and I finally have you all to myself."

Ignoring his grumpy mood I said, "I'm looking forward to it too. I can't deny that you appeal to me more than I ever dreamed possible. We'll both end up sorry about this. Of course Mother is upset. She thinks I should bring Sister Olga along. She also reminded me of certain mortal sins, but of course I reassured her that it wasn't necessary to worry. There are reasons why we can never be more that friends."

"What are those reasons, Susanna?"

"It isn't important to discuss them. You just need to remember that nothing romantic can ever come of our friendship."

His blue eyes glistened as he looked sadly at me. "You are so wrong, Susanna. I will eventually marry you and we're going to be happier than even Mama and Papa have been. You and I were born for each other. Except for those few short months when I must have been crazy, I've always known you were the only one for me." We stood on the edge of the street in the moonlight, with other people still out on the streets too, and he kissed me. "I love you, Susanna," he whispered.

As several soldiers yelled at us from a short distance away I said, "I love you too, but...."

"Shhh. We'll talk about everything after we get to Rome. For now, let's just enjoy the rest of the evening."

We sat in the garden for a while after we got back to the convent.

Joseph kept his arm around me and kissed me often, but I noticed he never moved his hands around on my body. It was nice having Joseph hold me and kiss me and I was glad I didn't have to worry about mortal sin with him.

The next morning we went to the 7:00 mass then headed for the train station with Mother Angelica quietly reminding me to be weary of the temptations of the devil before I left. I only had one small bag with my best dresses and few other possessions. Naturally Minnie went along with us. The truth was I could never have relaxed without Minnie at my side.

I only owned one battered pair of shoes and one extra pair of panties. Sister Maria Elizabeth had shown me how to bind my breasts so they wouldn't move when I walked when they first started getting large because I didn't own a corset. I washed out my only petticoat every night.

On the train we sat close together holding hands most of the time. Joseph caught me up on what all had happened at home. The housekeeper, Hannah, still cooked and kept house for them with Emily still her helper, but another maid and two nurses had also been hired. Papa was busy with government contracts for uniforms, blankets, socks, and even underwear! The war had been good for business. Mama was helping Dr. Barnes more since the war started than ever since her marriage. This was partly because the doctor needed the help but it was also because she needed something to take her mind off her three lost children. Papa had written that the war had been very hard on her, but Joseph believed it had been hardest on him. "You know what a mother hen he was about the three of us. I'm sure he has worried himself sick about us."

"When Tom was here, he said you were overly protective of me. He said I wouldn't have had a normal childhood if it hadn't been for him leading me off to see the world occasionally."

"I'm sure you wouldn't have gotten your bottom spanked nearly as often if it hadn't been for him either. Neither one of you could ever seem to get away with anything, but you never gave up trying. Papa always knew if anybody was doing anything they weren't supposed to."

"I never could figure out how he seemed to always know, and he seemed to always catch me at whatever little things I did. I remember the time Tom and I sneaked off to the drugstore for a Coke when you and Jacob were both out sick. Just as we went out the door to leave the drug store, we bumped right into him. It was always something." I sighed, "I wish I had acted better. I wish I could do it over again so they could remember me differently," I added with tears in my eyes.

"When we go home, you'll make new memories, but they'll always love the old ones too. Papa adored you and so did the others. You were their liebchen; they've never called anybody else that. You looked so much like Uncle Henry that we marveled every time we watched you smile. Papa became your father, but Henry Strashoffer's blood is in your veins."

I was embarrassed by what Joseph said. I looked at my hands and said nothing. I couldn't help wondering how it would have been if I had never gone to Luxembourg to visit. What if I had continued at the conservatory and none of this had happened. Would I have envied the people going off to the excitement of the war? My father and mother would have continued to love me and my body would have been whole. I would have been planning to marry Joseph before too much longer. I guessed it didn't matter anymore. Nothing really mattered.

When we checked in at the hotel, I noticed that Joseph registered us as Dr. and Mrs. Joseph Von Helldorf. I wondered why he didn't list us separately as Tom had done. The people at the hotel would have just assumed that we were brother and sister that way. It had always been impossible for us to call each other brother or sister, though. We both knew our relationship was different even when Joseph used to help me dress and do my hair when Papi had still been a widower, before he married Mother and they adopted me. Joseph used to help me into the car or up on my horse just as if I were a grown-up lady.

"Do you want to rest before dinner?" he asked, interrupting my thoughts.

"I'm not tired, are you?"

"Not really. What shall we do?"

"Want to walk around a look at things for a little while?"

"Sure, I keep forgetting that you know your way around here already."

"Well just from the trip Tom and I took. I never was here before that."

"Then let's walk around and look at everything. We may not get back here for a while and we don't want to miss anything."

That first afternoon we enjoyed the peace and beauty of Rome until we were ready to eat. It was as if there was no war as we strolled along the busy streets. At dinner I only ate a small amount of my food, explaining that every time I ate very much it made me sick. Though what I said seemed to worry him, Joseph, like all young soldiers in that war, was always hungry so he ate all he had and my leftovers too.

When we went back to our rooms, we both bathed and dressed in robes before returning to the little living room we would share for the next five days. Living together came naturally to us since we had been raised together. We talked until the wee hours again, but this time as it started to get late, Joseph's passion became slightly unleashed. He nuzzled my neck after we kissed, then his hands moved across my body

He whispered, "I love you so much. I want to possess all of you."

It was like having a glass of ice water poured over me. What was I doing? First of all, for years I could only count on God. He was all I had and He had taken care of me. Now, just because Joseph had shown up, I was ready to throw His wishes to the four corners of the earth, sentencing Joseph and myself to eternal hell! Second, Joseph would be appalled if he knew how disfigured my body was. It would sicken him to see the wide, still red scars that covered my body. He might love me, but he would never love me as a man loves a woman! I stopped him. With tears in my eyes I stood up and told him good night, then went to my own room and shut the door. I asked God why he allowed the people on the compound to mutilate my body and still allow me to live. I heard no voice in the night explaining it to me and felt abandoned.

I had wanted to stay with Josph all night and forever. Never had I felt so safe and warm even when I was with Sandro, but I knew I would never fit in with the family or the world that was waiting for him. I would have been ashamed for him to see my scarred body and the look on his face when he saw how disfigured I was. Only Alessandro would have been able to love me.

The next morning I left a note for Joseph before I took Minnie across the street to the park for a walk. It said:

Dear Joseph,
You always were a sleepyhead in the mornings. If you want some company, I'll be in the park across the street watching the children play and giving Minnie some time to stretch her legs. Come over. See you in a while!

Love,
Susanna

When he got to the park I was sitting on a park bench with my head leaning against a tree. I had my eyes shut and Minnie was sitting beneath the bench.

"Are you thinking of a song?" he asked.

No, I was just a million miles away thinking about things. What do you want to do today?" I asked looking up at the handsome blue-eyed blond- haired young man Joseph had become.

"First I want to talk. We need to get down to it."

I looked at him, dreading what would come next.

"We've always been able to talk about anything until now. I need to know what you're thinking. What happened last night? Were you scared to have me touch you because nobody ever has? Have I turned into your brother? Are you still too young or is it because of mortal sin? You know I want to marry you as soon as you consent. Have I lost you?"

I answered as I brushed a tear away and more rushed down to take its place. "I find myself thinking about what could have been, but never can be so often since you arrived. You just don't understand. Of course it is a mortal sin to do what you wanted to do. I've had to count on God for everything during these years when I have been alone. I can't turn my back on Him now."

His voice was quiet and his face serious as he questioned me. "But that isn't all of it. It's not the mortal sin that has made you so sad. What's the matter?"

"I can never love anybody and I certainly can never go back to Bayland," I cried.

He put his arms around me and held me.

"Why can't you love anybody? Did you love Alessandro so much that you can never love me?"

His question startled me. "I do love you, Joseph. I love you so much that it's killing me to think of the day I watch you pull out of the train station to go back to France. I don't know how I'll live without you, but it has to be that way."

"No it doesn't. You'll leave with me and we'll get Unc to marry us as soon as we get to France. He's in Paris most of the time."

"No! We can't do that!"

"We most certainly can and will!"

"You don't understand!"

"Make me understand. What happened? Were you raped? If that's it, honey, I love you the same as if it never happened. Nothing in this life will ever change my love for you."

I was shocked that he would think I had been raped! "I wasn't raped," I protested. "I've never even been with anybody--not even Alessandro." I clarified as Joseph smiled at the way I had put it. "But I have a very bad past just the same. You deserve a nice wife who has never experienced so many things and who has never done a horrible thing or lived as badly as I have. You also need a wife Mama and Papi can be proud of. They're so perfect. If they knew about me, they wouldn't ever want to see me again."

"You're so wrong."

"You just don't know and I'm ashamed to tell you."

"Tell me from the beginning exactly what happened, but I guarantee it won't change anything."

I was still crying, but when I could talk I said, "All right. You want to know about it, I'll tell you, but as soon as I do, I want you to get on a train and head for France and I never want you to tell anybody you ever saw me. It hurts too much to keep running into all of you."

"Tell me the story," he encouraged.

It took me a long time to get through it. I started by telling about my year in the mountains and the soldiers who found me. I explained about how the soldiers had planned to rape me until Major Altoviti had rescued me. Between sobs I told about the cold and the hunger while I lived in the cave and how tempted I had been to just sleep myself away had it not been for Minnie. I wept as I told how relieved I had been to find the garbage cans to eat out of. As I went through the story of my life for the past four years I spoke of Alessandro listening to me play and leaving the plate of food for me on the trashcan. More tears came as I told of Mother Maria Elizabeth cutting my hair to get the lice out and how I wore a nun's habit both because I no longer had clothes that fit and to protect me from the soldiers. Then I told of my conviction for being a traitor and at that point I couldn't go on.

As I cried my whole body shook. He held me tight, but told me I had to finish my story. His eyes were filled with tears as he watched me grieve over my past.

When I could talk again I continued, "I really was a traitor. I couldn't stand to have that boy shot. I wondered which side you and Tom and Papi were on. I didn't know who was right back then. All I cared about was saving people and practicing all the things I had read about in my books. That soldier looked a lot like you and Tom. I still don't know if I could turn somebody in. You are fighting for the Americans and you're sure, but I don't want to fight with anybody. I still don't have a side…"

"I would have probably done the same thing you did. You didn't do anything wrong," he said softly.

"It gets worse. They put the soldier in the middle of the compound and me with the executioners and made me watch them shoot him. The people in the compound cheered when he fell. When the hood fell off of his head, you could see brain tissue and bone pouring over the grass with his blood streaming over it." I was quickly getting hysterical at the thought of that dark and tragic day. "They stripped me except for my drawers and a little cover for my chest that fell off as soon as they tied my hands up, and they whipped me. I thought

I was on fire!" I felt the blood drain from my face as I remembered. Staring straight ahead I was silent as I relived the scene that ticked along in my mind. In a few minutes I went on, "I don't remember much after that, but Mother Maria said I went limp and they kept beating me. She said they cut me down and just left me lying in the middle of the compound to die. She and Sandro went out to see if I was still alive. When they saw that I was, she wrapped me in a sheet and he carried me away. They hid me in the hospital and Sandro sutured whatever he could, gave me some I.V. fluids, and cleaned my wounds. I didn't really respond very much for several days. As soon as Sandro could get away from the compound he and Sister Olga moved me here to Verona and Mother Angelica took me in."

Joseph was crying too as he buried his head into my hair and kneaded my shoulder. He whispered, "It's horrible, my God, but I still don't see why you can't marry me."

At that I went on to finish my story about thinking the scars would fade at first, but they hadn't and how Alessandro knew exactly how bad they were, but didn't mind because he knew ahead of time about them. Suddenly I shouted at him, "I'm disfigured, Joseph! I'm not a good person! I've lived in a cave like a wild animal, I've had lice, I've been filthy dirty, I've been a traitor, the worst of all sins! Now will you go back to France so I can just be alone?"

He surprised me by saying, "No, I won't. I love you and I plan to make the rest of your life as perfect as I can. You'll be a doctor if that's what you want and we'll share a practice, we'll have as many children as you want, and I'll love you forever." Softly he added, "There's nobody anywhere in this world like you. I can't love anybody else. Don't you see?"

I looked at him with tears still running down my cheeks, "I don't remember you being so hard-headed." I stood up and took his hand. "Come with me. I'm going to end this once and for all. Then you can go."

We walked back across the street and up to our suite. I locked the door. "You're hard to convince. I swore I would never show this to anybody, but you can't marry me and then find out. You'd never be able to stand to look at me," I sobbed as I unbuttoned my dress and let it drop to the floor. Next came the slip and then the binder I wore around my breasts. As the sun streamed through the window and shined upon my disfigured body, I stood before him only in the ragged drawers Mother Angelica had given me that were, as Mother had said, indecently made, and showed most of my body. Then I shouted at him, "Look at me! I'm scarred forever! You never planned to marry somebody with scars from her neck to her ankles! They're everywhere! There are suture lines everywhere!"

He looked at me solemnly, then a tear rolled down his cheek and he said, very softly, "My beautiful Susanna, if you don't want me to be all over you in about a minute, you had better put some clothes on fast. You have scars, but your body is beautiful and I want it. Those scars are a sad reminder of what people are capable of doing to each other, but they don't change my love for you. You're the smartest, most beautiful young woman I've ever seen and I love you with all of my soul. The scars don't change your beauty."

I was shocked! I had expected him to turn away and run for the door, but he didn't. In a weak voice I asked, "They don't make you sick?"

"No they don't. Now please, put your clothes back on quickly and let's go for a walk or something…hurry. I shouldn't be feeling the way I am."

Suddenly I felt embarrassed standing in front of him almost naked. He seemed to understand and turned with his back to me. He said, "I'm starving. Hurry up. You always were the slowest dresser I have ever known. When we get home, you'll have to learn to hurry. You're going to be pretty busy being my wife, a medical student, and giving the family the attention they're going to demand.

I felt a sudden stab in my stomach at the thought of going back to Bayland and facing our family. It was as if he had put a wall up between us. I couldn't go home. I couldn't stand the thought of it! I felt so worthless and vacant and I knew I couldn't put up a front to them because they would know something was wrong. They could always tell when I was bothered by something and these days I was bothered pretty often. At lunch I couldn't swallow with the lump that had formed in my throat. As I looked at my handsome Joseph who was obviously filled with love for me, I felt deep sorrow for a love I was sure to lose.

"What's the matter Susanna?" He asked.

"Nothing," I answered as I looked down at my plate to avoid his eyes.

"You might as well tell me what it is. I know you're upset. It started back at the hotel while you were dressing. Don't you love me anymore?"

"Of course I love you. I've told you that before! I always did! It's just that your love for me is so conditional! You only want me if I go home and you won't listen when I tell you I can't do that! Please stay here with me. We can go into practice here. You can see what need there is! We can be happy and Mother and Papi have their new children and Tom. They won't miss us. If they do, you can go visit."

Joseph reached across the table and held my hand. Very firmly he said, "No we're going home after the war, both of us. We'll come back here often, but we need to live at home. Mama and Papa love you. At first it'll be tough because they're not going to know what to say, but when they get used to the knowledge of everything that you have experienced and stop feeling so guilty about letting it happen to you, then life will settle down. Papa may be a little mad about me marrying you so soon, but he'll get over it and Mother will love you the same as always."

"I hope you're right, but I don't know. Maybe nobody should know what happened. I don't want everybody whispering about my scars or watching me to see if I act normal after 'being through so much.'"

"Well, Tom already knows most of it. Dr. Andretti told him."

I was horrified and suddenly angry, "You both knew? You made me go through all that and you already knew?"

"If you hadn't told me in your own words, that wall you mentioned would have always been between us. I would have never understood how you felt about everything that happened and I would have never understood about you and Alessandro." He bit his lower lip and added, "He must have been quite a man. I'm grateful he was there for you when you needed him so much, but now we're going to do exactly what he told you to do. We are going to get a fresh new start and we'll go on with the best part of our lives."

Joseph

When I was engaged to Carolyn Smitheson I knew I was making a mistake. A nagging feeling inside wouldn't let me rest. When Susanna protested my impending marriage and reminded me of her own assets and of the woman she was going to become, I tried to shut her out and then I felt worse. As I looked into Susanna's sparkling green eyes, I wondered why I had betrayed Carolyn and Susanna and myself. I suppose at the time it seemed so long until Susanna would be grown that my biological needs were making choices for me. What a mistake that had been!

The time I spent with her in Verona and in Rome brought back to me what I had always known. There could never be another woman so intelligent, so gifted, and so strong anywhere ever and I had to have her. It was that determination bursting inside me that made me desperate enough to do whatever was possible to convince her to marry me. I didn't want to wait and I wondered if I should have tried to seduce her while we were in Rome so she might have to marry me quickly. Only the strict moral upbringing we had and the possibility that I might compromise her love for me if I pushed too hard had kept me from ravishing her. I wondered what I could do if she refused to go back to France with me when my leave was up. What if she didn't want to marry me?

Chapter 9

During the week we spent together we went out to the cafes to eat several times a day even though I still could only eat small amounts at a time without getting sick. This worried Joseph, but he tried not to act concerned. We weren't really interested in seeing the sights, but incorporated our alone time with sight seeing as we got to know each other as adults.

The morning we left to return to Verona he told me I was radiant as I followed him out of the hotel dressed in new clothes from inside out. We were both happy and content as we steamed north toward Verona. I would do my show the next night and announce that it would be the last one and we would leave for France on Monday. I was still nervous about seeing my grandparents, aunts and uncles, but Joseph assured me that they had also had their share of hardships. He didn't tell me that Unc and several of the other members of the family, including our grandfather, were working for intelligence. He thought it would be better for me not to be worrying about anybody.

As I sat with my head on Joseph's shoulder I asked, "Do you think Tom made it home safely?"

"He should have gotten home a couple of weeks ago. I hope they're not killing him with kindness."

"I do too. You don't think he told everybody about the things that happened to me do you?"

"He said he wouldn't. He thought it would be best for them not to know. I disagree. They should know so we all understand each other."

"So we tell them--what then? They'll feel like it was their fault for sending me to Luxembourg. Then they'll make everybody be nice to me and the little boys will soon hate me or think I'm crazy. Everybody will look at me and wonder about the scars...."

"I won't ever say anything unless you give me permission, but I still think it would be best. We're not talking about your mother-in-law and your father-in-law. We're talking about the mother and father who loved you enough to adopt you and raise you like their own. You need to reconsider. I can tell them while you're doing something else and you never need to discuss it."

I was quiet while I thought about it, but didn't give an answer.

That night, in Verona, after we ate in the garden at the convent, we talked to Mother Angelica. She had tears in her eyes, but agreed that it was time for me to leave Italy and get on with my life.

"I told you once that I thought you came here because it was the one place God knew you would be able to share all your talents. Now that the war will soon be over, morale is better and casualties are fewer too. It is almost time for you to go home. You children should get married quickly. I see that you love each other very much and I wish you Godspeed."

She embraced us both and I cried. "I've loved you like a mother and I'll pray for you every day. Isn't it great that we're all under the same heaven so we're all together?"

"Yes dear, it is. You know, if Joseph hadn't come along, I believe you would have made a wonderful sister!"

"No Mother, I'm not nearly good enough to be a sister. I would never measure up."

"None of us are perfect, child. God doesn't ask that of us and your faith is as pure as any I have ever seen."

I cried when she said that for I was convinced that I was anything but good. After all, I had been guilty of a treasonous act and I had sinful thoughts about Alessandro and now about Joseph. They were so sinful that I hadn't even confessed them because I was afraid the priest would be shocked and might throw me out of the church. Only very bad people ever thought the things that had crossed my mind.

Mother said nothing only giving Joseph a sober look as she stood and left us alone. After she was gone, Joseph kissed me and left for his hotel.

We spent Saturday getting things ready for the trip to France. After Alessandro had been killed, Dr. Andretti had brought my guns to me. Between the two of us we dismantled them and packed them in a separate bag Joseph had bought in Rome. I had one small bag with the clothes Tom had bought for me and the clothes Joseph had bought and that was all. Joseph said he felt sad when he saw the few worldly goods I possessed, but I reminded him that I had nothing when I came into the world and would have nothing when I left the world. I had all that I needed.

"One time Papi told me I have a lot of money and Opa was constantly reminding me that I am the wealthiest woman in the world, but what difference does it make? It didn't save me from starving and it didn't save me from loneliness, and it didn't save me from being beaten almost to death. I may have money, but it hasn't done me much good has it? The truth is there isn't anything I want that I don't have since you and Tom bought me a few of life's necessities. I was pretty thread-bare before you came along, but now I'm fine."

He looked at me with adoration, "You are the most pure and sweet person I have ever known. Mother Angelica is right, you would have been the perfect nun, but I'll always thank God for giving you back to me instead. I promise to never take you for granted."

When everything was ready, we went for a stroll in the garden. I noticed that it needed weeding. I had been so busy with Joseph that I hadn't been taking care of it properly. "I hope the sisters don't let it go after I'm gone," I worried. "They never had enough to eat before they had the garden."

"Don't fret. They got along before you came."

"They did, but everybody went hungry. They couldn't even feed themselves let alone help the poor. There were starving women and children everywhere. It's better now."

"Did you show them how to do things?"

"Just Sister Genevieve. She was the only one I could be sure would take care of it every day."

"Well see, there is somebody to carry on," he said optimistically. I guess he still worried that I would change my mind about going and he wanted to keep everything looking up. "Come sit on our bench," he coaxed. "I have something for you. I want you to have it before your show tonight."

I laughed as he pulled my hand to direct me to the back corner of the garden. "Don't you want to look at the tomatoes?" I asked.

"Yes, yes, in a few minutes. Right now I have more pressing business. Come quickly!"

When we got to the bench we both sat down and he kissed me then he looked straight into my eyes. "I want to do this properly. I thought of giving it to you while we were in Rome, but then I was afraid you would turn me down and I couldn't have stood that. I love you so much, you know. Since the day Uncle Henry put you in my arms...the day you were born, I have always known that someday I would marry you. I was the kid carrying the baby girl around all over the house and at every school program and at every church function. When you were a little girl, I would have rather spent a day with you than with my friends or anybody else. You were a little spoiled and when you got into trouble with the adults of the family, I used to beg them not to disapline you," he sighed "...though it rarely helped. I only wish I could have protected you from everything that has happened in the past four years," he said dropping his voice. "Now that I've found you, I never want to be without you for a day. I want you to be my wife." He knelt down beside the bench as he held my hand. "Will you marry me, Susanna?" he asked as his eyes shined.

I had tears in my eyes. I did love him with all my heart and our love was pure and honest. "Yes, Joseph, I will marry you. I love you and I trust you and I'll never make you sad, I promise."

At that moment he reached into his pocket and pulled out a small velvet covered box. He opened it and took out a delicate white gold ring with a large emerald cut diamond with rubies clustered around it and he slipped it onto my left ring finger. As soon as we get to France we'll have Unc marry us and then we'll add this plain band to it," he said as he held up the wedding ring, "then we really will be one forever.

I was overwhelmed. "This is the happiest time in my life, "I said earnestly as I looked into his eyes wondering how it could be that I did love him so much when I had been in love with Alessandro less than a year before. It didn't seem loyal of me to accept his ring when it had been less than a year since I had accepted Alessandro's ring. "Are you sure you couldn't love someone else more?" I asked nervously.

He was sure. "I couldn't love anybody else even half as much as I love you. Do you have doubts, Susanna?"

"No, I don't have doubts, but I worry that I can love you so much when I loved Alessandro so much too. Maybe I shouldn't love you."

"Alessandro would want you to love me. You told me so yourself, besides, we have loved each other all our lives. We just went in different directions for a while, but we never stopped loving each other."

"That's true," I sighed. I always thought of you with sadness because you stopped loving me and if Alessandro hadn't been so special, I would have never loved anybody ever again. Who would have ever thought you would come back into my life again? It just goes to show you, nobody ever knows what's just around the corner. Sometimes it's pleasant to think about and other times it can be frightening." I could feel my voice trembling now. "With every happiness there is also sadness. I'm going to have trouble saying good-by to the sisters and I guess I'll need to write a letter to Dr. Andretti. I wish I could have seen him before leaving. Do you think I have enough money back home to be able to surprise the sisters with a gift for the convent and maybe to send something special to Dr. Andretti?"

Joseph smiled. He knew how much money I had and understood that I could buy anything I ever wanted, but I still didn't have any knowledge of my wealth. He told me, "Papa never wanted any of us to ever feel wealthy and he was very careful not to let us act spoiled, but the Von Helldorf's are well-to-do and you, Susanna, are one of the richest girls in the world. You can give them anything you think they'll need and I'll support you on any decision you make. These good women risked their own lives to take care of you and give you a home and we owe them everything. As for your Dr. Andretti, I can't imagine why you would ever want to do anything for him, but there must be something special about him if he could be responsible for you being almost beaten to death and still you care about him. I trust your judgment."

"I'm glad you understand. Some day you'll meet him and then you'll understand."

That night at the beginning of the show I told my audience that it would be my last performance. I would be moving to France, somewhere around Paris, to get married. After the war, my husband

and I would be moving home to Ohio in the United States. The crowd was hushed then people could be heard crying. I handled it well, telling them we needed to have fun together one last time. Soon we were singing some of the popular American songs that everybody knew. The program lasted longer than usual and the gathering of young men and a few women outside was larger than ever before. People seemed to just want to touch me.

I spent extra time shaking hands and signing pictures that somebody had made. The pictures were signed simply, "Love, Luciana."

When we finally got away, Joseph said, "I believe Mother Angelica's right; it was meant to be that you ended up in Verona where you could make such a difference. I don't know if you'll ever be satisfied practicing as a doctor in an ordinary place after all this!"

"Opportunity knocks everyday no matter where you are. You must answer to stay happy. I did plan to stay here where I thought I could do the most good, but the husbands will soon return and things will be a little better. Since God went to a lot of trouble to get us back together, I guess He'll show me what to do next." I surprised him by what I asked next because he thought I had completely given up the idea of staying in Italy. I looked at him with eyes of deepest hope and I begged him, "Are you sure there is no way we can stay here? We could be so happy. Joseph I don't want to leave and I don't want you to go without me! Please don't make me go!"

He put his arms around me and held me tightly. "You have to trust me, Susanna. It's best that we go home. You're scared, but you can never be whole again if you don't face up to this. You wonder what God wants? I think He wants you to return to the family He gave to you. He only loaned you to the Italians because when He gave you all your talents He didn't want them wasted. Italy was the only place He could send you for the war, but now that it's going to be over soon, you need to go home. Your talents will never be wasted. You'll surely find your way and I'll be at your side to help."

The next morning I went to the 6:00 mass with Mother Angelica, Sister Olga, and Sister Genevieve. By the time we got back to the convent Joseph was pacing. He had been afraid I might have changed my mind and left. He jumped at me when he saw me. "Thank God you're back! It's time to go!"

"I know, but I had to go to mass with the sisters one last time and I needed to say good-by to Dr. Bonfiglio."

"You never did have any concept of time," he complained. "Let me get your things. I've got Minnie tied outside."

"I turned to the three nuns with tears in my eyes. I owe you my life. If ever there's anything you need, I can help more than you know." I took three pieces of paper out of my pocket and gave one to each of them. "Write to me and I'll help you. Don't forget me and I'll visit as soon as I can. I'll write from France."

We embraced and I turned quickly to go, crying quietly. Joseph embraced them too and promised to take care of me, and then he helped me into the waiting carriage to take me to the train. I had asked the sisters not to go to the train station with us. I knew it would be too hard to say good-by to them there. Joseph assured me that I had made the right choice to go with him. I hoped he was right and I thought that leaving the sisters wasn't nearly as traumatic as it would have been to watch Joseph leave without me.

The train was crowded and smelly. It was packed mostly with soldiers and I could see that it would be even more unpleasant traveling without a male companion. I was careful not to drink much so I could relieve myself only at planned stops. Minnie was a model traveler as she curled up between the window and me and slept most of the day.

Joseph had the trip planned so we could stop off at hotels most of the nights rather than travel all night long. He always registered us as Dr. and Mrs. Joseph Von Helldorf but we never did anything to be ashamed of. We shared a room with Joseph insisting that he sleep on the floor beside the bed.

As soon as we arrived in Paris we rented a hotel and went out to find Uncle Pierre, our mother's twin brother, the priest who seemed never to be in the same place twice according to Joseph. It took most of the day to catch up with him. When we finally located him, he was in a private meeting in the basement of an old stone church. It seemed strange to me that there were guards on both sides of the door where he was meeting, but these were strange times so I didn't question it.

At first we were told that he couldn't come out, but Joseph wrote a note for them to take to him and he was out in seconds. When he came through the door and saw us, tears welled up in his eyes. He didn't move for a moment and then he let out a loud sob and ran to me and put his arms around me. "We never thought we would ever see you again, child!" Without concern for those looking on, he sobbed openly.

Pierre soon had Joseph wrapped in his arms too, and then he said, "I must cancel my meeting. We need to get out in the sunshine so I can see you better."

I was dwarfed by Joseph who was 6'2" tall and Unc who was 6' tall as I left the church, walking between them with my arms around them and theirs around me. We talked a mile a minute even though I hadn't used my French much in the past few years. Our first stop was at a large cafe where Unc ordered too much for me to eat and Joseph ordered not enough for himself, knowing he would end up finishing my food.

Joseph approached Unc as we were eating. "You remember that Susanna and I were betrothed when she was a baby?"

Unc, who instinctively knew what was going to come next stifled it by saying, "Yes, I remember you stayed betrothed until you broke the engagement and became engaged to one of the older girls in your church back home."

Silenced momentarily by that, he was quiet before starting again. "That was a mistake. I knew it almost as soon as it happened." He put down his fork and continued, "What I'm trying to say is that Susanna and I want to get married, today if possible. We love each other more than ever."

I was smiling until Unc quietly and simply said, "No."

I felt my smile immediately disappear. "What do you mean 'no'?" I asked.

"I mean just what I said, 'no'."

"...but why?" Joseph asked with his voice raised.

"You've already shown yourself to be unsure of what you want, Joseph. How long has it been since you first saw Susanna, a couple of weeks? What do you know of each other? Susanna is a child barely 16 years old and you're almost 25 years old."

Joseph was angry, "I know I made a mistake years ago, but not many people love somebody from childhood without making one mistake and I tried to resolve it as soon as I could. I've always loved her."

"No matter, there will be no marriage," he said matter-of-factly.

I spoke up next, "I'm not just barely 16. You don't know anything about me! I've been on my own for four terrible years and I can do whatever I want!"

Without raising his voice Unc said, "Your childish reaction only reinforces my belief that you are still a child. Next thing you'll burst into tears." He touched my cheek gently then added, "I don't know what happened to you, but whatever it was I know it's been pretty bad. This is no time to be making lifetime decisions. Enjoy your life for a while. Your grandparents can take care of you and when the war is over, I'll take you home."

"I don't ever want to go home! The only reason I ever consented to come this far was to be with Joseph! You don't know anything!" I said again. I looked at Joseph and said, "I should have stayed in Italy. This was a mistake." As I said it a tear slipped down my cheek.

"It wasn't a mistake. We'll find somebody else to marry us. Unc isn't the last priest in the world," he said angrily.

In a loud angry voice Pierre said, "Your marriage won't be valid if I have already turned you down." Then his voice softened, "I'm not trying to be difficult. I love you both and I love your parents. Are you being fair to marry without even talking to them first?"

"I loved them very much when I was a child," I said quietly, "but that was in another time. I still love them, but they're no longer part of my life and they never can be again so what's the need to consult them about my marriage?"

Pierre gave me a worried look. "For you to be like this, you must have come through hell. No child was ever more devoted to her parents than you were. Marriage at this time could be the biggest mistake of your life. They still love you the same as ever. Don't do this to them."

"If they still love me, it's only temporary. I'm not the same as I was. Once they see that, they'll settle back and enjoy their real children and realize that I'm not worth their thoughts." I stood up and said, "Please excuse me. I'm going over to your little chapel to think for a while. I've lost my appetite."

As I walked away I heard Pierre say, "I could kill you for doing this to her, Joseph."

"Me? She was perfectly happy till you started in."

"You put ideas in her mind about marriage when anybody can see that she shouldn't be making decisions about anything. Have you slept with her too?"

I waited around the corner to hear the answer to his question. Joseph was obviously taken back by his uncle's question when he shouted, "I don't think that's any of your business!"

"I think it is. You know you've both committed a mortal sin. At sixteen and with you an experienced 25 year-old-man, I doubt that Susanna resisted you at all. You should be ashamed of yourself. Did you ever think about what it might do to that child to become pregnant? You'll get shipped out when the war's over, but it's hard to tell when she'll be able to leave and she isn't even sure she wants to go. After you leave, maybe she'll decide to go back to Italy. What then? She'll be pregnant, unmarried, and disgraced. She appears very fragile both physically and emotionally. You'd better start thinking of her instead of your own desires."

"Her desire is to be with me. She loves me and she needs me and besides, I haven't slept with her. I love her and would never do anything to disgrace her or cause her to mar the strong faith she has cultured in the years she has been gone. What do you think I am?"

"I think you are selfish and you want to marry her so you can have her for yourself. She needs you, but she also needs the rest of the family. She doesn't need a husband and children and if you marry her now you will be living in sin and, neither of you will be welcome in the homes of your mother's family. No Jude will want anything to do with you. When you report back to headquarters, do you plan for her to live alone in some hotel full of Russian immigrants or what? No convent's going to want her. What are you going to do when you ship out at the end of the war? You'd better do some heavy thinking."

"You're wrong!" he flared as he stood and left to join me in the chapel. I hurried ahead, not wanting him to know that I had never broken my habit of eavesdropping. I ran into the chapel and knelt in a pew just before I heard the big wooden door to the chapel open and close again. He found me and knelt beside me and took my hand. "It'll be all right. Let's go talk to the chaplain at the camp where I'm stationed. We'll get him to marry us."

On the way out he asked, "Do you have any doubts? Did Unc make you see things differently?"

"No, I've never been more sure of anything in my life," I answered.

He smiled confidently and said, "Here's my plan, we'll get the Protestant chaplain to marry us then our love for each other is legal and binding. Later we'll get the marriage blessed in the Church whenever we can. We won't tell any of the family about the marriage unless we have to, but we'll know. I don't care what anybody says. You can stay with Grand-pere and Grand-mere and nobody needs to know anything."

"For the past four years I've taken care of myself, I don't need them."

"Yes you do. Some of what he said was right, you do need the love of our family and I'm going to be sure I don't ruin anything. There's a good possibility that I could get shipped out without you someday and I'll want you with family. He's right about some other things too, but I can take care of them."

"I'm beginning to think you aren't hearing me. I never want to stay with Grand-pere. I don't want to see him and I never want to see Unc again as long as I live. I want nothing to do with Mama's family or anybody else! This is just the beginning. I'm never going to fit in with any of them ever."

"You won't if you keep that attitude. Remember, life hasn't been that good for them either. Let's go talk to the chaplain and see what we can work out and we'll take the other things as we go."

We went together to the chaplain's office to talk to The Reverend Murray who Joseph told me had always seemed a kindly sort as he worked with the injured soldiers. The Reverend Murray wondered why we hadn't gone to a Catholic chaplain and we told him the truth. We told him our background, about the betrothal of Joseph to Carolyn and me to Alessandro, the adoption, all that had happened the past four years, and about Unc's refusal to marry us.

"We have to get married," Joseph told him. "Not because of the reasons most people would think, but because we love each other so much and always have. Susanna stopped being a child when Luxembourg was invaded. I'll take care of her and love her, and I swear I'll always encourage her to do the things she wants to do." His eyes were earnest

"You've explained your case well, Major Von Helldorf, but I need to talk to Susanna now. Are you comfortable speaking in English?" he asked.

"Yes sir, I've been speaking English quite a lot since the Americans came to Italy."

"A woman needs to obey her husband. You're only 16 years old. Are you going to be happy having Joseph's babies and answering to him for the rest of your life? If you're an accomplished musician as Joseph says, won't you hate leaving that?"

"I won't leave it. God will show me some unhappy people somewhere and I'll play for them. There's always a place for music. I had two years of college, one at Bayland College and one at Western Reserve by the time I was 12 years old. Joseph and I plan for me to go to medical school then to find a practice somewhere in an area where there's poverty. My life will be quite full and happy with Joseph because we come from like backgrounds and we have the same goals."

"What happens when the children start coming? How do you plan to do everything you want to do if you have a house full of children? They're going to need your attention. You'll be pulled between your need to do what you want to do and their needs."

Then I took a line from Alessandro, "I had a nurse when I was little and I loved her. Joseph and I will search till we find a nice older lady to be nurse to our children."

"And Joseph would agree to this?"

"Yes."

"You do sound like you have your head screwed on straight." He looked at me and then at Joseph, "Here are the papers that need to be filled out. They have to pend for three days. If they're approved and I'm sure they will be since you're both Americans, I'll marry you in three days at 2:00 in the afternoon. How would that be?"

I breathed a noticeable sigh of relief and the three of us laughed. Joseph put his arm around me, smiling from ear to ear. "That would be perfect! We'll be married before I have to report to duty again. I don't know when I'll get another leave. It'll be very comforting to know we have everything taken care of."

That evening Joseph very carefully began speaking of the future. He started out by saying, "After we get married Sunday, I need to take you to Rouen before I report for duty the next morning."

"No, Joseph. I won't go!"

"You have to."

"I won't go. You can't make me!" I panicked.

"What will you do in Paris all alone?"

"I'll go to the nearest convent and volunteer my services for room and board. Maybe they need a musician at the church or for their choir or somebody to clean or cook. I swear to you Joseph, I'll do anything to keep from ever having to see anybody else in the family," I said with my voice shaking.

He took me in his arms. "Susanna, you make me feel so bad," he said as he held me tightly. "What am I supposed to do? I'll just say bye, Susanna, in the morning when I leave to report for duty, then leave you to shift for yourself?"

"Yes."

"I'll go AWOL. I'm not leaving you."

"You can't do that!"

"Yes I can. I'm not leaving you on the streets of Paris. I swore to myself that I would never let anything else happen to you and I don't intend to!"

"Joseph please!" I cried. "They'll shoot you for desertion!"

"They'll have to find me. I'm not leaving you."

"They always find everybody. I've seen people shot for that!"

"Well, I'm not leaving you unless it's in Grand-pere's hands where you'll be safe and that's final."

I walked to the window and stared out. I could feel myself turning to ice as I went through emotional withdrawal, but I guess Joseph decided to act like he didn't notice. He said nothing. I reenacted the horrible scene when I witnessed the Austrian spy being executed before a firing squad and put Joseph in his place. The thought of it took my breath away. Finally I agreed to go to Rouen after the marriage ceremony.

"Promise you won't get upset and leave if Unc visits? If there's any chance that you're not going to stay, I won't leave you."

"I promise. I'd rather do anything than run the risk of having you shot," I choked.

Chapter 10

During the three-day wait, Joseph and I spent every minute together. In many ways it was as if the past four years had never happened. He taught me how to laugh again and I teased him and played with him while we were out and about town. We felt married already in most ways. Both of us tried to put the idea of mortal sin by marrying outside of the Church out of our minds. Not once did we see Unc anywhere even though we thought we might when we attended mass each evening. Neither of us took communion since we both knew we would be soon be committing what we believed would be a serious sin. The thought of it hurt us terribly.

Sunday afternoon we were at the chaplain's office by 1:00 just to be sure nothing would happen to keep us from being there on time. Our old friend Jacob Yoder, Joseph and Tom's companion from school, acted as a witness. His lady friend, Laure, was to be the other witness. Before being sent to Luxembourg, Jacob and I had become like siblings just as Joseph and Tom and Jacob had been. I could never remember our house back home without Jacob. When the boys and Jacob were graduated from college, Papi bought a new Peerless Roadster for each of the three of them. Evidently the relationship between them had never changed after I was taken out of the equation.

Jacob, unlike the Von Helldorf's was a husky red-faced young man who stood 5'10" tall. He had been raised a Brethren in a family of pious hardworking farmers who could never understand why he couldn't conform with the rest of them. Since the Brethren are pacifists, they disowned him when he joined the army. Jacob had left Dr. Barnes' practice in Bayland, Ohio as soon as the United States joined the war and requested to go to Paris to be near Joseph and Tom.

When Jacob saw me he put his arms around me and gave me a brotherly hug. "I'm glad you're all right, Liebchen," he said with tears in his eyes. "We were all worried about you, but somehow, I could never believe you wouldn't be back someday. I think I recognized some of your stitchery on a soldier who came in from Verona. He said a beautiful woman doctor had stitched him up. You did a first class job on him, but then I always knew you would be a great doctor some day." He hugged me again, this time burying his face in my shoulder and he cried. Laure looked on probably wondering what was the matter with us.

Breaking the ice with tears still in his eyes, he said, "I finally converted to Catholicism! As a physician for the U.S. Army and a man of thirty-one years, I decided I should do what I wanted to do for a change. I've been shunned by the entire Brethren community and my family forever for joining the army so I had nothing to lose. Besides, I had to do it."

"They didn't shun us and we were always Catholic," I said innocently.

"That's just it, you were always Catholic. They'll think I should know better. Oh well, I always wanted to be Catholic ever since I used to have to take Tom and Joseph to their religion classes. It made so much sense. Joining the army made sense too. I couldn't stand by and watch our men die without doing something to help," he explained.

"Does this Protestant wedding make sense to you then?" I asked.

"Not exactly, but I understand why you're doing it. Old Unc'll soften eventually and bless it. In the meantime," he added very seriously, "don't do anything that would put you in mortal sin."

I blushed and Joseph reprimanded him jokingly for embarrassing his bride.

As we waited, I realized that Jacob's girl friend spoke almost no English and Jacob's French wasn't much better than it had been back home. He always spoke excellent German, but rarely used the French he had painstakingly learned in college.

I finally asked, "How do you and Laure communicate with the language barrier?"

"Communication isn't necessary. I've never known anybody so gentle and sweet, unless it was you, and you were way too young for me," he grinned. "We get along just fine together. I thought there would never be anybody for me, but I was wrong."

"It sounds serious. Are you going to get married?"

"I hope so, but she doesn't want to leave her family here and I want to go home to the U.S. I miss the Barnes family and yours and the people we saw as patients." He didn't say he missed his own people and I knew they had always looked upon him as the black sheep of the family ever since he had started taking care of the boys and had enrolled in college. "She has to change her mind. I know she'll hit it off just great with your ma."

I felt ashamed of myself. I never wanted to go home and I certainly never wanted to see any more of my family than I already had. "You can probably change her mind. If she loves you enough she'll leave here even if she's scared to death to go."

Joseph looked at me knowingly because he knew I was scared to death to go to Bayland. He also knew he would be taking me there even if I cried every mile I got closer to it. He strongly believed that we had to go home or it would break our parent's hearts.

It was finally 2:00 when Chaplain Murray shook hands with the men and bowed to Laure and me. We walked into the quiet makeshift chapel and started the short ceremony. I had on a green dress that I hoped made my eyes look more green than ever and wondered if the hot flushing of my face was as my adoptive mother's had been ten years before on her wedding day. We said our vows with such love and sincerity that even Laure who didn't understand the words still filled up with tears as she listened and watched. When it was over, Joseph kissed me tenderly then we all hugged. I admired the small, plain wedding band resting below the elegant engagement ring.

Jacob hugged us again then looked at me as he said, "Mrs. Von Helldorf, I could see the special relationship you and Joseph had way back when I first met you. In case you have forgotten, you were five and Joseph was fourteen. Your father had that ruptured gall bladder and we didn't think he was going to make it. You were both scared to death that he was going to die, but you were also so gentle and concerned for each other that I thought you acted like a little old married couple even then. It was always that way between the two of you. If two people ever deserved to be together, it's you."

Joseph gave the chaplain a hundred-dollar bill then we all went out to eat the best cuisine we could find. When we finished eating, Joseph and I went back to our hotel. He was the most gentle groom a bride ever had and by morning I loved him even more than before. It was a poor way to start a marriage, but we had to rise early in the morning to make the trip to Rouen. After we were both dressed he suggested that we go downstairs to the lobby for breakfast. While we waited for our food to come he said, "The marriage has been consummated and because of that no one can have it annulled. We truly are married forever. I love you so much and last night was the most special night of my life, but you must see a priest as soon as you possibly can and get absolution for what we did. I never wanted to cause you to sin but there was no other way to assure that Papa couldn't annul our marriage. He's not going to be happy about this, you know." He added, "Until our marriage is properly blessed by the Church, I will not touch you in that way again."

Suddenly I felt the impact of what we had done and felt sick. The night before it had all seemed so right to be with my husband, but the thought of disappointing my God who had seen me through the past four-and-a-half years made my whole body feel weighted down. I angrily said, "I've been on my own for four-and-a-half years and I don't need Papi telling me what I can and cannot do! He doesn't know anything about me!" Then I went on to say, "I hope God will forgive me for last night if it was wrong, but He knows my heart and knows that I wouldn't willingly do anything to disappoint Him. If it had to happen to assure that our marriage vows are sealed, it couldn't be so wrong. As for Papi, I don't care what he wants or doesn't want. He isn't a part of my life anymore."

My tone seemed to shock Joseph. "You don't think it will bother you to go against our father's will? It used to be very important for you to have his favor."

"I realized a few years ago that I had been deluding myself when I was a child. I thought I really was exactly the same as a daughter to him, but I know now I wasn't. I needed a home and he gave it to me and I'm grateful. Where would I have been without him? On the other hand, he has six sons of his own blood. Do you really think he would have not found a way to find one of you if you had been lost? It wasn't that hard to put me out of his mind and to get on to other things when I came up missing. The only thing I worry about is whether he will think that I am good enough to be married to his oldest son. He cared enough to pay a few investigators to look for me, but I don't think he put forth much effort to find me."

Joseph turned his back to me and said nothing. I was quiet. I had had my say and there was nothing more to be said. It was time to take me to Rouen. He collected our bags and I followed him downstairs to a borrowed army truck not unlike the ones Alessandro had used when he came to Verona to visit.

The trip to Rouen seemed only to take minutes even though Joseph barely said a word the whole way. Just outside of Rouen he pulled to the side of the road and stopped to have a few minutes to talk. "You know I'd never leave you for a minute if there were any other way," he said.

"I know." I answered, and then hopefully added, "There's still time to turn it around. I know I'd do fine in Paris on my own. Maybe I could even stay with Laure."

He was firm with me, I guess because he wanted to squelch any ideas of my returning to Paris, "Her family is from around Verdun. They had to flee years ago and since then they live in terrible conditions with about three other families and a bunch of children, half of them bastards. It kills Jacob to have her living like that, but she refuses to go to our grandparents' house to stay because she wants to be near her family."

In my panic I suggested, "I could live in the hotel where we stayed."

Now he was cross with me, "We've been through this a dozen times, Susanna! I won't have it! It would be just a matter of time till the men seeing you coming and going unescorted would be after you and I couldn't stand that…besides, it wouldn't be safe. Soldiers are always chasing tail. That's the way they are."

I said no more, wiped away the tears and turned forward to show that I was ready to face whatever happened. Now I would be alone again.

The farm looked run down when we arrived. The usually well-kept yard was uncut and there were no flowers. No livestock could be seen in the stockyard. It looked like nobody lived there.

"It looks bad!" I said, surprised.

"All Frenchmen are suffering. The war has probably devastated France a lot more than it did Italy. You were just in a bad place."

When we stopped, our grandmother came out on the porch to see who was there. She walked toward the vehicle when she recognized Joseph, but it was as if Grand-mere, Amalie, was looking at a ghost when she first looked at me. She looked at Joseph then back at me then she screamed my name, ran the rest of the way, pulled open the heavy door as if it weighed nothing, and threw her arms around me. I felt loved, not adopted. I responded stiffly, not with the same vigor I had shown in childhood. Already I was anticipating problems. Joseph read my behavior and winced. I guess he hoped I would warm up to the Jude's in the same way as I had to Tom and Jacob, but these were the adults who had been in my life and they were the ones who would be the judges of my worth. I didn't feel very worthy. I felt that I had been abandoned by the adults of the family who had failed to rescue me from the years of estrangement I had endured in Italy. I didn't think I would ever be able to freely give my love to the people who had been responsible for everything that had happened.

Amalie immediately started to fuss as she complained that nobody was there except her. She quickly assumed that I would be staying and happily looked for my bags. Joseph went for them while Grand-mere hugged me again. "I said a rosary for you every day since you disappeared and prayed to St. Anthony to help you be found!"

She offered to feed us, but Joseph had told me that they hardly ever had enough to eat so we declined the invitation. Since her daughter, Gabrielle's sister Helene, and her children had been forced to move in with them, things had been worse than ever. He told me that Grand-mere always said, "We just add a little more water to the soup then there's enough for everybody," but he knew they went to bed with empty bellies more often than not.

Joseph brought in a box of supplies that he had been gathering since his last visit out to the farm. It wasn't very big, but anytime he found anything he thought they could use; he picked it up and saved it for them. Papa had sent them money, but there was nothing to buy so in most cases it did no good to have it.

Before he left, Joseph kissed me, and then looked at me longingly. "I'll be back as soon as I can and I'll write every day, even if it's just a couple lines. The mail in France is bad. Don't think I'm not thinking of you if you don't get a letter. I'm going to send a telegram to Mama and Papa to tell them you're safe with Grand-mere. Be sure you see a priest and remember a confession does no good unless your conscience is contrite so think about what we did because it surely was a sin."

I opened my mouth to protest, but Joseph gently put his hands on my shoulders and looked into my eyes very seriously and repeated himself, "I'm going to send a telegram to Mama and Papa to tell them you're safe with Grand-mere. Get to a priest soon. "

"What about your soul Joseph? Can you be sorry for consummating our marriage?" I asked with a shaky voice.

"That will take some thinking and praying over, but I'll speak to a priest and try to work it out. I've got to go. I love you. Please wait for me."

"I'll wait," I choked. "You're the only reason I'm here."

I looked straight ahead without a tear in my eye as he quickly got into the little truck and drove away, leaving only a trail of dust behind him. I seemed to have lost the ability to cry after Alessandro's death. As I stood there like a wooden statue with no movement and no emotion, Grand-mere tried to comfort me, though she had no knowledge of my life the past four years except for what little Tom had chosen to tell her when he had stopped over. I guess no words could take away the sorrow and fear I was experiencing and she knew it so the old woman simply told me, "Whatever it is, I'll try to help you begin to heal. I'm your grandmother and I love you."

Looking at my adoptive grandmother's earnest, wrinkled old face, I wondered if I had been wrong about my feelings for the family. As a child I had loved all the Jude's except for Isabel who always seemed jealous of my mother and never seemed to like any of the Von Helldorf's. Instead of rejecting my grandmother as I had planned to do, I accepted her offer and responded saying only, "Thank you Grand-mere."

Amalie was a tiny spunky little woman with long white hair twisted in a knot at her neck. She sounded strong and not the least bit defeated when she said, "This war has tried to ruin everybody in Europe, but we're not going to let it get any of us down!"

I had to smile at my little grandmother as she put a pot of water on the stove for some tea and laid out some of the cookies Joseph had brought. She didn't ask about what had happened over the past four years, I guess realizing that it must have been a painful time. The glee that had always been with me just waiting to bubble to the surface was gone. Instead we talked about shortages and how bad my clothing situation had been after I grew tall and womanly and found myself with nothing to wear. Grand-mere laughed when she heard that I had worn a nun's habit for almost two years for lack of anything else to wear.

"I suppose it protected me from the soldiers. They would never use bad language or do anything too disgraceful around a nun. After living the life of a sister, I have to say, it was very safe and comforting. The habit couldn't protect me from everything though," I said as I remembered it being striped off before I had been led out to be beaten almost to death.

"No, I suppose not."

"Have you written to your mother?"

I looked down at my cup, "No, I wouldn't know what to say. There isn't much good to write about and I don't want to worry her. Do you write to her?"

"Yes. It's my duty to keep her from worrying."

"What kinds of things do you say?"

"This fall I've mentioned how beautiful the leaves are and I often talk about the grandchildren, especially Helene's brood since they live here now. Children are not so affected by things. I mention how much I love them all. A page can be filled without ever saying much of anything. I doubt that she has any idea what it's really been like."

"I doubt I can ever do anything like that. You always were such a good person, but I'm different. I have all I can do to keep myself from thinking about things myself. The last thing I need to do is write chitchat to Mama. I guess I'm too selfish."

"You're not selfish. You just have too heavy of a burden to carry someone else's too. I can help you when you're ready. It would mean so much to her and to your father, but I understand if you need more time."

"Maybe I'll do it someday. I can't think about it now."

Throughout the afternoon and evening the family came in. First it was Helene and the four children, then Guillaume, my grandfather. Each time the reunion was tearful for them and each time I seemed to feel nothing. That night the house was filled with love and caring. Nobody pried or asked about my time in Italy except to mention the shows Tom had told them about. They wished they had a piano so I could play any time I wanted to. Their love and kindness made me sad because I couldn't seem to relate to it.

Helene shyly mentioned, "Mama and I volunteer at the field hospital in town and they have a piano in the old YMCA building.

Sometimes they have little programs for the soldiers there. Usually they aren't too good. Do you think you might like to go there to use the piano while we're helping out at the hospital? It's probably not a very good one, but at least you could play sometimes."

I felt a surge of excitement. "I'd love that. I'd like to help at the hospital too if they could use another hand sometimes."

"There's never enough help. It's better since the Americans took it over, but some of those American nurses!" she shook her head.

"I've heard that the only people cockier than the Americans are the Australians, but I haven't dealt with the Australians yet so I don't know. With my background, I don't really know what I am, American or something else." I said in an effort to seem cheerful.

I managed to be friendly throughout the evening without really giving of myself. That night, in the bed that had belonged to my mother many years ago, I tossed and turned as I had done so many times at the convent. I thought of Opa, and Alessandro, and Mother Maria Elizabeth, and Niccolo and the screaming soldiers who had been killed or maimed or executed for simply doing what they thought they had to do. I worried that I was not sorry for giving Joseph, my husband, the love he had demanded of me and wondered how I would confess allowing such a thing without remorse. I wondered if eternal hell was waiting for me now that I had sinned in such a way.

The next morning no one mentioned hearing me thrash about in the squeaky bed so I assumed they had slept through it and I was thankful.

I was like a caged animal by the time I had been with my grandparents three days. I was used to every waking moment being busy and suddenly there was little to do. I cleaned every inch of the house and washed all the bedding and replaced it. The furniture was polished and all the cupboards cleaned out. When nothing was left to do inside the normally tidy old farmhouse, I started working outside.

The barn had already been cleaned out when the last of the animals were taken away. I was cutting all the weeds down with a sickle one day when a voice behind me said, "That's an odd waste of time for a famous entertainer like Luciana to be engaged in."

I jumped and turned around to see Unc grinning at me. "Oh, it's you! What do you want to tell me what a sinful person I am or are you just here to tell everybody else? I didn't want to come here. Joseph said he would desert if I didn't and I didn't want him shot."

My uncle smiled again, "He told me. He also said he found a chaplain to marry you, but of course you're still living in sin."

"He said we weren't going to tell anybody! Anyway, I guess I'm not living in sin anymore, unless God stopped forgiving people for certain sins that are worse than others. I went to confession and told the priest I had slept with a man. It took me the rest of the day to do all the penance he assigned to me and I haven't seen Joseph since the day we got married. I wish you'd change your mind."

"Well I won't. At least not until you're home with your parents and we talk to them."

"So if I never go home, our marriage will never be blessed," I gasped. "I always thought you liked us. Mama always thought you were such a nice person," I added as a betrayed look must have crossed my face.

"I know you think I'm the meanest man in the world, but you're wrong. I do love you and Joseph, and that's why I'm not going to stand by and let you jump into something I don't believe you're ready for. There's a lot more to marriage than sharing the same bed. You're a child and you must have had some very bad experiences in the past few years. You're not a candidate for marriage yet and Joseph should be hung for what he has done to you," he said firmly.

"Well, I think you should turn it over to a priest who isn't so partial. We should have gone to somebody else, besides, Joseph says our marriage can never be annulled now that we…!'"

"…Now that you committed a mortal sin! Your marriage is not valid and if your father has any sense he will most definitely have it annulled! I'm not going to turn your case over to someone who knows nothing about you and I'll not change my mind. I'm going to do everything in my power to see that there's no more indecency between the two of you until we get you home to your mother and father and you've had a few months to be sure of what you want and I will pray that your father sees fit to annul it as quickly as possible."

"What does Joseph say?"

"I think I've finally talked some sense into him."

I felt as if somebody had knocked the wind out of me. "He regrets the marriage?" I asked. "His letters haven't indicated a change of feelings."

"He still wants the marriage blessed," he said as he realized what I was thinking. "He loves you as always, but I think I've convinced him that if he doesn't care about himself, he at least should care about you and the feelings of your parents and the sinful state of your lives."

"Did he say when he would be coming?" I asked, changing the subject.

"It'll probably be a long time. He's at the hospital almost constantly. There's no letup in sight. That's what I came to talk to you about. Mama says you're at loose ends. She says you're cleaning, pulling weeds and everything else. You need something to do and they're not letting you do enough in the hospital. Tom and Joseph both say you were very successful when you did your show in Verona, Miss Luciana. Would you like me to take you to Paris to do a show this weekend? You could visit Joseph, not alone, but you could see him and talk to him and you could make some people happy."

"I'd love to!" I answered with the first genuine smile I had given him.

"Good! You don't have much time. Let me take you over to the YMCA to practice. I'll wait for you and tomorrow we'll head for Paris." He paused and added, "Don't get any ideas. Joseph will be working in the hospital all day Friday and you'll need to practice. I'll have two of the sisters with you at all times. You'll do your show, sleep at the convent and Sunday evening I'll bring you back here. We were so sure you were going to be willing to do this program that we've already advertised it. You should have a great turnout. Believe it or not, some of the soldiers have heard of Luciana."

"I'm still going to be billed as Luciana?"

"Yes. That was Joseph's idea. He thought it would be less personal than having the soldiers drooling over his, 'wife'. He's more than a little jealous, you know."

"No, I didn't know," I answered with a contented smile.

While I practiced all afternoon and into the evening at the YMCA building, military personnel came and went, much as they had done during my first days at the compound. By evening the building was packed. I ended up getting them to sing with me and soon had an enthusiastic audience that stayed until midnight when Unc ordered me to come along. I teased my uncle in front of the group about ending our fun…wasn't that just like a priest? We left together happily. This was the first time Pierre and I hadn't been at odds with each other since about 20 minutes after we had met in Paris.

We left early the next morning and had an uneventful trip. The sisters at the convent were cordial, as they looked me over carefully to see what kind of girl Father's niece was. They seemed to like me. Over the years I had lived with nuns so much that I fell into their ways instantly. I was quiet, polite, and serious, being careful to observe the rules of the house. That evening I observed silence and went to vespers with them, and then later I played for them. I played my own compositions as well as the religious and classical pieces that

I particularly loved. By Saturday morning I had won them over.

Joseph came to see me when he got off duty that morning. He had taken the time to shave and change clothes before coming, but it was obvious that he hadn't slept in a long time. Conversation was careful because two sisters were assigned to sit with us just as Unc had ordered. Joseph wondered what he thought was going to happen in a convent, but later he realized the wisdom of it and said he was determined never to put my soul on the line again.

I beamed a glassy smile as I looked at him. I didn't care what the sisters thought when I said, "I still love you. I'm glad to see you no matter what the rules are."

"I love you too. You look beautiful! Farm life must agree with you. Maybe instead of a doctor you need to be a farmer. I already know what you can do with a garden," he teased.

"I'll be a gardener in a big way, but I'll practice medicine with my husband. Nobody will ever need a doctor and not have one because of money ever again."

The nuns smiled at my comment, reminding me that they were listening to every word either of us said. It must have been obvious that we were very much in love as we talked.

"When the war is over you can enroll at Bayland College for spring semester if you get back soon enough, then you'll only have one semester to go till you can apply for medical school. If you don't have too many problems because of being female, you could possibly be in the class that starts in 1920."

"I'll be so old by the time I finish," I said wistfully.

"You won't be old for about 40 years!"

I smiled. "Did you send that telegram?"

"Yes. They answered it and wondered why you don't write. They think you blame them for everything that happened. They say you're right to feel that way. You have to do something."

Deep down inside I did blame them, but I tried not to let it show too often. Somehow I believed that they required their children to be perfect, and then sentenced me to a life that made me very imperfect and I resented them for it. I said, "Grand-mere says that too. Maybe enough good things have happened that I can write about the garden in Verona and how well fed we were." My voice became dreamy as I went on, thinking of the sisters in Verona. "I guess I could say something about Luciana and her shows too." Then, becoming sarcastic I added, "I'll reassure them that things have been great for me and that even though I've missed them it has been a rewarding experience."

"Susanna what are you saying? Just tell them you love them, miss them, and can't wait to see them again and that you don't blame them for everything that has happened!"

"They don't know anything about the war over here and they won't ever know anything about what happened to me! I don't miss them and I never want to see them again. I can't be perfect enough for them anymore...I guess I never could be what they wanted even before this happened! Do you remember how often Papi used to get after me when I was growing up? I was always in trouble!"

Joseph shook his head and sighed, "You made your own trouble. Look at Tom! He got in as much trouble as you did. Did Papa ever spare the rod on him? You are so wrong! They have always loved you and maybe Papa made some mistakes raising you, but he never showed favoritism and he always loved you. As for your experiences over here, they know about the war and how it has taken it's toll on the European people, you always have thought they were just a little stupid even though they never let you get away with much. They read the newspapers and have a fair idea about things. Make your letter a friendly little note and tell them you love them, if you still do."

I felt deeply saddened when he said that and shouted, "Of course

I try not to have hard feelings toward them. They took care of me when I had no one and I loved them, but I have no feelings for them now. I try not to think about them at all, then I don't have to feel anything. I'm very grateful that they gave me a home and tried to make me feel like one of the family. Mama was never mean to me and Papa did what he thought was right and I'm grateful for that too."

"Well, sometime real soon you need show some of that gratitude and sit down by yourself and decide exactly what you do feel. When you figure it out, you need to write the letter. They need to hear from you."

Joseph finally, though reluctantly, left to get some sleep. He gave me a tender kiss on the cheek and promised to try to get to my show that evening if he could find anybody to cover for him. "I love you, baby," he said in English so hopefully the nuns wouldn't understand.

"I love you too. Sleep well."

I practiced all day without stopping until the sisters reminded me that I needed to go back to the convent for vespers and to eat before the program. It would have been like me to never notice the time of day and play right up to performance time. Nothing else ever mattered when I was playing.

That evening Joseph, Jacob, and Laure met me backstage before the show started.

Joseph said, "I practically got down on my hands and knees and begged my commander to give me the time to come to this. I told him you were my wife, but he didn't believe it because I don't speak Italian. He says everybody knows Luciana is Italian. Thank God Jacob came to my rescue and collaborated my story or I never would have gotten off. As it turns out, he gave me the whole night off, thinking we actually live like married people.

I squeezed his hand then we held each other till one of the sisters cleared her throat loudly.

"This must be the most frustrating experience there ever was to have a wife you're not ever allowed to even touch!" he complained.

Just as he opened his mouth to say more, I was called on stage. When the applause started, I suddenly felt full of energy and like the weight of the world had lifted off of me. The crowd was polite, but not enthusiastic like when I performed in Verona. I was a stranger here, but that only lasted a few minutes. First I played a cheery piece from Handel, then a medley of popular tunes with all the power the grand piano could bring forth. The crowd vigorously applauded at the end of each number.

After playing several selections, I got up from the piano and greeted them in perfect English and perfect French. I explained that I never did a show without the assistance of my audience. For a moment I paced back and forth across the stage. The audience wondered if I had forgotten what to do next and there was total silence as they wondered what was going to happen. Finally I picked a young soldier who had a big smile and an air of assurance about him and I and asked him to help. He didn't want to come and even though he had seemed exactly like the one I was looking for, I was concerned when his face turned crimson and he refused to come. Before I could turn away to look for somebody else, two of his buddies picked him up and carried him to the front, exactly as it had happened when it all began out on the post in Northern Italy so long ago. For a second I was frozen in my tracks, but the crowd didn't seem to notice. Everybody cheered. He looked terrified. By the time they reached me I had recovered sufficiently to be able to proceed with the fun. I insisted that all three of them stay. "There's safety in numbers…right?" I asked the audience. Next I turned to my three recruits and asked them what songs they liked. All the while I talked to the audience as if they were co-conspirators.

"Alright, you two, stand over here by the piano and sing along with me," I ordered. Then I pointed at the nervous one and ordered him to sit beside me on the piano bench. In seconds I taught the man sitting with me how to play several notes simultaneously, then I started to sing with the other two and I played the tune while the soldier repeated his notes as part of the duet. It sounded great and the audience loved it because it was coming from their own friends. When we finished, the applause shook the building. I assured them that anybody can be a performer if they just sit back and enjoy it. By the time we had performed several numbers all three men were having fun with me and acted as if they would be happy to stay with me for the rest of the show.

After they were finally dismissed to return to their seats, I sat down and played for thirty minutes nonstop. I never liked to have breaks in a show. I took requests, had more people up to help me and at the end thanked them all for coming. Three encores followed.

I think Unc, Jacob, Laure, and the two nuns were surprised at the crowd's response to the show. All of them, but Laure knew I could play well, but they never thought for a moment that the crowd would be so enthusiastic. Joseph was beaming with pride until we got ready to leave and he saw the crowd of men waiting outside. I could feel his change of mood and see the change of his face from an expression of pure happiness to one of anger as his jaw set and he began to complain about the soldiers waiting like a pack of dogs.

"We can't wade out past all those men. They look pretty rowdy-- not like the ones in Verona," he said.

"Maybe we'd do better just walking out the front door and disappearing somewhere," I suggested.

"You will disappear back to the convent," Unc ordered without a smile or a glimmer in his eye.

Pease Uncle Pierre, can't we go out and celebrate? I'm not a baby," I said angrily.

"You are a child barely 16 and you need to go to bed."

Just as I opened my mouth to protest more violently, Joseph stepped in. "Look, nobody could sleep after giving a performance like that. Why don't you excuse the two sisters, we'll take them back to the convent, and the five of us can go out and celebrate for a while. You can be sure I won't lay a hand on my wife."

"She's not your wife and you know it," he argued gruffly, "but that does sound like a reasonable compromise. We'll all go out together."

At the cafe, before the party began, Jacob carefully asked Unc if he would consider marrying he and Laure. They discussed the language problem and the fact that Laure didn't want to move to the U.S., but finally he said he would marry them if they could work out those problems. Joseph and I both bristled at that. I said, "I don't understand! Joseph and I have known and loved each other all our lives! I told you we were going to get married someday back when I was five years old, but you won't marry us. Why is it that you'll marry them? It isn't fair!"

"It would seem obvious why," he was becoming irritated with my constant challenges. "Jacob just told me he is 31 years old. Laure is 25. They are a grown up couple and they know what they want. Don't spoil this great evening by acting even younger than you are. I'm not going to argue with a child!"

I wondered how I could have ever loved my uncle. He had just embarrassed me in front of everybody and made me feel like a baby. I hated him!

Joseph took my hand and gave it a little squeeze as if to say, it's all right, just let it go for now. Jacob and Laure said no more about getting married and the subject was changed to the war and when it would finally be over. Bulgaria had signed an armistice on September 29 and it looked like the Ottoman Empire would fall soon.

"I wonder how long it'll take us to get home?" Jacob sighed. "I'm gonna be so glad to get back on U.S. soil. I'll bring Laure back here to visit her parents, but I hope I never have to stay for long!"

Laure, Pierre, and I all looked dark after that. It was Laure's home, I didn't want to go home, and Pierre was French to the core. Jacob looked at us and didn't understand what he had said wrong. "What's the matter with everybody? What did I say?"

I looked at him, understanding completely and loving him for his innocence and said kindly, "You said nothing wrong. You just love your country. I wish I felt that way about some place."

People were dancing, so to change the atmosphere to something happier, I asked if Joseph and I could dance together. I was elated when Unc gave his consent. In minutes we had our arms around each other and I had my head against his chest.

Joseph whispered, "It's so good to hold you in my arms. It's been so long since we've been together...I can't sleep at night. I miss you so much."

I asked, "Do you wish you hadn't gotten into this? I'm sure lots of women would love to marry you and you work with those nurses every day. Grand-mere says they're different than most young women."

He was smiling as he answered me with a back handed question, "And you have hundreds of young men falling all over you when you do your shows, but you don't want to spend time with them? My beautiful Susanna, I'll never even look at anybody but you for the rest of my life even it takes five years to convince Unc to marry us. You have to know how much I love you. There isn't anybody anywhere as smart and gifted and beautiful as you."

We had danced over to the darkest corner of the floor by now. Thinking nobody would see us, he kissed me with all the passion he had in him, and then we held each other. I laid my head down on his chest again and we had our arms around each other, barely moving our feet to the music when two hands pulled me away from him. It was Unc again! He said angrily, "Susanna, you are going back to the convent and Joseph, you should be ashamed of yourself!"

"I'm not ashamed of myself," Joseph declared. "I should be able to hold and love my own wife without her being hostage to your wishes! Believe me I have no intention of causing either of us to live in mortal sin, but you could help our souls by simply blessing our marriage!"

"I'm not blessing your marriage because there is no marriage and as for trusting you with my niece's virtue, I don't see why I should. You haven't been proven to be trustworthy up until now!" He took my arm very gently and, lowering his voice to almost a whisper he said, "Come along child, it's time for you to be in bed."

Looking back on it I remember that we had a good time that night, even with Unc along. He always had been fun. It was for that reason he had been our favorite uncle as we were growing up. All of us had drank just enough wine to be in high spirits, but not drunk. Unc fussed that I should not be drinking wine, but conceded when he saw the dark look both Joseph and I gave him. Later, at the convent door, Joseph said he knew better than to do more than hold my hand and give me a quick hug and a peck of a kiss. He said, "It is only because of my love for you that I have dropped you off at the convent. Unc will stick to his word. He would see that you aren't welcome to stay with his parents or anybody else if we disobey him and I want you tucked safely in the love and protection of our mother's parents." As he turned unhappily to leave, he gave me a wad of money. "You might need this for something. I'll give you more the next time I see you."

"I don't need this. There's nothing to buy!"

"Something might come up. I want you to have some money."

Unc was watching as he gave me another gentle kiss on the cheek and said, "Goodnight."

LINDA STEELE

Gran-Pere

*I*first met my granddaughter when I visited the United States in 1908 when she was five-and-a-half years old. My daughter Gabrielle was marrying widower, Rolf VonHelldorf, the father of two young sons. After the wedding ceremony my daughter adopted his two sons and together she and Rolf adopted Susanna, the orphaned daughter of Rolf's best friend. She was such a ray of sunshine! I've never seen a happier child.

The young lady who came to me and to my wife, Amalie in the summer of 1918 was not the same person. I can only imagine the horrors she must have experienced. I must say, my grandson, Tom, had warned me but I had to see it to believe it.

Susanna was beautiful! Her dark, curly hair was pulled back away from her face and her complexion was flawless. I've always been a man who liked a woman with some meat on her bones, but my poor Susanna was shockingly thin. Food was short everywhere and I wished we could fatten her up. There wouldn't be much hope of that, but I thought maybe we could help.

As a little girl she would have run to us with hugs and kisses, but this time when Joseph helped her out of an old borrowed sedan, she obviously didn't want to see us. I wasn't there at the time, but Amalie told me that she ran to her and was soon wrapping her arms around our precious girl.

I noticed that she seemed to have an intimate relationship with young Joseph, almost like husband and wife as they demonstrated concern for each other and understanding of different expressions that needed no words. I also noticed animosity between Susanna and my son, Pierre and I wondered what had happened. He had always been her favorite uncle. Pierre seemed to have special understanding of her peculiar ways and of her incredible genius. The rest of us loved her and accepted her, but we didn't come close *to understanding her.*

After Joseph left to go back to Paris, we tried to get to know her, but she was so quiet. The joy that had lived in her soul seemed to have dried up and blown away. We knew about the beating she had taken and about the horrible death of her man friend. Amalie and I wondered if there was nothing left inside of her until I took her to town with me one day. She found an old piano while she waited for me at the church. It was out of tune, but she was transformed. When we heard the music, the meeting was concluded. By the time we got to her, a crowd had already gathered. She was laughing; they were singing; and I knew that my beautiful granddaughter was going to make it. The road to health would be a long one, but we would help her. After all, love can cure anything, can it not?

Chapter 11

It was October 15 and the weather was getting cold in France. I had no coat so one day my grandparents took me to Rouen to look for one. Clothes were so scarce they weren't sure they would be able to find anything. It was a cool, crisp day with the leaves turned red and orange and the sun shining brightly. We looked everywhere for an adequate coat, but were unable to find anything.

Grand-mere thought it was unusual for a girl my age not to be upset about not finding what I wanted. She just didn't have any idea what a small thing finding a coat was to me. I didn't want to be cold because that would be inconveneint, but I wouldn't freeze to death and eventually I knew we would find something for me to use. Unfortunately I knew my grandmother was beginning to understand some of what had happened to me because one day she walked into my room when I was undressed and I know she saw my scars. I think we were both horrified. We stared at each other and then I put on my veneer of normalcy and acted as if the scars weren't there. I never discussed how I had gotten them and I didn't complain. I still didn't know if my mother's family would disown me for being a traitor or not.

Both of my grandparents coaxed me to write to my parents. "Your mother and father have both written to you a number of times. Even your other grandparents have written almost every day, but you still remain silent. What is your explanation for this?" Guillaume, my grandfather, gently demanded.

"Please don't ask me. I can't talk about it. This is such a beautiful day. We need to enjoy it. My parents have four little boys plus Joseph and Tom. They're just fine."

"Susanna, you are a joy to us and we would like you to stay with us forever, but that would break your parent's hearts. We had eight children, but when we lost Andre and Paul, they left a vacuum that can never be filled. We'll never be whole again even though we have six other children and many grandchildren," Guillaume explained.

"But I'm adopted and that's different."

"You didn't think it was different when you were a small child. You thought your father hung the moon and your mother hung the stars. Do you blame them for what happened?"

I squirmed. I did find them responsible, but was afraid for anyone to know. "No," I lied, "I don't, but I just don't fit in their world anymore. You can't understand, but I just can't go back ever. I can't explain it. When the war is over I don't know what I'll do about Joseph. I love him so much, but I know I can't follow him home. It's too much to ask of me."

"This doesn't sound like you. Can't is a word you never used to use. I don't know what all happened to you, but surely you can overcome it. Joseph wants to go home so much and he thinks you'll go too. Our son, Pierre, must know more than we gave him credit for. You aren't ready for marriage if you don't intend to go with him."

That hurt like a slap! "He could stay here. He might not like it there either. After all, he hasn't been home in years."

"He loves his country. He'll want to go home."

I felt numbed by his comment because I didn't want to go and yet I suddenly realized how much it meant to Joseph to be home.

Grand-pere said, "Since we are in the house together, we will sit down and have tea together. We need to talk. Do you trust us, child?"

"Yes," I answered, not entirely sure that I was telling the truth.

"Tell us about it. Let us help."

"Nobody can help," I said sadly. "I'm ruined inside."

Grand-pere was gentle. "Even St. Dismus wasn't ruined. He had been a criminal all his life, but he changed while up on the cross with our Lord and went to heaven on that very day. If he could do that, nobody on this earth is ruined. Tell us about it."

We talked all afternoon. I still believed I had been a traitor no matter what reassurance Joseph, Alessandro and the sisters had given me that I was not. My grandparents reassured me by telling me about their work for intelligence. "Would I tell you that if I didn't trust you, child?" Grand-pere asked.

I knew he had taken great risk by telling me that. Truly he must be willing to stake his life on my innocence. I nodded my head, agreeing that, indeed, he must believe that I hadn't been a traitor. "The problem is how do I go home where everything is perfect, where I'm expected to be perfect and act like nothing ever happened? I can't do it. I have a sadness inside that I can't get rid of. It feels so heavy on me..." I stopped till I could talk again "...that sometimes I can hardly breathe. Only you who have been here know about the suffering all around us. What about Papi leaving me here all this time by myself? Now I'm asked to act as if nothing ever happened! I have a story and so does everybody else, but my story has ruined me."

Grand-pere was stern. "Your father and your brother and all the rest of us, including Joseph searched everywhere for you! Until Tom notified us that you had been found, your father had investigators looking for you every day since the war started, but we could never find a trace of you. Why didn't you contact us? We could have come!"

"I didn't contact you because by the time it was possible to correspond, I was already ruined. After that I went downhill every day. I couldn't stand for any of you to see what had happened to me."

"Now you see that it was nonsense for you to have felt that way. Love accepts the good with the bad and, besides, you never did anything wrong. What you did was save the lives of many people and put a spot of joy in their lives at the same time."

Doggedly, he went on. "We are now back to the place where your parents love you and want you to come home. Your grandmother and I do understand about the hurt, but we need to find a solution to your problem. You don't want to disappoint Joseph by failing to join him in America after the war and surely you don't want to hurt your mother and father either," he continued. "We will not discuss the possibility of your father not loving you enough to come for you because that, of course, is nonsense."

Then he asked, "Why don't I write a long letter to your parents? I'll tell them what happened and how you feel now. They'll cry and they'll feel guilty because they sent you over here in the first place. I don't doubt that they will miss more than a few meals over it, but after all, we've all missed more than a few meals here in France and you almost starved to death at one time. Their suffering will help them understand yours and ours and everybody else's. It's what needs to be done. You know Tom has to be having a hard time of it too."

I looked at Grand-mere, "What do you think?"

"I agree with your grandfather. It all needs to come out in the open. The people in America have no idea how things have been and nobody would ever dream everything that's happened to you."

"I don't want anybody feeling sorry for me."

"Nor do we, but how can we pull our lives back together if we have no understanding of each other?"

I thought a minute then finally said, "Let me talk to Joseph about it when I do my show this weekend. If it might help Tom or you or

Joseph, then you should do it. Possibly it would be best not to tell them everything about me since it sounds bad and we don't know how they might react. Just tell them enough so they understand why I can't write or go home then tell them about yourselves and the poor soldiers. I really am handling things just fine."

"Yes, you have held together remarkably well considering everything," Grand-pere agreed as he rested his hand on my arm. "You are a remarkable young girl."

The next weekend I was unusually bright and happy when the sisters and I met with Joseph. I told him about the letter and asked his opinion. To me, the letter would free me of all possibility of ever having to contact my family again. Joseph could see where I was coming from and reminded me that as his wife, it was my duty to stand by his side wherever he lived whether it was in Italy, France, or the United States. Then he reminded me that I would be going to the United States. I was crushed, but covered it up so nobody would notice. Joseph noticed everything. He said, "You make me worry that after I'm shipped out, you won't follow me. I need you, Susanna, and I don't want to have to be concerned that your love for me is so superficial that as soon as I'm gone you'll forget all about me."

"I could never forget all about you," I cried. "I love you, but my love for you is not conditional. I don't require you to stay with me in order to love you. I'll love you till the day I die."

"This long separation hasn't been good for us." He was angry. I hadn't seen him like that since we were children. "My love is not conditional either, but two people who love each other should live together and I want to go home…to our home!"

"And I don't want to go to your home. It isn't my home anymore. I wouldn't fit in. Can't you see? I'm not a Von Helldorf and I don't fit the mold and I never did!"

Unc walked up and looked from Joseph to me. "Having a lovers quarrel? Maybe now you are getting some sense. Susanna, it is time for you to go back to Rouen and Joseph, you need to be looking for a woman your own age."

Joseph's eyes shot fire when he said, "If this marriage doesn't work out I'll hold you responsible for the rest of my life! You have done everything in your power to put a wall between us, but I don't care if I live to be a hundred years old, I'll never love anybody else till the day I die! Do you understand?"

Unc sighed and looked down at the ground. "Yes, unfortunately, I understand more than you think. Come along child," he ordered as he took my arm and led me to the waiting vehicle.

I refused to talk to my uncle on the way back to Rouen and for most of the next two days I had nothing to say. The only way I could have Joesph in my life was to live in Bayland. The thought of pulling into the Bayland train station and seeing my family made me so depressed that I could almost feel my body become heavier until I thought I couldn't move.

One sunny afternoon while I was sitting on a broken down tree limb in the pasture a long distance from the house Grand-pere said "You seem to have a lot on your mind, little one. What's the matter?"

Joseph wants to go back to Bayland. I wish he'd stay here or go to Italy. People over here need good doctors so much."

"Everybody needs a good doctor. He wants to go home. You should understand that."

"I should, I know, but what I know and what I feel are two different things. We had an argument and he was angry when I left Paris. I don't think I'll see him again. I shouldn't have married him. It wasn't in the Church so maybe he can get the marriage annulled."

"Mon chere, I don't think he will be discouraged that easily. He will be back into your life as soon as you return to Paris. I understand from your grand-mere that you will be playing for the soldiers again very soon. Many think the armistice is near. You will have many things to talk about and you must straighten things out then."

"I don't see how we can. Unc won't allow us to be alone for even a minute and Joseph is unreasonable about going back to Bayland. He won't consider staying here."

"Then you must consider returning to the States and trying to make yourself at home there once again. If you are not happy, then Joseph can get his annulment and you can return to France to live with us and you will have lost nothing."

"I never thought about it that way. Maybe I could just go over for a little while to be near him for a little longer."

"Indeed, that is a very good idea," he agreed wisely.

I was in Paris to do a show November 9. I had already made a name for myself and everybody in the city knew about Luciana. Spirits were soaring everywhere. Austria signed an armistice November 3 and just that day Kaiser Wilhelm II of Germany had abdicated. Unc had agreed to let me stay until after the festivities of the armistice, and then I would go back to Rouen.

I hadn't seen or heard from Joseph since my last trip several weeks before. It seemed as if I had lost another important person in my life and my heart was heavy. My music was the only happiness I could find and even my music told a story of sorrow. My practice reflected the constant sorrow I carried. The afternoon of the concert as I played, a voice from the auditorium said, "If you play that at the concert, everybody will go home."

I knew the voice, but stopped playing and turned to see if it was real. By now he was standing at front stage with his arms stretched up for me to jump down into them. Not caring what the nuns who were waiting for me thought, I ran to him and did jump into his waiting arms. Without saying a word he carried me up the aisle and out the door. Outside he kissed me soundly and took my hand. Let's get out of here and go where we can be alone to talk. He guided me to a hotel room and ordered me inside.

He said, "I've missed you so much. I can't live this way any longer. You are my wife and I'm a grown man. Somehow we have to straighten things out. Do you still love me?"

My heart was pounding. "Of course I do. You are my world. There's nothing but my music left in it since you haven't written. I wrote to you but you never answered."

"I'm sorry. At first I wanted to teach you a lesson and then I was ashamed and then I was sad. Finally, I knew I had to do something to clear things up because I couldn't stand losing you again."

We spent the afternoon together, alone, as friends, not as husband and wife. When it was time for my show, he escorted me directly to the auditorium. Unc looked at us disapprovingly, but said nothing. He knew it wouldn't be wise to get me upset right before a show and though I was afraid of what action he would take because of the unchaperoned time Joseph and I had spent together, I felt light and happy. I supposed later I would not be so happy, but for the moment all was well.

My show was met with enthusiasm and my own spirits were high until afterwards when Unc gave me a tongue-lashing like I had never had before. He left me in the chapel to pray over my sins then later dragged me to a priest who could be unbiased to hear my confession. I told the priest that I was sorry to have sinned, but I didn't think I had committed one except for being married outside of the Church. We had not been together in the flesh since the night of our marriage. Could marrying outside of the church possibly be so terribly sinful? He assured me that as long as Joseph and I didn't spend time together as man and wife, we hadn't sinned.

Germany signed the armistice on Monday. People were so happy they were dancing in the streets. The town was in an uproar. Joseph said it was hard to even keep his mind on his work. All he wanted to do was pick up his things and his wife and head for home. Soldiers would start being sent out soon and each ship would have a doctor on it. It would be a while before civilians would be able to leave Europe so he planned to try to stay as long as possible or go back and forth if he could.

I was glad to have the war over. I had helped in the hospital in Rouen some, but the American doctors were very particular about who did what and I hadn't been able to do much more than dress feet that were decayed with trench foot or hold the hands of the dying men. These were important duties, but when I saw the hatchet jobs the young men were given as the busy doctors repaired facial wounds, it pained me that I didn't have my credentials now. Oh well, none of it mattered anymore. The war was over. Maybe there would never be another war. People said it was the war to end all wars. I hoped so. It had left such destruction in its wake.

When I left Paris, Joseph promised to come as soon as possible. He also promised to try to stay as long as he could, but we both knew when the orders came he would move out fast and there would be little he could do about it. I was relieved that Unc had not refused for me to stay with my grandparents because of what he thought Joseph and I had done. He had been so angry at both of us that I wondered if he would become violent. I wondered if God ever became angry like that too.

The farm was bleak and cold. I spent more and more time outside. Sometimes I just walked and other times I found little chores to do. My parents were writing every day, though the letters came in bundles some days and none at all other days. Sometimes I read them and other times it hurt too much. Finally, without permission, Guillaume wrote a detailed letter that I read years later while going through my mother's things after her death. She saved it at the bottom of her handkerchief box for many years along with several other letters that had been dear to her. The letter from Guillaume told about everything that had happened to me. He told them about the feelings I had shared with he and Amalie and asked Rolf if there was any possibility that he could come for me. "The child needs you very much. She just can't face the normalcy you can provide for her and I'm afraid it's tearing her apart a little more each day. She has promised Joseph she will allow Pierre to take her over to the States, but I fear she never will no matter how much she loves your son."

Two weeks after Guillaume sent the letter, Joseph showed up at the farm. I knew without him telling me that he had gotten orders to leave. I turned my back to him so he wouldn't see the sadness on my face when he told me he would be going in three days.

"That's good," I said, determined to sound cheerful. "I know how much you have looked forward to going home. Will you get to go straight to Bayland or what?"

"I'll be stationed in New York City to check out the men before they're discharged and sent home. I may be able to spend a day or so in Bayland if the train schedules work out right. I have ten days to report for duty after I arrive in the country."

"That's good. Be sure and tell everybody hello for me. I guess Paul and the twins won't know you either. Tell Tom I love him." I couldn't find any words after that.

"Seeing them won't be nearly as good as being with you. Promise you'll come."

"I'll try."

"You'll try?" He gave me a little shake and said loudly, "Susanna, come on! Promise!" He didn't care if his grandparents and Helene and the children did hear. "You've got to promise!"

"I'll do the best I can!" I almost screamed.

"Grand-pere, do something!" he begged in desperation.

"I already have. I wrote a detailed letter to your father and told him everything that happened in the last four years, not only to Susanna, but to everybody else too. I told him why Susanna never wrote and how she felt about things and how this problem with going home was affecting the relationship between you two. He sent a telegram right away and should be over here sometime in the next two weeks. Evidently it's easy to come here--just hard to get back over there. I have no doubt that he'll be able to take care of everything." He turned to me and said, "It's going to break my heart to lose you, little one, but it's best for you."

I was still in a state of shock. My grandfather was usually quiet and not one to get forceful about things. "You told him everything?"

"Yes. He wrote a long letter right after that; I just got it. He was pretty upset, but it's like I told you little one, it'll be good for he and my daughter to be upset. They need to know. We've sent those rosy little letters too many times. It's time to tell the truth."

I was already worried, "I know you did what you thought was best, but I don't know what I'll ever say to him. I don't want to see him, not ever and for sure I never wanted him to know about all of this. What'll he think of me?"

"First of all, it shouldn't be necessary to say much. I already told him everything in my letter."

Joseph spent all three days of his leave in Rouen. On the third day Joseph thanked his grandfather for taking matters into his own hands. He held me and kissed with all his love, then with tears in his eyes he embraced each member of the family and left. We stood watching him till his little truck went over the horizon. Grand-mere hurried everybody into the house for tea, as she said, "Before we all freeze to death, we must have some tea." Nobody talked about Joseph or Rolf, though they were on the minds of each of us.

Grand-pere and I discussed the garden he would plant and he made me promise to send plenty of good seeds, but I promised to help him find seeds in France. I also promised to help him plant it and keep it free of weeds. Grandfather ignored the message I was sending. We went on to talk about fertilizer and how he needed a few cattle just for that purpose. He hoped to get the farm operational by spring and I suggested that we go out and get started repairing fences. He could see that I needed to be busy even more than usual so he took me up on my offer to help.

That night as I lay in bed, I thought of Joseph moving farther and farther away from me. It was all over now. He wouldn't be back. I didn't have any tears left as I tossed and turned sleeplessly. I hoped Papi had changed his mind and decided to stay home in Bayland with his wife and four little sons. Before the sun was up, Minnie and I were up and about. I had to be busy to keep from thinking. Loud, sad music pounded in my head till I could hardly think! I scrubbed the kitchen floor and washed the windows, then started in on the large living room floor, humming the sad refrain as I worked.

"I don't believe this house has ever been as clean as it has since you came to stay with us," Helene said as she looked around. "Maybe I need to do more cleaning to take things off my mind like you do. We all know you aren't happy even though you always act like you are. At least you have a choice to go on with your life if you want to. You still have Joseph. My wonderful Edouard is gone forever. As soon as you get the chance, go to him. The two of you can work out your problems. What's worse? Living here without him or living there with him and a bunch of people who love you but don't know how to treat you? I'd go to China if I thought Edouard would be there waiting for me."

It was as if a curtain had come up and suddenly I could see very clearly. It was true that Helene had no idea the extent of my physical and emotional devastation in the past, but Joseph was my anchor and being with him would be worth anything. After thinking for a few seconds I said, "I never thought of it that way. Thanks Aunt Helene." I hugged her. "Want go out for a walk? The kids can take care of themselves for a while."

It was the first time I had ever really talked to my aunt since I had moved in three months before. I chatted with her almost like I used to talk to my mother. Edouard had died almost four years ago and Helene didn't think she would ever marry again although there was a man she had met at the hospital who seemed interested in her. She told me that she hated to be disloyal to her husband by allowing herself to love another man. I told her about Alessandro and the things Mother Angelica had said. That day we became good friends, finding a common ground and helping each other to overcome our troubles.

I accompanied Grand-mere, who was a midwife, just like my mother, on most of her deliveries and most of them were uneventful. She was always proud of me as we worked together. It was hard for her to imagine a 16 year-old-girl knowing so much about delivering babies, though I had told her of my experiences in Italy.

In three short months I had gotten to know most of Rouen through my piano playing and my trips with grand-mere to deliver babies. I tried to always be friendly to people and felt genuine interest in their well-being. I never actually gave away anything about myself to them, but I had already learned that people are basically self-centered and if you are a good listener, they will like you. I also knew that if I kept them focused on themselves they wouldn't be particularly interested in me. That worked for everybody but the people I lived with. They constantly tried to get inside of me to see how I was feeling, what I wanted, how they could make me happy. It had taken all these months for me to warm up to them. They often said that they wondered what was going on inside of me.

I wrote to Joseph every day and often sent letters to Tom now. When the letters for Tom started arriving in Bayland, it made Gabrielle cry. She thought that I didn't care about her or my father anymore. She blamed Papi and herself for sending me to Luxembourg and especially blamed herself because she had been the one who had told Papi to stop worrying. With her parents only 200 miles from Herr Strashoffer, she had been certain that I would be safe. After receiving Grand-pere's letter she was sure that I blamed her and Papi for everything.

One day Tom found Mother crying all by herself in the library because she was sure she had lost me forever. He stayed with her long enough to have a cup of tea and some cake to calm her down then he left the house, plunging through the snow on his crutches with his stump swinging. Gabrielle watched him go.

He got Jim, the farm manager, to help him up on his horse and hung his crutches down on the side. In minutes he was off to the Western Union station. Dismounting was hard, but his old horse was patient and seemed to understand that he needed a little help as he always stood dead still for Tom, patiently waiting for him until he was ready to go.

That afternoon he sent a telegram to Rouen. It was addressed to Susanna Von Helldorf and said:

SUSANNA =
WRITE TO MAMA =
YOU NEED TO STOP THINKING OF ONLY YOURSELF =
YOU ARE BREAKING HER HEART =
TOM.

I was outside with Grand-pere when the telegram came. It scared me at first because telegrams usually meant something bad. When I read it, I couldn't understand how I could possibly be breaking anybody's heart, but Grand-pere, who was always insightful, explained it to me. I didn't believe it.

"She must be grieving for you if Tom thought it necessary to send a telegram. You'd better go in and write to her right now. I don't care what you say as long as you tell her you love her. We'll take it into town as soon as you finish...go on!" he said with a firm tone to his voice. "You can't put it off any longer."

In my letter I marveled over the fact that I had a three-year-old brother I had never seen. I mentioned that everybody was well, including Minnie who was my constant companion. I told them that in the spring I was planning to help Grand-pere with his garden and that I had the reputation of having a green thumb among my friends in Italy. There was mention of my shows and how I missed them now. Only once did anything touch on the negative and that was when I mentioned that sometimes things had been a little tough in the past four years, but all that was behind me and I was a better person because of everything that had happened.

I never dreamed the sadness that would overcome my mother by what I wrote next, though I never meant for it to cause unhappiness. I explained why I hadn't written by saying, "I'm sorry I haven't written, but I have been gone so long, I didn't think you would still care. I've always loved you so much that I try not to think about you. It's important not to think about anything that's sad and I feel sad knowing we'll probably never see each other again." I signed it simply Susanna.

Evidently Grand-pere and I passed Papi on the road into town, but never recognized him. Posting the letter seemed to take a burden off my shoulders. I even managed to get Grand-pere to sing along with me on the way back to the farm. We were in good spirits as we hurried through the slush and snow into the house. I was bent over taking my wet shoes off when I saw a pair of legs standing in front of me. I froze as I looked up to see who it was. Seeing that it was Papi, I crouched down towards the floor without speaking, in shock. All along I had managed to convince myself that he would never come and now he was standing right in front of me!

He came down to me and on his knees he pulled me to him. "Liebchen," he said gently. "It's all over now. Shhh." My whole body convulsed with emotion.

"Oh Papi, I used to pray that Mr. Switzer would tell you where we were and you would come for me. When the snow melted in the mountains I used to think I heard you calling, then I knew you'd never come. So many times I wanted to ask you what to do."

He held me at arm's length so he could see me. I wore my shabby new plaid coat that was about six sizes too big and I knew that my curly brown hair was sticking up everywhere as it always had done when the weather was damp, but in spite of it all, he said, "You have grown up to be a beautiful young woman. Tom didn't exaggerate when he said you were every man's dream."

After looking me over, he hugged me again and he cried. When we stood up, he was amazed at how tall I was. "Your mother was just a little bitty thing!" he exclaimed as he held his hand out at waist length. "Look at you. You must be 5'5" or maybe 5'6"?"

"You're very good, I'm 5'5" tall, and when things are going good I weigh 105 pounds, but sometimes I go below a hundred and then I eat everything in sight to fatten up," I lied, knowing the weight loss always came with hard times when there wasn't enough to eat. I stared at him so long that a worried look crossed his face. When I realized what I was doing I said, "Sorry, Papi. I just can't seem to get over seeing you. Grand-pere said you were coming, but somehow I was sure you wouldn't." I didn't mean to hurt him, but when I said that, I did.

He looked at me sadly and said, "That stings all the way to the center of my being. I have loved you as much as I have loved any of my sons. You are the last living remnant of your father, Henry, the best friend I have ever had in my life. You are what is left of the world Tom and Joseph and I shared with you and your parents for so many years and you are my daughter as much as you were Henry's daughter and as much as my sons are sons. I will always love you dearly"

All the Jude's had tears in their eyes and smiles on their faces as they left us alone to go make a pot of tea, but I could only wonder if he would have left one of his beloved sons alone for four-and-a-half years through an entire war.

I showed him the crumpled telegram I had received that day and wondered about it out loud, "I can't imagine why Mama would care if I wrote or not. She must be busy with four little boys of her own and now she has Tom back, but Grand-pere thought I should send a letter right away. That's where we were, posting the letter."

I could see his shoulders slump forward slightly as another look of sadness crossed his face. "I'm sad to think you might believe we love you less than the other children. Did you think we loved you any less when Henry or the twins were born?"

"Well, not when Henry came along, but everybody was so busy when the twins were born and then I was sent to Luxembourg and nobody ever came for me...."

I could feel him watching me when I turned sideways so he couldn't see my face. "We talked to Switzer and he swore he had no idea where you were. I told him I'd kill him if he was lying to me. Nobody knew where your grandfather had taken you and when you wrote those two letters, you never said where you were. They were post-marked Rome and the return address on the second envelope was so badly damaged that we couldn't make it out. My detectives even went to the compound where you...where all that happened and nobody ever claimed to have ever heard of you or seen you. "I would have come. I swear to you, if I had to take a canoe across the ocean. I would have come."

I couldn't help but smile as I thought of him paddling across the ocean, then I got serious, "Grand-pere said he wrote everything about me in his letter. I'm not good anymore like the rest of the family. Why did you come?"

"My God, Liebchen, what are you talking about? Anybody less than you would never have survived it at all! I'm proud of you!"

"He must not have told you everything," I said suspiciously. "Did he say I lived in a cave, worse than a dog? Did he tell you I ate out of garbage cans and felt lucky to find food that didn't smell too bad! If the stuff in them looked good enough, sometimes I ate with both hands! I didn't bathe either, and I had lice. My hair had to be cut... CUT! It was so dirty and matted and full of lice that Mother Maria Elizabeth had to cut it!" I was almost screaming now. "I was tried for treason and convicted! I was guilty! I don't have more than a few inches on my body that aren't scarred from the beating I got--and deserved for hiding an Austrian spy! I've watched people be executed and I've hated, and I've had men swear at me and use language I never dreamed existed! I am dirty trash Papi! You shouldn't have come!" I stood up and took my coat off the hook and put it back on. "I'll go outside while you try to decide what to do. I know you can't leave for a while, but I can probably stay in Paris while you're here. I know you won't want anything to do with me now that you know all about it. I'm sorry you came all this way, Papi."

I ran out of the house and kept on running till I was several miles away. When I was finally exhausted I sat down under a tree, bare of leaves, closed my eyes, and tried hard not to think of anything. It was very quiet there. The only sounds were of the wind blowing the creaking limbs of the tree and the drops of rain hitting the leaf covered ground. When thoughts started creeping back into my conscious, I asked myself what I was going to do. I hadn't brought anything with me. Even Minnie hadn't had time to escape out the door with me! I didn't see how I could ever face my father again. His rejection would be more than I could take. I knew he would be polite to me, but his opinion of me would be so much less than it had been when I was a child. After all that had happened, how could it be anything else?

The temperature plummeted as the sun set and a cold wind took my breath away. If I sat there without any shelter all night I would surely die. To have lived through so much and then commit suicide at the end seemed wrong, besides, there were things I wanted to do in my life. Finally I decided that I would go back to the house, be polite, and try not to get upset by anything. Papi didn't mean anything to me anymore anyway. I'd get a hot bath and go to bed. In the morning I would get up early and go to Paris. It was time for me to start making my own way. I couldn't stay with the Jude's any more.

Papi was sitting in the living room by the door waiting for me when I entered the house. "I decided I would stay here forever waiting for you if necessary," he said gently.

I took my wet shoes off and rubbed my red hands together, stalling for time. "It's getting cold outside," I said. "Would you like to come with me into the kitchen for a cup of hot tea? I'm freezing."

"That sounds good." He put his arm around my shoulders and for some reason it felt good. "Can we start over again, Liebchen?"

"If you still want to," I answered shyly, wondering why suddenly I didn't feel like running away anymore. "I just wanted to be sure you understood."

"I understand. You're still my daughter and I still love you the same as always or maybe more because now I know how empty life is without you and I know what a strong person you are."

"Thanks, Papi." There was suddenly a lump in my throat and I could hardly breathe.

Over our tea we talked about everybody in Bayland, including my best friend Ilona, and I filled him in on Jacob and Laure. She's waiting for passage to Ohio. Joseph told her she could stay at our house till Jacob gets discharged. He seemed sure you wouldn't mind. He's been pushing me pretty hard to go home and I think he had an idea that I would feel obligated to go to help Laure. She's 25 years old and just now got married, isn't that something?"

"Your mama didn't marry me till she was 28."

"That was different. She was a nun and we had to persuade her to leave the convent first." I hesitated, and then added, "I can understand being a nun now. Living in a convent is pretty nice. It's safe and peaceful and the sisters all stick together. They never say or do anything mean to each other."

Papi looked concerned, "You're not thinking of anything like that, are you?"

I laughed, "No. Mother Angelica said I would make a good nun, but it takes a better person than me to be worthy of something like that. I plan to go to medical school as soon as I get accepted. There are Joseph and Minnie to consider too. I don't think any convent will let me bring both of them and I couldn't go alone."

"What about you and Joseph? I still haven't seen him."

"We still love each other, but it's a little different sort of thing now that we're both grown. He wants me to go home and I haven't wanted to because of everything that's happened. I'm afraid I'll be even more of a misfit than ever. The last two times we've been together we've argued, but I guess all marriages survive problems like that. He knows I love him, but I don't see why we can't live here."

"He loves home. Once you get back, you'll love it too. What I don't understand is your comment about marriage. You two aren't thinking of getting married yet, are you? I wouldn't rush things. You're still very young and you've been through so much. Let your mother and I take care of you for a while."

"You sound like Unc," I teased, "He's been a real grouch ever since I came here. Joseph and I haven't been allowed to be alone together for a minute ever. When I went to Paris to do my shows two nuns were assigned to be with me every second and if we came near each other one of them would clear her throat loud enough to cause an echo," I giggled.

After that, there was no more talk of anybody moving out of the Jude house and my father and I quickly started picking up where we had left off four-and-a-half years before. Sometimes we laughed together and other times we had serious discussions about whether it is a sin to execute a prisoner or kill somebody during a time of war. We talked about triage and hopeless cases and how that had upset me in the beginning yet didn't seem to bother me much in the end. I wondered if I had become too hardened.

"People do what they have to in order to survive. You never would have gotten anything done if you had cried and mourned over every woman's son who came through your hospitals. When you live in normal circumstances, you'll be able to respond more normally, those were extreme situations," he reassured.

I told him about Alessandro, "He was the most kind, gentle man. When I think about him, I know I'll always love him for everything he was to me. Sometimes I wonder how I can love him and still love Joseph so much. I know it's what he would have wanted because he said so right before he died. ...Still, I wonder."

"I had the same situation when your Aunt Catherine died. I spent twelve years raising the boys without a wife. Of course, your parents were always at my side helping me, but it still wasn't the same as having a wife. Never once in those twelve years did I ever see anybody I would ever want to marry until Gaabrielle came along. She was so pure and good. For three years I tried to ignore her, but then after your parents were killed, we kept getting thrown together one way or another until I couldn't turn my back on my love for her any longer. I felt guilty too, but then I realized that maybe it was right that I not be alone forever and I've never regretted marrying again for a moment. Out of that marriage we have been so happy, you and the boys got a mother, and together we produced four more fine sons! It was right and it's probably right for you to love Joseph. Nobody will ever love you more, though you need to wait a while before you even think of marriage."

Slowly things began to straighten themselves out in my mind. We went for long walks, frequently including Amalia and Guillaume and occasionally even Helene, though she was becoming more involved with the gentleman she had mentioned to me the day we became friends. Lately all her free time was spent with him.

We visited Laure in Paris one day and agreed to get her ticket for passage on the same ship as ours. Papi was sure Jacob would want her traveling with us. She looked pale and thin and finally confided in me that she was pregnant and wasn't sure how she was going to make the trip, but was desperate to be with Jacob again. She hugged me and cried when we left. We promised to keep her informed of our progress in getting the tickets.

Afterwards Papi said, "She's a pretty girl, but she doesn't look very healthy. It's probably because she has to live in that dark, damp old building."

"No Papi, it's because she's carrying Jacob's child. She must have gotten pregnant as soon as she and Jacob were married and now she's really sick. I hope we get to take her home soon. She hadn't wanted to leave her family, but they're so poor, the only thing they have to give her is love. Love is important, but she needs to be with Jacob." I thought to myself, and I need to be with Joseph.

Unc visited several times, but never discussed the fact that Joseph and I had gotten married out of the church. He told me that I needed to tell him about it, but things were going so well that I never did. Papi asked if the ring I was wearing was an engagement ring and I happily admitted it. Grand-mere told me it was a disgrace not to tell him that the ring underneath it was a wedding ring, but I was afraid of upsetting him.

At mass in Paris one Sunday Unc refused to give me communion. Papi was irritated, not with me, but with Pierre for denying me. "What could the child have possibly done wrong?" he asked.

Later, when Pierre had me alone he scolded me. "I know you and Joseph got together after the concerts at least once when you visited here and don't tell me you didn't! You should be spanked, but Joseph is just as bad as you are. You've both pushed me to the limit. Did you get together in my father's house too?"

"No!" I protested.

"I don't believe you!" he said harshly. As soon as we get you home we're going to have a family meeting and get this straightened out once and for all! Either the marriage will be blessed or you two need to be sent off in opposite directions."

"Opposite directions?" I asked. "You're the one who keeps screaming that I need to go home! I never wanted to go home. You're also the one who refused to marry us and to this day refuses to bless our marriage. What do you want?" My face was hot and I knew it was flushed when Papi joined us.

"What's going on?" he asked as he looked from one to the other.

"Unc is being his usual disagreeable self," I answered.

Pierre said nothing, but it was easy to see that he was mad too.

"You two used to get along so well, now I'm not sure if you love each other or hate each other."

ROLF

I'm afraid I didn't adjust to having a grown daughter very well. Susanna had been through terrible things and had grown up without any guidance. She had done her best, under the worst of circumstances, but deep down inside of me, I couldn't quite forgive her for it. I felt cheated and I wanted my little girl back.

One day she said, "Papi, you need to understand that I love Joseph and I plan to spend my life with him."

Purposly trying not to understand I told her, "We all love him and, Lord willing, the whole family will get back together and we'll never be very far apart again."

She didn't argue. All she did was walk away, withdrawing into her shell where it was safe. And then I felt angry. Sixteen was too young to be talking of love; I huffed to myself. The child hand't even finished her education. Anyway, what did she know of love?

Understanding my daughter was troublesome to me. Most of the time I saw a serious girl who behaved like a 40-year old woman, very matter-of-fact, rarely displaying happiness or looking forward to the future. Then on the trip back to the States, when she performed for a large crowd of people on the ship, I saw her laugh, sing, and rattle the walls and everything else in the ballroom with her sometimes bawdy and other times spine-chilling music. As she presented her show under the name of Luciana, I saw the lovliest young woman I had ever laid my eyes on! After her show I wanted to trounce every young buck who came near her drooling and panting. Couldn't they see that she was only a child?

My emotions were in such turmoil that I lost all sensitivity and common sense!

Later, when we met up with the rest of the family in New York City, and I realized that my one son had already trespassed on her virtues, I thought I would die!!

Chapter 12

I wrote to Joseph every day and to my mother and Tom several times a week. I sent little one-page messages to my other grandparents too. I truly was making an effort to reach out to them, though I still had misgivings about ever fitting into the VonHelldorf family again. As the weeks went by, the false cheerfulness I worked hard to display was being replaced by genuine happiness. When letters came from home, I read them out loud to everybody and commented on them. Tom and Joseph had both given our mother pictures of me that had been taken when they were with me in Verona, and Papi sent pictures of all the Jude's as well as pictures of me. In turn, Mother sent pictures of herself, the grandparents, and of the four little boys. She told little details about each child to help me get to know them. I was elated, but still wondered if the little boys would like me or if they would ever see me as their sister.

Christmas was hard on everybody but me. It was the only one I had actually celebrated in years even though I, of course, had gone to the Christmas masses when I lived in Verona. I would have liked to be with Joseph, but was glad to be with Papi, my French grandparents, and the rest of the Jude family. Gabrielle said she was very lonely even though she had most of her family together and she knew we were safe. Since their courtship, she and Papi had never been separated for such a long time. He missed her and the little boys terribly and he missed Tom and Joseph, but he said he was so grateful to have me back that he was comforted beyond words. What was left of the war torn Jude family got together to celebrate. The dinner was festive even though it was modest.

Papi quickly learned what I had been trying to tell him, that money couldn't buy what didn't exist. "You can't imagine how glad we were to finally find a coat for me," I told him. "It was the first of November and had already snowed a little and I still didn't own a coat! Joseph found this one in Paris. It's big, but warm."

Finally in mid-January we got the news that we would be heading home on the Olympus on February 1. We sent word to Pierre and Laure in Paris immediately and sent a telegram to Joseph and one to Mother. Joseph made arrangements to be on leave for a week after we arrived and made reservations for everybody at a hotel. He and I would have adjoining rooms. Jacob was planning to be there too.

Guillaume and Amalie were more and more quiet as the departure day for Uncle Pierre, Papi, and I approached. They were particularly fond of me, I knew. Finally one day Papi asked them if maybe they would like to go along. They brightened right away. Tickets were hard to come by, but he was able to pay extra and a room was found for them. More telegrams were sent and soon everything was set up for them to go too. There were now six people traveling together. Helene said we were going to make her jealous if we kept acting so happy, but the truth was, she would have never left France now that she had Gregoire, her new friend.

When the day finally came to leave Rouen, it wasn't traumatic as I thought it would be. I hugged Helene and left without a tear. After all, the grandparents I loved so much were coming along and so was Unc. Even though he scolded me and had treated me like a baby, I still loved him. Papi had made home look good to me and my mother's warm, loving letters convinced me that I was as loved as ever. I no longer felt like I was going to be a stranger when I got there.

We took a train to LeHavre and then a boat to England, and then boarded the ship there. The ship was large and elegant and we quickly made ourselves comfortable in our suites. Grand-mere and Grand-pere had a suite alone and Papi, Laure, Pierre, and I shared one. We each had a room and were happy sharing a sitting room. Papi was used to luxury, but the rest of us were used to every discomfort imaginable. Laure was still sick, but even she seemed to relax and rest once we were safely on the ship.

We stayed to ourselves most of the time the first two days until I found a grand piano that wasn't used during the day and spent the whole morning of the third day playing one piece after another. I always seemed to draw a crowd and soon the captain asked if I would do a performance that night. I agreed to do it, then decided out of courtesy that I should ask Papi for permission. I would have done it whether he wanted me to or not, but I thought it might make him feel good if I asked.

They billed me as Luciana, for Joseph, and I did one of my usual fun performances. Papi beamed when I introduced him as my father and made him play a duet with me. During a break I introduced the rest of my family. I played until midnight when everybody in my family was exhausted, but I promised to return the next night if anybody wanted to come again.

The time on the ship flew and soon we were sailing into New York Harbor. I didn't go out on the deck till we were close because I didn't want my hair to curl up before Joseph saw me. Finally I couldn't stand it anymore and I scampered outside with the rest of the family and Laure. A huge crowd was waiting, but as much as we strained to see, we couldn't locate Jacob or Joseph. It wasn't until we moved down the gangplank and looked through the crowd that two arms grabbed Papi and me from behind. It was Joseph! He hadn't seen his father in three-and-a-half years and he hadn't seen me in two-and-a-half months. He hugged us, squeezed us and couldn't seem to let go of either of us.

"Papa," he shouted, "You look great! France must agree with you!" Then he looked down at me, "You look beautiful as always." He said tenderly. He put his arms around me and kissed me with all his love, and then he held me and kissed me again.

"Joseph," Papi exclaimed. "She's just a child. Now I understand why your uncle assigned the nuns to watch over you! That isn't appropriate!"

Joseph paid no attention and though I heard it, I didn't pay any attention either. Joseph turned and embraced Grand-mere and Grand-pere. Jacob only had eyes for Laure when he saw her. There was no doubt of his love for the pretty Frenchwoman he had married. When the excitement had died down we went through all the formalities of collecting Minnie and our baggage, showing papers and so on. By the time we headed for a taxi to go to the hotel, we were tired and hungry and all talking at once.

At the hotel Unc carefully scanned the sleeping arrangements. "Ah ha!" he said, "Just as I thought. Excuse me Rolf, but this needs to be changed. You need to take the room adjoining Susanna's." Then, he added, "A young unmarried girl shouldn't be staying in a hotel by herself. You can move Joseph down the hall to the room that was assigned to you."

I could see that Joseph was burned to the core. He hadn't seen me in months and now we were going to have to sneak around just to have a little time alone. I actually think that he was beginning to hate his uncle. Though he said nothing, he slapped his gloves against the reception desk with a loud snap as he stalked off. My grandparents and I looked on as he fell into one of the lobby chairs.

Papi innocently said, "Well, it wouldn't have been as if she would have been alone, since Joseph would have been just next door," then he stopped, probably realizing what was going on. None of us could ever fool him about anything. He looked at Joseph sulking over in his chair in the lobby and said, "...I see what you mean. Yes I probably do need to be in the adjoining room."

In the confusion we never noticed any other familiar names in the guest book as we signed in. Only Joseph and Jacob knew about those, although Pierre had just ruined the effect of the surprise.

Even though Joseph and I were disappointed at not having adjoining rooms and everybody in our group was exhausted, we were still in good spirits. Before we went to our rooms to freshen up for lunch, all of us hugged and kissed each other as if we would never see each other again.

As soon as Papi and I were in our rooms there was a knock on his door. The doors between our rooms were open so I could see that it was Joseph. He said, "Papa, you need to come to my room. There's something important you need to see."

My father looked perplexed. He had just left Joseph a minute ago and already there was an urgent problem to be settled. Joseph hurried him down the hall with his arm around his shoulders to speed him along. I followed, out of curiosity, to see what could possibly be so urgent. The door was open when we got there. I watched them enter the room and saw my mother standing by the window, as beautiful and stately as ever.

"Rolf!" she cried, "I couldn't wait till you got to Bayland! Tom's here too." She had tears in her eyes as he hurried to embrace her.

Joseph turned and shut the door with a smile on his face. He grabbed my hand and led me up the hall back to my own room. When we were in the room with the door shut he said, "I think we're safe for a few minutes," and put his arms around me. "You can't imagine how much I've missed you!"

We were so glad to be together that we didn't move, instead we just held each other.

I finally started worrying that Papi would bring Mother to see me and asked, "Do we have time for this? They may come bursting in here any moment."

"I know, but I couldn't wait to have you to myself."

There was a knock on the door. "Just a minute!" I called as I reached for the dressing gown Joseph had given me in Paris.

He ran into Papi's room and shut the door before I opened mine. When I opened it, there stood Papi, Tom, and my mother. As I stood and looked at them, not knowing what to say, Joseph walked up behind them to watch.

"Mama! I missed you so much!" I cried. They were so overwhelmed that all they could do was smile teary smiles and look at me. The original family, Gabrielle, Rolf, Joseph, Tom, and I were finally all back together after close to five years.

Mother and I stood back and looked at each other again. She said admiringly, "You've grown up to be a beautiful young lady!"

"Well not too beautiful," I answered as I pointed at some of the scars showing below the short-sleeved dressing gown and at the revealing neckline.

"Your beauty shines right through, little one."

"Thank you, Mother; you always have had a way of making me feel wonderful. You haven't changed any since I left. I bet Grandmother is still fussing that you need to be fattened up."

"Right now she's pretty busy doting over Tom. Since he got home, she's completely driven to coddling him," she laughed.

"Are the babies with her and Grandfather?"

"Yes. It wouldn't be a vacation to travel with those little monsters!"

"Henry's close to the age I was when I left. He must be very grown up."

"He is. As a matter-of-fact, all four boys are much more mature for their ages than other children. It may be because we've been older parents or possibly it's due to the mood the family has been in over the years. I'm afraid there hasn't been much cheer with all of you gone and never knowing from day to day..." she teared up and couldn't say any more.

"Oh Mother, I'm so sorry. I never meant to make you sad," I said as I reached out to her. While we stood at the doorway holding each other and she cried some more, the others got in on the act and soon all of them were huddled together with teary eyes. I felt love for them, but still couldn't cry. A little part of me seemed numb and I wondered what was the matter with me. Other visitors in the hotel must have wondered what was going on as they watched us standing in the hallway crying, with all of us hugging, and speaking in three different languages as I tried to smile and tried to feel. Finally, after a long time, we left each other once again to get ready for lunch.

There was another emotional gathering when Mother found her parents. She hadn't seen them in six years. The war had brought Tom, Joseph, and I closer to our French family, but our mother had been left out of the loop. Until the war, we had only known our mother's family as guests in our home and had only visited France once. Now we were closer to them than to our father's parents who had almost always lived next door to us.

Mother immediately fell in love with Laure. Jacob had practically been part of the family since before she had married my father and she had always thought of him as a younger brother. She talked excitedly to the young woman about how wonderful it would be to have her in the family. Now she would have somebody else to speak French to!

We had lunch and talked for two hours afterwards. Back at the hotel Jacob and Laure excused themselves so Laure could rest for a while. In the past week her nausea had left her even though she had been on a ship, but she was still tired all the time. The rest of the group just moved from one room to another.

When Joseph and I got Tom alone, we told him about our marriage and our problems with Unc.

"You'd better be careful tonight with Unc and Papa both here at the same time. They'll be laying for you to make a wrong move," Tom said as he looked at me. "Papa obviously still thinks of you as his little girl. I can see it written all over his face. He'll kill you both if he suspects anything."

"We go through a whole war with people blowing things up around us constantly for years then have to come home to die!" I laughed. "At least I'll die happy. I never thought I'd be happy again and now, at this very moment, all my dreams have come true. I'm not afraid of Papi or Unc. I've lived through worse than their ire, though I have to admit, I'd hate to have them turn their backs to me."

Not wanting things to get too serious, Tom smiled and said, "I happen to have a serious lady friend. They said it would never happen to Bayland's most eligible bachelor, but I am very seriously thinking of buying the lady in question an engagement ring."

"Who is she? Anybody we know? You sure work fast!" Joseph noted.

"Not as fast as you two. Joseph rolls into Italy and the two of you get married three weeks later. Now that's fast!"

Joseph defended us, "But we knew each other all our lives! That was different!"

"Who are you seeing, Tom?" I asked. "I hope I like her. You know I don't like many women. Thank goodness I like Laure."

"You both know this young lady and, Susanna, you like her very much."

"Are you in love with Emily?"

Tom sat up looking confused, "Emily who?"

"Emily the cleaning lady, Hannah's helper. She's the only single female I can think of who I like. It must be her," I teased.

We were all laughing at the thought of Tom marrying poor old Emily.

"No it isn't Emily," he said rolling his eyes and looking perturbed. "It's your best friend in the whole world. Remember Ilona? Cute little Ilona? Well, right after I got back I was in Cleveland getting fitted for my new leg and afterwards I was eating at that little diner close to the conservatory and who should come in and sit right down beside me but Ilona. She's 18 now and really beautiful. As a child she was so plain, but now, I bet she has to beat the guys off with a stick! ...Anyway, I bought her lunch, then she asked me out...brassy little thing. I offered to take her dancing, but she said she hated to dance," he added with a twinkle in his eye. "We've been seeing each other ever since.

"I can only think of Ilona the way she was when I left," I said, remembering how she had looked when I waved to her from the back window of a taxi as I left the conservatory for the last time that day so long ago. "She was getting prettier, but she had a hair problem too. With the new permanent waves, she can have hair that's just the way it's supposed to be--not too curly and not too straight." Shaking my own mass of curls that refused to stay up in the ladylike twist I had put them in, I added, "I'll bet she is pretty! We always used to wish we were sisters! You have to marry her, but not before Joseph and I are officially married or we'll never forgive you."

That night after dinner, the members of the group slowly went their separate ways. It had been a long, exhausting day. Jacob and Laure were the first to leave, then Grand-pere and Grand-mere. Joseph and I were hoping Pierre would leave soon, but he stayed close occasionally giving a suspicious eye to us both. Finally Papi suggested that we call it a day.

After Pierre went down the hall to his room and was out of hearing distance, Joseph asked Papi, "I thought since Mama is here, you might like to have my suite. It's much nicer and more private than the room you have. I don't know why Unc insisted on changing the rooms. I can take care of Susanna if there are any problems."

"I appreciate your offer, but where we are is just fine. If Susanna needs anything, we want to be able to take care of her."

"She's not a baby. Remember, she's been on her own for over four years! If she needs anything I can take care of it."

I almost laughed. Papi pretended not to notice the smile I was choking down and was beginning to seem a little irritable. "We'll stay where we are." he said firmly.

"Well, goodnight, then," he sighed as he turned to go to his own room alone.

I hugged my parents, and then retired to my room. I figured my parents would close their door and that would allow me to slip out without them ever noticing. As a child they had always slept with their door closed. This night, though, they left the door open. Now I would have to be careful they were asleep before I went to Joseph's room.

I took my time getting ready for bed with a long, hot bath and a shampoo, and then turned out my light. When I thought I heard them breathing as if in sleep, I tiptoed in and checked on them. They definitely looked asleep so I went back into my room, opened the door that went out to the hallway, and met Joseph who had been waiting for me.

Just as we were hurrying down the hall arm in arm Unc stepped out of his room and stood in front of us with his arms crossed. At the same time we heard a gruff voice call, "Get back here this minute!" from behind us.

We stopped in our tracks. "Oh Joseph, he hasn't lost his touch. He'll kill us and disown me, only now we have Unc to contend with too!"

"You heard me, come here now!"

Neither of us had ever seen our father look more angry as he stood in the middle of the hallway with his hands on his hips. When we got up to him he gestured for us to enter his room. Unc followed. I tried to cover myself tighter as I stood in front of my mother and father and Unc with tears of embarrassment rolling down my cheeks.

Throughout our childhoods neither of us ever remembered our father raising his voice to us, even when we had done something really bad and were about to be punished. This time he roared.

"What's the matter with you two?"

Joseph put his arm around me.

"Take your hands off her! Have you both lost all your morals?" He looked at me, "Didn't your mother ever teach you anything?"

Tears were flowing freely down my cheeks as I yelled back at him, "I was only 11 years old the last time I saw my mother! She never had a chance!"

"So you just figured everything out for yourself, of course with Joseph's help! Joseph, how could you think of such a thing! I didn't raise you to take advantage of this little girl!"

"She's not a little girl! She is a grown up woman--my wife!" Joseph yelled.

Unc yelled, "She's not your wife!"

Everything was quiet as Mother cried and I stood with a burning angry face looking back and forth at my father and then at my uncle. Papi just looked at his son and then at me. "Your wife? What do you mean wife?" he asked quietly.

"She is not his wife!" Unc yelled again.

"Well, she's sort of my wife."

"There's no such thing as sort of. Either she is or she isn't your wife, now which is it?"

"They have both made a mockery of the sacrament of marriage," Unc added angrily.

"Let's sit down and talk without yelling at each other," Joseph suggested.

We all sat down and he started. "Do you remember the day Susanna was born? Uncle Henry put her in my arms. She was so perfect. As I held her I said, 'Someday I'm going to marry her.' I never treated her any way but as my girl, even when she was five. Remember I didn't want the adoption because I was afraid it would get in the way of our betrothal? You assured me if it was meant to be it would be. You said Susanna needed a family and for her welfare, you needed to adopt her. She never was my sister. I worked hard to make sure that she never saw me as anything but a future husband. The only time I got stupid was right before she left for Luxembourg. You'll remember I realized my mistake right away. I almost lost her because I was stupid and then while she was in Italy she became engaged to a good man, Dr. Alessandro Adami. If he hadn't been killed, I would have lost her forever.

"When Tom told me where she was, I told him I planned to marry her as soon as she would consent. I wasn't about to risk losing her again so I took an engagement ring to Italy with me. It took some doing, but in two weeks I managed to convince her not only to go back to France with me, but also to be my wife."

"He also convinced her to climb into his bed!" Unc interrupted angrily.

"Unc! I did not! I would have never have done anything like that to Susanna," Joseph growled.

"Go on Joseph," Papi ordered as his face grew crimson.

"Susanna could have had her pick of the men. They used to

swarm all around her when she did her shows. I wanted to kill every one of them!"

Joseph continued, "The first thing we did when we got to Paris was ask Unc to marry us. He refused. He said we hadn't been together long enough; Susanna was just a child; she had been through too much; it wasn't fair to you and Mama. You name it, and if it was negative, he said it! She had been on her own for all those years and he had the nerve to say she was still a child! It made me so mad I never wanted to see him again.

"I told him we would go to another priest, but he said it wouldn't be valid because we had already been refused. We had to get married. I had to know that she was finally mine and I knew she loved me, so we went to a Protestant army chaplain and three days later, on September 8, we got married."

Gabrielle put her hand to her mouth and gasped in horror.

"Unc had said he would be sure Susanna wasn't welcome in any of the Jude homes if we consummated our marriage and I didn't want her to stay in Paris without me. I had to be at headquarters almost constantly and I knew I'd have to watch her every minute to keep her out of trouble there. Paris was pretty rowdy."

"I took her to Rouen without talking to him about it. I told Grand-pere and Grand-mere about the marriage and Grand-pere was firm about the fact that we might be legally married, but there was to be no fooling around until it was right in God's eyes. They were happy to have Susanna, but I had to swear I'd go AWOL to keep her from staying in Paris. She didn't want any contact with the family because she didn't think she could fit in anymore and she didn't want to be away from me." He lowered his voice when he said, "She didn't think she was good enough to be a part of this family and the only reason she finally stayed with them was because she had seen soldiers shot for desertion and she was afraid I'd be shot."

"So you saw each other when Susanna went to Paris to do her shows and then again just before you left for New York?"

"Yes."

"And in all that time you never consummated your marriage?" He looked Joseph straight in the eye.

The room was deadly quiet as they looked at each other with one set of crystal blue eyes staring into the other. I watched in silence, sure this was the end of our happy family. My father was going to kill us both if Joseph told the truth.

Finally Joseph answered, "Yes, we consummated it on our wedding night as would be expected."

"And a few times before that," Unc added.

"That's not true! Mind your own business, Unc! I'm sick of you interfering all the time!"

"You and Susanna are my business and I won't have it!" he yelled shaking his finger at the two of us.

"We have no regrets, except for Unc's failure to bless our marriage. "It seems that he thinks we're the last two people who could ever be happy together!" he shouted as he glared at his mother's brother.

"Well, by God, I have some regrets!" Papi yelled as he glared at Joseph and me.

Mother crossed herself when she heard her husband curse. None of them had ever heard him say a curse word before.

He looked at Joseph and said, "A twenty-five year old man taking advantage of a little sixteen-year-old girl! I'm ashamed for you!" Then he looked at me and asked, "Didn't you know it's up to the girl to control things like that? Do you know what they call a woman who climbs into a man's bed before marriage?"

With that Susanna stood up ready for a fight. "Yes, even I have heard about whores and I guess that's what you think of me. Well, I believe that I am married and that God has blessed my marriage to

Joseph. If you are right then it may be that I am a whore because your son didn't take advantage of me," I said in an icy-cold voice. "Much as I regret it, I had to give up my childhood the day Opa died. When you're out on your own trying to survive in the middle of a war zone, you grow up real fast! There was no one around to ask for advice. It seemed to me that I had been entirely forgotten by those who were supposed to love me. I made a lot of mistakes, but nothing I did with Joseph was a mistake except, probably marrying him. I knew it would be wrong to have contact with any of you and I knew if I married Joseph he would insist on my coming back to the States. I never wanted to come because I knew it would mean more heartbreak for everybody. I have to admit, I hadn't expected to be called a whore for loving and marrying Joseph and for wanting to express my love for him in the most intimate way I could. Don't worry; you shouldn't have any trouble getting an annulment so he can find a suitable wife later. As for me, Opa was always telling me how rich I am. If that's true, I'll need just enough money to get me back to Italy and I'll never bother any of you ever again!" With that I turned, went into my room and slammed the door.

I quickly dressed, put on my coat and led Minnie down the hall and out of the hotel. As I passed my parent's room I could still hear Joseph, Unc, Papi, and now even my mother yelling at each other. All I wanted to do was get out of there as quickly as possible.

I caught a passing cab in front of the hotel and directed the driver to take me to the nearest Catholic Church. Catholic churches were never locked and they always had pianos. He took me to a small church several blocks from the hotel and left me on the sidewalk after I paid for my fare with money Joseph had given me that day in Paris.

Nobody was in the church at that time of the night so I walked to the front and sat down on the piano bench to play. I played all night as Minnie sat alertly under the bench guarding me.

Joseph told me later that he left his parents and uncle in a rage that only became more intense when he tried to enter my room and was unable to gain admittance. The hotel clerk gave him a key while giving him a knowing look. He had claimed that he didn't want to wake his wife by knocking, but needed to get into the room. When he found the room empty, he looked all over the hotel for me, then got a coat and started searching the area around the hotel. He looked everywhere for me until morning when he went back to the hotel to see if I had come back.

Though he never wanted to ever see his parents again, he knocked on their door and told them that I was gone without even leaving a note. "I'm going to keep looking for her and I'll call back here every hour to see if you have any news of her, if you don't mind too much," he added coldly.

Papi apologized. He said, "I'm sorry, son. I handled it all very badly. I would give anything if I could take back my words."

Joseph was unforgiving when he responded with, "Well, unfortunately you can't take them back. None of us will ever forget them, but what I can't understand is how you could stand there and be so self-righteous when I know my mother must have been at least four or maybe even five months pregnant for me when you married her. I saw the certificate you had from the church when you married her. I doubt that you two had been married by a Protestant minister or even had an agreement when I was conceived. Was she a whore too? I guess I'm a bastard so what could you expect of me? At least I tried to marry Susanna to make things right first."

Mother told me about the circumstances of Papi's first marriage once, years later. She said that he had loved Catherine with all his heart. He had told her that just hearing Joseph use the word whore in connection with her had made him wince.

Papi was visibly shaken by what Joseph had said about his first wife. He told him, "I can't say my behavior before I married your mother was a mistake because it resulted in your birth, but I know we should have been married before we slept together. Your mother was a wonderful young girl who probably should never have had anything to do with me, but she did and she paid dearly for it. Her father gave her a whipping and threw her out of the house the day he found out she was pregnant. He told her he never wanted to lay eyes on her again and he never did. I was so sorry to have caused her so much grief. We were so young. Now I see Susanna making the same mistakes."

"Why is it such a big mistake for us to love each other and be married? I just don't understand it!"

He became angry again. "She couldn't possibly know what she wants right now. If she gets stuck with a husband and children before she's ready, she'll never be happy. She's sixteen-years-old and already sleeping with a grown man. Tell me you would want that for your daughter when she is a mere sixteen-years-old."

"I wouldn't want anything that's happened to Susanna to happen to my daughter, including what happened last night. Unfortunately it all did happen to your daughter and now she's somewhere roaming around New York City feeling like the loneliest person who ever lived. If I find her, I'm going to promise her anything she wants. I'll move to Italy or France or wherever she wants to live and hopefully I can protect her from anything like this ever happening again. She was right. She never should have come back and all of you should have just left her alone."

"You're wrong. I was mad and what I said was unforgivable, but I love her and so does your uncle. We're just upset by her choices. She committed adultery!"

"So did you! So did I! So does Tom! ...So did my mother. It's not an unforgivable sin! It's human nature to want to make love to the one you love and she was in such need of love when I found her, but even then, we waited until we were married. We would have liked to have the Church's blessing but she wouldn't give it to us so we did what we could to make our union right in God's eyes and I truly believe that we have God's blessing if no one else's."

"And you were only too happy to convince her to marry you knowing that it would be without our blessings," he said sarcastically.

"Yes. At the first sight of her all I wanted to do was put my arms around her and never let her go. Papa, don't you understand how much I love her?"

Our father hung he head and hesitated before finally answering, "Yes, I guess I do. The truth is you've always loved her. I'm so sorry I handled it all so badly, but I wish you could have waited before getting into all of that. Why couldn't you have waited?" Without waiting for an answer he added, "I hope you can forgive me."

"I don't know if Susanna will ever forgive you."

"Will you?"

"I don't know yet. I'm sorry, but I'm too worried to think about it right now."

"Well, let me help you look for her and we'll get your mother to stand by the telephone."

That morning I was still playing as people filed into the church for the 6:00 mass. My music was being played from the heart, deep and meaningful. I was startled when the regular musician for the church interrupted me to see if I planned to play for the mass.

I stood up and looked at the man and felt as if I had just been wakened from a deep sleep. "I'm sorry. I guess I lost track of the time. I just came in to use the piano for a while. Excuse me."

It was time for seclusion. As I walked to the back of the church I noticed the confessionals, a private place to grieve until I got it all out of my system and decided what to do. I didn't want anybody to see me. I needed privacy.

Minnie and I went inside one of them and shut the door. I sat and stared at the wall for a long time, then I closed my eyes and tried to commune with God without thoughts, only with feelings.

Later I heard a voice speaking in Italian, of all things say, "Whoever it is has been in there since early this morning. Maybe she needs to talk to somebody."

The little Italian priest knocked quietly on the door. "Would you like to talk?" he asked in broken English.

"I don't think it would do any good," I answered in Italian.

"Come out and let's see," he coaxed, again with a heavy Italian accent.

Slowly I opened the door stood there holding my big coat and Minnie's leash. Tears were still streaming down my cheeks for the first time since I recovered from Alessandro's death.

"Come with me to my office where we can sit down."

We followed him obediently.

When we were in his office, we sat down in front of his warm-crackling fireplace. "Now tell me what this is all about."

I spoke to him in Italian, telling him everything about my life from the time my parents had been killed when I was five years old up to the present. When I finished I said, "I've decided to go down to the harbor to find out when I can get passage back to either France or England. I'll tell Joseph I want the marriage annulled, and I'll go to medical school and practice in Verona like I always planned. I'm so sorry for the things I've done. I wish I had been a better person."

"You are thinking of what you should do, but you give no thought of your husband. What makes you think he will want an annulment? Does it occur to you that he might really love you? What about your parents? Your father said some bad things, but he was angry and disappointed in you and Joseph. Maybe he didn't mean what he said.

He might be grieving over his own mistakes by now. Could you ever forgive him?"

"I forgive him now, but I think I killed his love for me and I couldn't stand to have him not like me anymore and I don't want to come between him and Joseph. I think men do bad things all the time. It doesn't seem to be the same kind of sin for them."

The little priest smiled, "My dear, you must understand that it is indeed the same sin for men as it is for women. It's just that men usually don't suffer here on earth the same way women do. Their suffering comes in eternity if they don't change their ways first."

After discussing the issue completely, we went together to check on the departures for Europe and I wrote them down. By the time we did that, it was 5:00 in the evening.

"Allow me escort you back to your hotel. You need some rest. Promise to stay there until I return in the morning. Don't run off again no matter what happens and you must refuse to sleep with your husband again until the marriage is blessed." He looked into my eyes kindly as he extracted the promise from me.

"I promise, Father. You helped me so much just by listening and not making me feel so bad about myself. You're not so emotional about things."

Once I was in my room I made sure both doors were locked. I took a hot bath and crawled into bed and was in an exhausted sleep in minutes.

Father Adamophilos went straight to my parent's room and found Mother waiting for the phone to ring. She told me later that she was so relieved when he told her I was in my room that she hugged him. "Do you think she'll go back to Italy?" she asked. "Have we lost her?"

She said he answered her truthfully by saying, "I don't know. She has a tremendous capacity for forgiveness. If all of you can accept her for the way she is, everything will probably be all right, but if you cannot, she will know and you will lose her. Right now, she is exhausted. Why do you not let her sleep and deal with it tomorrow when she is finally rested?" As he started out the door he added, "She has promised not to live with her husband as man and wife until the marriage is blessed. I would not wait too long to allow the blessing to take place. She is a good girl, but I do believe she is in love with her husband and will have problems denying him anything he requests."

Joseph told me the next morning that soon after Father Adamophilos left our mother he called and Mother told him that I was back. They met in the lobby of the hotel. As soon as he saw Papi he told him, "I'm spending the night with Susanna whether you like it or not. She needs me."

Papi said nothing.

Joseph showered and shaved in his own suite, then crept quietly into my room. I never stirred as he put his arms around me and fell into his own peaceful slumber.

In the morning I couldn't figure out what was happening when I awoke with those arms around me. Looking over the covers at me, grinning, he said, "You always were such a sleepyhead."

"I was never a sleepyhead! Remember, I was always the first one up every morning! You shouldn't be here. I promised, besides, your father will be upset." I wasn't claiming him as my father.

"I don't care. The only thing I'm ever going to care about ever again is you."

I hadn't expected him to say anything like that. What I expected was that he and the rest of the family would have had a meeting of the minds and would have decided to get an annulment so we could wait till later to see if Joseph and I were right for each other. I looked at him darkly and complained, "Why is it that every time I get everything figured out, you show up and get me all mixed up again?"

"Because you always make your plans without consulting me and

I have my own ideas about things. It isn't fair for you to make plans without including your husband."

"I can't live with the whole family looking at me like a black sheep. I just want to be left alone to live my life with no judgment passed. I'm going back to Verona day after tomorrow."

"No, you aren't going back to Verona, unless all that business last night has made you sorry you married me. I won't be discharged for a while and I'll have to stay here." He grinned, "You wouldn't want me to be shot for desertion at this late stage of the game would you? We want the same things in life. I too want to be left alone with no judgment passed. I'm a grown man and nobody is going to tell me what to do. I want to live my life with you and have a family with you and if Papa and Unc can't tolerate that, then I'm ready to head to Verona with you."

"Do you really mean that?"

"I really do," he answered as he held me close.

After we cuddled a few minutes, I again remembered my promise to Father Adamophilos. I sat up in bed and wrapped the covers around me. "We can't be in this bed together. I have to talk to you."

I told him about Father Adamophilos and my promise along with my plans to sail back to Europe in two days. When I finished, I popped out of bed before things could get out of control and ran to shower and got dressed.

While I was struggling with my hair, there was a knock on the door. I looked around the corner and saw that it was our parents. They were holding hands and looking grave. Gabrielle asked, "May we come in?"

Papi said, "I have to talk to both of you. Where's Susanna?" he asked, sounding worried as if he thought I had run away again.

"She's in the bathroom doing her hair. I think she's more anxious to see a beautician to have it thinned than she is to buy some better clothes."

When I came out I teared up. I stood looking at them, not sure what to do. "Do you want to sit down?" I asked them.

Papi started talking without taking a seat, "I don't expect you to ever forgive me for the way I acted the other night. It was inexcusable. I just want to tell you what made me do it. When Joseph said you were married, I felt cheated and deceived. I know you didn't tell me about it in the months while we were in France together because you knew I'd behave just the way I did. It's just that you were my little girl and I never got the chance to finish raising you. I only had you for such a short time and then you were gone. After Tom found you, I imagined you coming back home and life picking up right where things had left off four-and-a-half years ago. When I saw you, intellectually I knew you were grown up, but I made myself think you were still a child because I couldn't think I had lost the child in you. It all came slamming down on me when Joseph admitted that you had slept together and you told me you had wanted him to make love to you. I knew then that things would never be the same. I only got to be your father for six short years and you were gone!" He had tears in his eyes. "The last thing I ever want is to lose you forever. Please try to forgive me. I've made more mistakes in my life than you ever dreamed of and I promise you I have only the highest opinion of the two of you."

Without a word I walked over to my father and embraced him. "Of course I forgive you. There's nothing to forgive. I love you. Where would I have been without you?"

About that time, my vision started to black out. I had been fighting it off since I had crawled out of bed. "Susanna!" I heard him shout as he laid me down on the sofa. "My God what now?"

I came out of it almost as soon as my head hit the sofa. With a gravelly voice I mumbled, "It's okay. I just do this when I haven't eaten for a while, although it usually takes me longer than this to pass out. I'm all right now."

"Could you be pregnant?" Gabrielle asked gently.

"No Mama," I sighed, embarrassed. "I'm not pregnant."

"You're sure?"

"I'm positive."

Gabrielle looked at Joseph. He answered, "She's right, there's no way."

Papi seemed disgusted that Joseph would have knowledge of such a personal nature to be able to answer a question like that and gruffly asked, "When did you last eat something?"

"The other night…. Don't look at me like that. Only in the United States do people eat every day. I've gone for days without eating just like everybody else in Europe. It's nothing to pass out. Afterwards it seems like you get a second wind."

Mother took charge. "Well, there will be no more second winds for you, young lady. From now on, you will eat three times a day until we get you strong and healthy! Normally, people in Europe eat regularly too. You were just there at an unusual time. People everywhere eat two or three times a day."

Breakfast for the four of us was brought to the room. While we ate we agreed that Joseph and I were indeed married, but would not live like a married couple until the marriage was blessed, after Joseph's discharge from the army. I would go on to Bayland to stay with our parents until then. It would give me time to adjust to the family and to restore my health. It would also give Papi time to adjust to having a grownup daughter. He and Mother would take care of Unc and would explain the agreement to him and we all hoped he would bless the marriage before he left again for France.

Pierre

*S*usanna, Joseph, and I finally settled our differences before we left Joseph in New York and headed for Bayland with the rest of the family. I loved those two children and Tom as if they were my own. I had other nieces and nephews, but those three were special and though I never had the opportunity to spend as much time with them as I did with my French family, I had a special love for them. As the young people today say, we were on the same wave length, that is, until I found out that Joesph and Susanna had defied me by getting married in a Protestant ceremony! When it looked like Susanna and Joseph might never forgive me, I wondered if I had made a mistake. I wouldn't be the first priest to use poor judgment. Still, it only seemed like common sense for a young girl who had been through what Susanna had, to wait for a year or two before making any lifetime decisions. I still hadn't forgotten that she and Joseph had parted on bad terms when she had left the United States just before her twelfth birthday and headed for Luxembourg. They needed time to get to know each other as adults. I wasn't wrong!

It was with misgivings that I agreed to bless the wedding that spring. Seeing them together reminded me of an old married couple. They weren't giddy or silly about their love. It was matter-of-fact and it was right. They respected each other and seemed to want to take care of each other. By the time the month of May finally rolled around, I had not only resigned myself to it, but had started to believe that it was one marriage that would honestly be blessed by God Himself!

When Susanna walked down the aisle she glowed. The guests in the *pews were speechless; you could hear a pin drop as they looked up and saw her slowly walking on her father's arm to her husband. She was confident and walked with purpose She and Joseph would be devoted to each other forever. Everybody there could see it.*

Chapter 13

It was May 3, 1919 and the day our marriage was finally going to be blessed. Uncle Pierre and Father Adamophilos, who had helped us through our crisis, would perform the service. Joseph had been discharged from the army the week before. Though it was to be a private gathering of family and close friends, the church was more than half full. I didn't realize that so many people still cared about us.

Tom, who carried a mahogany cane and walked with a slight limp, stood beside his brother and Jacob stood beside him. My best friend, Ilona, stood beside me. I was dressed in an elegant off-white dress with a large matching lace mantilla the nuns had sent me from Italy. Laure, who was now blooming with her pregnancy stood next to Ilona. It was customary for young ladies who were expecting a baby to stay behind closed doors, but I wouldn't hear of it.

The ceremony was short compared to the long, formal mass and adoption ceremony our parents had gone through just eleven years and one day before, but never have two people said their vows with more love and passion than we did. Our marriage was one made in heaven, right from the start. We had happy times and some sad ones, but our love for each other is still strong to this day and I know that Joseph waits for me now on the other side of life where we truly will live happily ever after.

THE END

CPSIA information can be obtained
at www.ICGtesting.com
Printed in the USA
BVHW031949210622
640332BV00003B/161